The French Baker's War

MICHAEL WHATLING

MORTAL COIL BOOKS

THE FRENCH BAKER'S WAR
Copyright © 2021 by Michael Whatling

Excerpt from *Le Petit Prince* by Antoine de Saint-Exupéry, 1943.

Spot a typo? Send it to: Typo@MortalCoilBooks.com

ISBN 978-1-7775699-2-1 (pbk.)
ISBN 978-1-7775699-3-8 (ebk.)
ISBN 978-1-7775699-4-5 (hbk.)

FIRST EDITION

9 8 7 6 5 4 3 2 1e

"The guilty one is not he who commits the sin, but the one who causes the darkness."

– Victor Hugo

Inspired by a true story.

Part I

A Disappearance

ONE

Tuesday, October 19, 1943
Early Morning

Ever the optimist, Mireille Albert believes a beautiful day or two can still be squeezed out of a season already spoiled by rain. She sits on the windowsill, face tilted towards the sun, body swaying in its warmth. How wonderful it is to push aside the blackout curtain and discover an unblemished sky.

A low rumbling draws her eyes down, but the street's empty, too early for shops with little to sell to be open, or for customers in threadbare overcoats to be lining up, clutching ration books. The sound rises from somewhere behind the buildings across the way, but Mireille can't pinpoint what's making it.

"Come back to bed for a few more minutes," her husband groans.

There's a flash at the top of the street. The indistinct shape of a man looms inside Saint-Joachim's bell tower. Mireille's eyes narrow. Another flash, a signal with a mirror to someone at the edge of town. Who'd be so foolish in daytime? It can't be Père Blais, he never risks going up there. "I'm close enough to God," she overheard him say once after Easter mass. Then she recognizes the shock of blond hair catching the sunlight. Mireille scans the windows opposite, and when she looks back, he's gone. She can't repress a shiver. What started as a pebble in a shoe, soon will be the size of a rock under the surface of a calm sea waiting to cause shipwrecks.

Mireille shuts the window and joins André in their narrow bed. Tiny hands push down the covers to reveal their son, his face wide with excitement.

"Oh! This isn't your bed!" She exaggerates her playful rebuke, knowing how much it pleases the boy. She gnarls her fingers into the claws of an imaginary creature and tickles him. Frédéric lets out a whoop and hides again. Giving her one of his boyish grins, André shifts to make room for her on the horsehair mattress. He peeks under the blankets and calls Frédéric's name as though trying to find him in a black cavern.

Before slipping in beside her family, Mireille glances at the window.

Mireille puts a record on the gramophone, and music flows down the stairs and fills the pâtisserie with a cheerful song. Today she's chosen Charles Trenet's whimsical *"Y'a d'la joie."* When the first notes begin, she pictures André downstairs humming along for a few bars, before returning to his baking. Fond as she is of teasing him for being a slave to habit, routine's what keeps their shop open. Every morning, André rolls up the sleeves of his white shirt, dons a white apron, and meticulously marshals his soldiers for battle: pans, sheets, bowls, utensils, and ingredients.

She dresses their son in a sailor's suit he insists on wearing, the why of which baffles her, and carries him into the shop. He holds up a red ball with two hands in veneration. André covers something on the worktable with a cloth, then takes Frédéric, gives him a twirl to the music, and sits the four-year-old on the floor. The boy offers the ball to his father.

"There'll be time to play later, *mon fils.*"

Frédéric's lip quivers, so André sets a large pot in front of him, averting impending tears. They've learned the hard way it's better to placate the child than endure one of his tantrums.

André examines the thermometer on the oven door. Concerned, he taps its glass face. Mireille has asked him what good that does dozens of times, but he always shrugs. Ironic it's one of his rituals she finds comforting as lying in his arms.

At the worktable, he breaks and separates two eggs, then whisks the whites until they form peaks, adding sugar as he goes. To check for stiffness, he holds the bowl upside down above his head. Only then does he allow himself a satisfied smile.

Mireille ties on a white apron, takes flour from deep in a large burlap bag sitting on the floor, and adds and removes some on one side of a scale until it matches the iron weight on the opposite side. Hopefully, there'll be enough for the next few days—there's never been so little. When she plops the last of the butter in a bowl, André raises an eyebrow, so she takes half out and carefully covers it again in its brown paper wrapping. He's right—they have to stretch it far as they can. But how long can they realistically go on like this? She presses her lips together with resolve.

André fills a metal piping syringe with meringue and makes perfect disks on a baking sheet. He puts the macarons aside to rest so a skin can form. He pulls out a tray of *biscuits au sucre* from the oven and lays it on the table to cool. There's the satisfying aroma of sugary edges starting to caramelize.

Checking to see if Frédéric is still playing, André removes the cloth to reveal a tiny marzipan creation: an almond paste boy and fox on an almond paste asteroid. Hands steady, eyes unblinking, he adds a last touch—a smile to the boy's face.

Mireille holds out two bowls. "Which one?"

André covers the figures again and points to the bowl on the left. He moves aside so she can shroud three petits fours in pink and pipe small delicate buttercream roses on them. Finished, she snaps to mock attention.

"Sous-lieutenant Mireille Albert, ready for inspection, *mon capitaine.*"

"Beautiful!" André gently nudges her arm, and she gives her head a shake as though exasperated with their little game. With reverence, he carries the petits fours to the display case.

The rumbling, now accompanied by the metallic clanking of some awful machine. Mireille meets André at the display, and they exchange looks. A tank lumbers into view, a swastika emblazoned on its side. They've seen plenty of their cars, and trucks, and jeeps, but this is a first.

The Alberts stand silently as the behemoth clatters out of town. Thankfully, Frédéric doesn't look up until it has rolled past. His fascination with all things military is the one thing that disturbs them about their son.

André goes back to positioning plates of pastries on the shelves, but Mireille doesn't move. "André," she says, but he doesn't hear her. She opens her mouth to say it again, but stops. How does he deserve what she's about to confess? She balls her hand into a fist and presses it against her abdomen, her thumb rubbing a knuckle.

Frédéric gives out a squawk, and Mireille looks around with a great sweep of her head and pretends to be surprised when she finds him hiding under the worktable. The boy giggles and covers his eyes. Her heart becomes lighter.

When they've made all the pastries they can for the day, André puts on his baker's whites. He fastens the last button and his back straightens. He dons a toque and ties a *foulard* around his neck, then checks they're not crooked in the glass of the display case.

Mireille and André take a last look around—the final inspection.

Their pâtisserie is typical of the pastry shops found in towns across France, simple and clean, but past its prime. Whenever customers comment on its décor, good or bad, Mireille always says, "It's exactly how we like it." The truth is, she doesn't have the heart to change anything from when her parents owned it. A customer from back then could walk in after all these years and not spot a single difference. It isn't the sweet smell of pastries Mireille breathes when they're baking, but memories of her childhood.

André goes to the front door and turns the sign in the window to OUVERT. Without looking, Mireille knows it can't be more than a hair before ten o'clock.

She uses the corner of her apron to wipe away the tinniest of smudges from the display's glass. With its dark cherry wood frame and thick beveled glass, the display case dominates the shop. This is where neighbours used to meet to share news, whether or not they were buying. But now with no jobs or money, not as many people come in. The scarcer the supplies, the fewer pastries the Alberts make, resulting in even less customers. Everyone's trapped in a vicious whirlpool as commerce withers.

When there is talk, it's dominated by war, food shortages, and Germans—*les maudits boches*. Where once those who gathered in their shop were certain the Nazi occupation wouldn't last long, these days they don't believe it will ever end.

TWO

Mireille steps out the side door, and music follows her into the alley. When the song becomes muted, she smiles. André has stuffed a rag in the gramophone's horn, a compromise between it being as loud as she likes and his desire for quiet.

She pours out a bucket of water she used to mop the floor and watches it snake away. So few customers, and still the floors don't stay clean. She goes back inside, returning a moment later with a broom.

On her way up the alley towards the street, she stops to pick up a discarded sardine can. The trace odour brings back the sea air where she and André spent a day for their honeymoon. There they relaxed in their love for the first time, as their meeting, courtship, and wedding had happened so fast. In stark contrast, when Mireille and André came home from their day away, all they had was time to be alone together—it took three interminable years to conceive Frédéric.

She peers inside the can, tips it, and jiggles it clean of a spider that scuttles away along the line of slate-grey water. She puts the can in her apron pocket and continues on.

The Alberts' shop stands on a street lined by trees dropping their colours. One of its windows proudly proclaims its name: PÂTISSERIE SAINT-LÉRY. At the top of the street, a church bathes in the morning light. So familiar are their neighbours with Saint-Joachim, most having grown up nearby, few have noticed the gargoyles hunched on its roof glowering down at them, demanding piety.

Across the road, Monsieur Hébert, the florist, arranges tansies and asters in a basket outside his shop, although Mireille can't imagine who's still buying flowers. He waves; she waves back. She hasn't much to do with the man, but she appreciates how he sends over a rose on her birthday, and how he complains boisterously and with wild facial expressions to André about the weather and his daughter who left with her new husband to live in Paris. Idle talk exasperates André, but he doesn't do a thing to avoid it. "Manners cost nothing." Mireille chuckles. Easy for him to say when he seldom has to deal with people.

How little the street changes. She knows every cobblestone, every crack and chip and the ones that are missing. André wouldn't notice, let alone care, if they were ripped up and re-placed with cabbages, as long as it doesn't prevent customers from coming into the shop.

Monsieur Lussier puts a few thin, gristly chops in the window of his *boucherie*. Already there's a long line outside anxious to buy them. He, too, gives Mireille a wave, and she returns it.

"Hello." The whispered word barely reaches her. Mireille looks around and doesn't see anyone except a passerby she doesn't know, more intent on not stepping in horse manure than offering greetings to strangers.

"Madame Albert, up here."

Mireille tilts her head. Madame Bujold, an old woman con-fined by her infirmities to a wheelchair and her second-floor flat, waves from a window, and Mireille obligingly nods. Only last week the shut-in had lamented her life was no different than being stranded on a desert island the size of a postage stamp. She's notorious for being the street's busybody—judge, jury, and executioner—blunting any sympathy her situation should elicit.

Pleasantries over, the two women resume their chores: Mireille to sweeping, and Madame Bujold to scrutinizing the street.

The music becomes loud again. André pulling the rag from the gramophone means only one thing. A moment later, the door opens with a tinkle of its bell, and he steps out, his baker whites and toque gone, a jacket and a hat in their place. Not one for shows of affection in public, he gives her a quick kiss on her temple. She smells vanilla. Before he can rush off, Mireille stops him. She unties the *foulard* from around his neck and stuffs it in his pocket.

"*Bon courage.*"

"I'll bring back something." André jerks his head towards the window and Frédéric on the other side watching them. In better times, André liked to surprise her with little gifts, too, each one somehow more thoughtful. This memory prompts her to kiss him on the cheek.

"What's that for?" He arches an eyebrow as if it was the oddest thing she could've done. Mireille shoos him away with a flick of her hand.

André looks to see if anyone is watching, then leans in to kiss her again, this time on the lips, and she impishly turns at the last moment so it lands next to her mouth. Dejected, he starts walking away. When she laughs, he looks back and winks.

Mireille watches him go, worry and awe warring inside her at how doggedly persistent her husband is despite all reason. She absently rubs the cross hanging from her neck between her fingers. Her mind's made up—she'll speak with him tonight.

With a quick shake of the broom as if warding off misfortune, she returns to sweeping.

Her mood sours when she spots a tiny shard of glass at her feet. She looks at the shop next door: one window boarded up, the other blackened by fire except where "Samuel" is still legible. A sign with a line drawing of a cobbler sways in the breeze above a door defaced with "JUIF" and a crude Star of David.

Mireille gnaws on her lower lip. Never underestimate how reprehensible people can be. How naïve for her to have thought the war was far away.

A distinguished, bespectacled older gentleman in a suit and hat walks up.

"Good morning, Mireille."

She greets him with a respectful "Monsieur Durand" as he kisses her on both cheeks. She looks back at the Samuels' shop. The smell of soot and leather closes her nose. The old man follows her gaze to the vandals' work.

"A terrible mess. Those poor souls were treated like vermin."

"Who would do such a thing?" Mireille lowers her voice. "The Germans?"

Monsieur Durand shakes his head and, taking the hint, speaks more quietly. "One of them."

They watch people pass and shopkeepers go about their business. The florist snips the bottoms of stems off flowers; a customer exits the *boucherie,* followed by the crisp chop of a cleaver; and the bread baker stomps on the cobbles outside his shop to scare off pigeons feasting on crumbs his customers drop when they leave with a baguette under their arms.

"Abraham and his family were well-advised to leave. It could only become worse for them." Monsieur Durand's glasses slide down his nose, and he peers at her over them.

"So we'll never know."

"This street can be mute if it wants. Silence is one way to survive." He scrubs his hands together as though cleaning them of disgust.

"And no one lifts a finger."

"Only a fist. People never lack the strength, only the will." He puts his arms behind his back, as if restraining himself from an untidy show of emotion.

Her stomach clenches for not going next door Sunday night when the cobbler's shop was attacked, having begged off by saying she had Frédéric to care for. Only André and Monsieur Durand helped Samuel and his family fight the fire and slip away in the night, the other neighbours rendered deaf and blind, sudden as a clap of thunder.

She'd been unable to move, her body heavy as a bag filled

with wet sand. She was painfully reminded of the fire in the pâtisserie when she was a girl—the old oven ignited, trapping her family by the flames that engulfed the stairs. Mireille vividly remembers how her father carried her down them, then went up for her mother. On their way back, a step crumbled, and they plummeted the rest of the way. Mireille's father broke his ankle, and her mother couldn't breathe from the smoke and was so disoriented she tried to go upstairs again. While her father soon healed, her mother had a stubborn cough that hastened her to her death at age thirty-nine. Not long after, Mireille's father died from no specific cause, as though without his wife, he gave up living.

When Mireille asks herself what the Samuels could've done to deserve what happened to them, she can only come up with one sorry, despicable answer: They're Jews. A reason so arbitrary it makes her question people's sanity.

"At least someone had the decency to board it up." She looks over at the Samuels' shop again. "Not that there's anything left to take."

"They were our neighbours." Monsieur Durand pushes his glasses up on his nose, and his sharp blue eyes appear larger and more sorrowful.

Mireille searches his face, but his dignified demeanour reveals nothing. Then she understands and nods. It's just like him to do that and not tell anyone. She feels tears forming. His selflessness rises in contrast with her sinking lack of it.

Monsieur Durand gallantly switches the subject. "How's business?" Mireille tips her head from side to side. "It'll change," he assures her. "Up. Down. These are the times. Never mind. We have perseverance."

"More than a lifetime's worth." She dilutes her words with a self-pitying sigh.

"That is how we triumph, no?"

She gives this sentiment a smile and peers through the window at Frédéric playing on the floor with his ball, the large pot, and now some pastry boxes. He's their *petit cadeau*, the only gift she and André ever wanted and will ever need: their beautiful boy.

Two German soldiers on patrol walk towards them, rifles across their backs. They stop to look in the *chapellerie*, and grin at the selection of hats like they're ready to trade in their field caps for fedoras. Pedestrians bustle over to the other side of the street.

Monsieur Durand whispers, "Now there's the true pestilence."

The soldiers nod to them as they pass.

The butcher's son, cigarette dangling from his mouth, his mop of blond hair falling over one eye, bursts out of his father's shop and loudly sings *La Marseillaise*.

Mireille's neck tightens and she can feel a scowl cloud her face. He's being reckless—he has to be drinking. And at this hour! She tries to warn him not to be stupid, but nothing comes out except a peep of a moan.

The Germans stop and look over at him with puzzled indifference. The butcher hobbles out and drags his son back in. With barely a raised eyebrow between them, the soldiers continue down the street.

Mireille shudders. It beggars belief how Gilles hasn't gotten himself killed. Had he been drunk last night? It's a miracle he didn't fall out of the bell tower.

"Oh! Madame Monchamp!" Monsieur Durand cries out.

They look up the street to his *librairie* where a portly older woman is waiting, dressed more formally than the time of day warrants. Even from where they're standing, they can see impatience painted on her face and her tapping a book against her palm as if counting the seconds she's been there.

"She browses for hours and never buys a thing," Monsieur Durand says in a hushed tone, although the woman's too far to hear. "I would be better off selling pencils on a street corner." The bookseller pauses, and when he speaks again, his voice is solemn as a eulogy. "Your parents would be proud to see you fighting to stay open."

Mireille bows her head and sweeps dried leaves into the gutter. Those words are the ones she most desires to hear. The old man shifts, and Mireille knows he didn't intend to invoke such a reaction. He touches the brim of his hat, and heads back to his bookstore.

She's grateful he's in their lives. Monsieur Durand has come to their aid more times than she can remember, often financially, even though taking money from him bothers André to no end. "For Frédéric's sake," the old man implores, and they relent, sometimes too readily. Their friend can be counted on, his discretion inviolable.

If he suspects what she's been up to, he hasn't said anything to her.

Mireille opens the door to go back in when the rattle of horse's hooves on the cobbles and the discordant creaking of a cart causes her to freeze. What's left of her smile dissolves.

The florist slinks into his shop and shuts the door. Madame Bujold closes the shutters with a decisive bang. Shopkeepers along the street poke their heads out, then slam their doors and lock them. Customers scurry away.

Mireille remains motionless, unable to look away from the horse and cart coming towards her.

The door behind her swings in and music spills out, but it can't silence the bone-rattling scream of a man crying out in pain.

THREE

Same Day Afternoon

In Saint-Léry d'Espoir's *place de ville*, dozens of townspeople, mostly women with baskets, ration books at the ready, line up under a sign announcing BEURRE - OEUFS - FROMAGE.

André darts across the square and joins the queue.

Mireille used to handle buying ingredients, but when the war began, suppliers faded away, and then Frédéric was born, it became André's chore to scrounge for what he could.

Venturing out is pure necessity—he hates being away from the shop for any length of time. The contradiction isn't lost on him. It wasn't that long ago when his younger self thought his world was much too small and confining and continuing to shrink. Now the world seems too large and expansive—he's only truly at ease in his own little corner. He thanks God every night as he falls asleep for having all the world he needs in Mireille, Frédéric, and the pâtisserie.

When a handful of customers exit, more push their way in, and André is swept along with them. He squeezes over to the shelf where the butter's supposed to be. It's empty. He removes his hat and runs his fingers through his hair. Now what? Everywhere he went looking for supplies has proven to be a waste of time. Last Friday, he overheard the fishmonger say with a laugh soon they'll have to ration the rations. Too absorbed with finding ingredients and thinking the man was telling another of his fishy tales, at first André missed the joke.

A cluster of women are arguing with the shopkeeper, a large, affable man with an overwhelmingly bushy moustache whose name André can't remember. Today the man undermines his usual cheerful disposition by feigning being devastated.

"Tragic. Completely tragic. I've been let down again. There are no words, Mesdames. But tomorrow... Certainly by week's end."

"You swore that to us every day this week, Monsieur." A tiny woman folds her arms, and disregarding both their sizes, plants herself solidly in front of him, blocking any escape the poor man might be considering. "And the week before!"

"There's still some cheese, Madame." The shopkeeper nervously tries to appease their anger, his lips appearing and disappearing through the curtain of facial hair. André smiles. The man does right to fear for his safety. Who knows what vengeance women with baskets hand out?

"We've already used our tickets for cheese," spits another woman. She holds a basket larger than anyone else's. André marvels at her optimism. Or is it foolishness? What does she plan to fill it with?

"We need milk." The woman shoves her oversized basket at the shopkeeper, who sputters and frantically looks around for help as more women surround him.

André pushes his way out of the shop and drags himself across the square. Why bother arguing? It won't make food appear.

A sickly looking man stops André as he passes by. He leans in conspiratorially and shows André a few dirty ration books. "For what you can give me," he whispers with a raspy voice. "Anything."

André reads the desperation on his face, etched raw and deep as though by acid. When André shakes his head, the man's eyes drop and his shoulders slump. The ration book is probably all he has of value to sell. For what reason, God only knows. A doctor? Medicine? He must be in such despair he'll give up eating. André deliberates whether to agree to the proposition, knowing it means taking food from the man's mouth to feed his own.

He digs a hand in his pocket and pulls out a few coins—all he has—and passes them over. As the man coughs his gratitude, still offering the ration book, André walks on, listless as a wounded animal. He can hear his father chiding him: "Kindness to strangers is always repaid by lashes from a whip."

André's mouth sets into a tight line, and he picks up his pace. He vowed long ago he'd never inherit any of the cynicisms his father spouts.

He stops dead. Damn! Now he has no money to buy Frédéric a *cadeau*. He'll have to make a treat for his son with whatever's left at home.

Outside the gendarmerie, André crosses the street and is almost hit by a truck covered with canvas. He jumps back and breathes out in relief as the vehicle brakes beside the station. Two gendarmes climb out of the cab, and two more exit from the back. Other passersby stop to watch the police pull out three badly beaten men.

A bald man smelling of stale beer stops beside André to gawk at the goings-on playing out in the sun's glare. "Black marketeers," he offers, without anyone asking. "*Maudits salauds!* They won't haggle their way out of the embrace of Madame La Guillotine." When the men are herded into the station, the man shrugs, and walks away with the air of someone who's bored by having seen it one too many times before.

Now the gendarmes are out of sight, a teenage boy lopes to the truck and climbs in. He emerges moments later with bags of flour and sugar, holding them above his head in triumph to the applause and cheers of the gathering crowd. But as he leaps out, he drops a sugar bag and it breaks open, covering the cobblestones in white. Without even a glance of regret at what he's lost, the boy sprints away, clutching what's left against his chest for dear life.

Envy floats in André like a dead fish. If only he could be so bold.

An old woman runs over with surprising agility and scoops up the loose sugar into the fold of her dress. As if on cue, the other onlookers swarm the truck. It's chaos. Each of them fights for possession of the marketeers' bounty. Some emerge victorious as the boy, arms full of goods, but it's short-lived when others snatch it from them.

André edges towards the vehicle. He rubs his bottom lip with his thumb. God expects everyone to be glad for what they have, even if it's next to nothing. But as fervently as André believes this, his steps quicken. In an instant, he climbs up and disappears inside the truck.

When André reappears, he's carrying blocks of butter, but has to fight to keep them because of people trying to rip them from his grasp, not much different from feral dogs fighting over a carcass. He shoulders his way past them and jumps to the ground.

Three gendarmes race out of the station and start yanking people from the truck, letting them fall unceremoniously to the street like sacks of potatoes. The policemen are overwhelmed by the throng, until one gendarme takes out his pistol and shoots in the air.

The crowd scatters.

André runs, but stumbles on an uneven cobblestone, and drops all the blocks of butter except one. He tries to retrieve them, but the mob tramples them in their panic to get away. André stares at the lost ingredient in spite of being bumped and jostled, cursing under his breath.

Carrying the only block of butter he saved, André makes his way home feeling ruined. Every so often, he looks behind, worrying gendarmes will materialize to arrest him for his crime. He grips the packet so tightly, his fingers dig into its mushy contents.

When André sees the modest spire of Saint-Joachim, his anxiety evaporates. He turns the corner to the pâtisserie, and his mouth goes dry. The door's wide open and Frédéric is chasing his bouncing ball towards the street.

André rushes over and folds his arms around his son. "Making a break for it, I see." He holds Frédéric to him for a moment, thankful there were no motorcars or trucks just then. The boy has never wandered outside on his own before. Frédéric points to the open door and makes an excited noise.

"Yes. Yes. We'll see what your maman has for our meal." André retrieves the ball, and carries his son inside.

The shop's empty. André puts Frédéric down and the boy goes back to playing: he drops the ball with a thump, and when it lazily rolls away, he patters after it and picks it up. The only other noise is from upstairs: the rhythmic clicking of the gramophone needle against the record's label.

Leaving the butter on the worktable, André crosses to the stairs. "Mireille?" No reply. Then more loudly: "Mireille?" Nothing.

He's about to go up and switch off the gramophone when the sounds of the ball hitting the floor and Frédéric's running feet stop. André turns and is startled to see his son holding out the red ball to a woman crouching behind the display case.

What in God's...

"May I help you?" André has never seen her before. Is she a customer who's fallen? Has Mireille gone for help? The hair on his arms stand up. It makes no sense for this woman to be cowering there on the floor, nothing more than a crumpled pile of clothes.

She turns her body, an arm stretched protectively across her chest. She's gaunt and pale and is wearing a faded and torn grey work uniform. A dirty rag covers her hair, and her face is streaked with grime. Under one eye, there's a yellow and purple bruise, and dried flakes of blood ring her nostrils.

"Is something— Are you hurt?" When the woman doesn't answer, André moves to help her up, but she flinches and shifts away from him. "I'm sorry. I don't..." He'd never hurt her— how can she think such a thing? "My wife's supposed to..." He stops. What's the point of telling her about Mireille? That if he has a wife, somehow it will reassure her he's a good person?

How can you prove to someone you don't know what's in your heart?

He's at a loss what to do. Call the gendarmes? They'd only overreact and end up dragging her out kicking and screaming. Mireille would never forgive him if he lets that happen. For a second he considers throwing the woman out himself, and his skin goes clammy. How is that any better than what the gendarmes will do? Mireille won't think much of that, either.

André watches Frédéric pad over to the stairs and plop down on the bottom step, his eyes riveted on the stranger.

"It's all right," André says gently to her as though talking to a child. He realizes that's wrong, too.

She lifts her head, her eyes swollen in fear. To emphasize he isn't a threat, André takes a step back and raises the palms of his hands to her in surrender. After a moment, she slowly stands, but falters and reaches for the display case to steady herself.

André spots the yellow badge she's been hiding—a Star of David with JUIF written on it.

"No! You can't be here." She has to go. André bounds to the front door and opens it.

Across the street, the butcher and the florist are outside the *boucherie*, and when they see him, they stop talking. Nosey bastards. André quickly shuts the door.

"You have to leave. This way." He pulls open the side door, and hurries back to her. "Go down the alley and—"

The woman whimpers, crouches again, and covers her head. Her reaction stops André cold. His throat closes and he starts to sweat.

Why did she pick this shop? The flower shop is more charming; the butcher's more popular; and in the bread shop, Monsieur Sylvestre gives away samples like a Pigalle prostitute does syphilis.

"I-I just want you to..." André turns to the door willing Mireille to walk in right then. If she went for help, she's taking her time. He goes to the window and looks out, hoping to see her up the street heading home. "Where is she?"

He looks back at the woman, trying to work out the mystery of how a Jew ended up in their shop. Her expression's blank as a plate. Is she a criminal? If she is, and if the state she's in is any indication, they've punished her for it. She's run away, that's obvious, but from where? André doesn't know many of the Jews in town, there's not many. The Samuels next door, of course, but they're gone now. And there was a journalist who wrote for *La Dépêche du Saint-Léry* who used to come in every Monday without fail to buy six macarons and six madeleines, but he left just after the war started when he was let go.

The Jews are not wanted here, especially now the Germans have arrived. André overhears what his neighbours say about them around the display case, though he tries not to listen, and would rather they'd buy their pastries in silence and go. Anyway, it's not any concern of his. He leaves debates about politics to Mireille and Monsieur Durand. He's a baker. He has no need to stray from that.

He concentrates on the star pinned to her—he heard Monsieur Durand speak of Jews in their ghettos in Paris having to wear it. He hasn't seen anyone with it here in Saint-Léry except for the Samuels. He didn't give it much thought when they were first required to put it on, although it bothered Mireille and their learnèd friend to no end. The law seemed reasonable enough to him—André had been hearing for years how Jews were causing problems in the city. How exactly, he's not sure. The Samuels had always been nice to him and his family, and that was good enough for him.

Now there's a woman hiding in their pâtisserie wearing that star. One of them. A Jew. André's pulse races. She has to leave.

The monotone sound of the gramophone needle continues clicking throughout the shop. It makes André think of a clock chipping seconds into dust, or a steady heartbeat ridiculing him for the fact his is racing sixteen to the dozen.

He circles back to the display case, careful not to pass too near to the woman. Her eyes track him as he goes. He finds it unsettling, but not as disturbing as how thin she is, as wretched as anyone he's ever seen. Maybe after she's had some food, she'll be gone. Then he can see what's keeping Mireille. André pulls out a plate of cakes and offers them to her.

"Here. Petits fours. Take them and go."

She steals a look but doesn't budge, so André places the plate on the display and backs away. "I have my family to worry about." He tries to make his tone conciliatory. "If you were found... Please understand."

He waits for her to say something. Anything. Pressure builds at his temple. Finally, he blurts out in frustration, "You can't...be...here."

Frédéric ambles over and offers the woman the ball again. She twists away and draws her arms closer.

André picks up the boy. "Come, *mon fils*. Papa will find you a treat." To the woman, he says, "I'm sorry," but he's not sure she heard him. He waits a bit for her to speak, and when she doesn't, he shakes his head and climbs the stairs with his son.

The woman gathers her strength and stands. She looks around, then picks up a cake, smells it, and eats ravenously. Above her, the noise from the gramophone needle stops.

The front door's bell jingles, and she ducks as a matronly woman struts to the display case. Despite the warm weather, she has on a heavy brown coat with a fox collar, the animal wrapped around her neck biting its own tail near her chin. She wears it like she's purchased it just yesterday from the finest furrier in Paris, but it's obviously well worn, so mottled that patches of bare hide are clearly visible.

André dashes in from the stairs. "Madame Monchamp." He greets his customer with a curt nod. Her lavender scent already permeates the room, overwhelming every other smell. Not an easy feat to accomplish in a pastry shop.

And still no Mireille.

He looks around for the Jewish woman and sees she's gone, too. Thank goodness!

Madame Monchamp vigourously taps the display with a finger. "These are made today?" She asks this every time she comes in. Maybe he'll stop her from doing it if he says they only have pastries excavated from Egyptian tombs.

"Of course, Madame. Fresh every day."

André spots the stranger hiding at the far end of the display. *Ça suffit!* He doesn't need this right now. Still, he stands in a way that shields her from Madame Monchamp's view, and distracts the older woman by offering her a plate of pastries. She inspects them with blatant disdain and exhales loudly as if the effort of just being there's too taxing. André is familiar with this sound from her. Mireille once devilishly compared it to the snort of a routing beast.

"My daughter and her husband will be dining with me. Not much of a selection. It appears I went out of my way for nothing."

"The war, Madame." Having to humour her drains André of the desire to live.

"Yes. I've heard." Her lips peel back as she decides if he's being facetious. She carries on, but her eyes are fixed on him like a cadaver. "I will have two *mille feuilles* and two, no three, macarons."

André bends to get a box. The stranger is gone again, and the door at the bottom of the display case has been slid open, pastry boxes exposed. He fights the urge to search for her on the other side, not wanting to alert Madame Monchamp.

He grabs one of the boxes and places the pastries inside as the meddlesome old cow moves along the display to the plate of half-eaten petits fours. Hovering over them, she turns up her nose, as if disappointed to see they're resting in a field of crumbs. Her head snaps, and she squints at the block of butter on the worktable. She begins to move over there like a child who's spotted candy.

André's spine stiffens. "Madame!" The old woman stops. "How about a gâteau as well?"

Madame Monchamp dismissively flaps her gloved hand, and André adeptly ties the box with string and passes it to her.

"Here, Madame. I trust you and your guests will enjoy these."

She drops coins onto the display, snatches the box, and leaves. Finally! André tracks the unpleasant woman as she walks past the window, crosses the street, and sails out of sight.

"It might be better if you didn't stay down here," he says to thin air. The way this Jew looks would frighten ghosts. Letting her stay down here in that state is a danger to them all.

After another silence, the stranger rises to her feet at the far end of the display and blinks at him with impossibly sad eyes.

André ladles a ragoût of root vegetables from a pot on the stove into a bowl. The Jewish woman sits at the table opposite Frédéric, who's nibbling at a biscuit and watching her with interest. How could he not feed her? He's seen feral dogs with more meat on them.

"My wife will be back soon." André brings over the bowl and a spoon, and pushes aside a ledger. He never did have a chance to go over the numbers. "She likes to look in on Madame Pelletier when the baking's done. She hasn't been well, the poor woman." He can't think of another plausible explanation for Mireille not being here, although it doesn't explain why she left Frédéric alone. She always takes him with her when she makes her rounds. Maybe she only expected to be out for a minute. Then where is she? If she's not back—he glances at the clock on the buffet—by the top of the hour, he'll go find her.

The stranger examines the bowl with wonder.

"Eat. Please. There isn't much meat in it, but Mireille always makes sure it's hearty enough." André doesn't tell the woman that yesterday they received a package from his parents all the way from their small vineyard in the countryside. Usually the mail's so slow, food arrives covered in maggots, and any meat has to be soaked in vinegar and boiled for hours to make it edible. But yesterday's package reached them miraculously fast.

The woman picks up the spoon and tastes the broth. She looks up, her eyes wary, unsure it's not a trick.

"Good, no? Go on. There's more."

She begins eating greedily, barely pausing to chew. Stray dogs are less hungry.

Downstairs, the shop's bell rings.

"Oh! There she is! Watch Frédéric for me. He'll try for another biscuit, the little greedy-guts." André jerks his head at a plate on the table as he tousles his son's light brown hair.

He vanishes down the stairs, and a moment later there are muffled voices from below.

When she finishes devouring the ragoût, she waits, her hands resting in her lap, an attempt to calm herself, but her fingers start to twitch, and the pain in her right hand throbs and shoots up her arm. The hand's a pulpy mess, purple and red and lumpy.

She can't stop her mind from spinning, demanding she be aware of everything around her. Giving in, she surveys the room: areas for eating—a stove, the table where she's sitting, a buffet—and sleeping—an armoire and two beds. A clawfoot bathtub, starkly white among the room's brown hues, peeks out from behind a folding screen. There's a closet-like structure in the corner, most likely a toilet, an addition probably built years after the original building. Near the stairs, a gramophone rests on a stand, and above it, a wooden crucifix, the head of its gold-paint Christ slumped to the side.

Her heart bumps. The stairs and a window on the other wall are the only ways out. She feels trapped, gasping for air under a bell jar.

The boy swallows the last of the biscuit and starts to cry. Instinctively she reaches out to him, but pauses, and withdraws her hand. She looks to the ceiling, helpless, as the child wails. The sound goes through her, and her lungs contract with an agonizing jolt.

From below, there's the solid ring of a cash register and the tinny sound of the shop bell again, then footsteps tramping up the stairs.

Her brain groans to a halt.

André sees his son's distress. "What's wrong, *mon petit chou*?" He picks up a hand puppet from a chair, a home-made Guignol, and shows it to the boy who instantly stops crying. "Magic!" André tells the woman.

He gives the puppet to Frédéric and goes to the window. "She must be held up by one of Madame Pelletier's stories." He breathes out a tiny sigh. "That woman could trap a wild boar with her tales."

André spots the empty bowl. He takes it to the stove, ladles more ragoût, and places it in front of her again. "Just a bit longer. I must see what's become of my wife."

He looks at Frédéric to see if the woman's presence is upsetting him, but the boy seems content now. But when André lifts his son up, he lets out a godawful screech. When Frédéric doesn't want to do something, he can be as stubborn as a red wine stain. André lets him back down. Yes, like Mireille always says, he gives in too easily. For always choosing appeasement over conflict, she jokingly calls him "Neville." André doesn't find it amusing since she's no better when it comes to indulging their son.

The woman looks harmless enough, more shell-shocked than anything else. Customers, strangers even, leave their children with them all the time to pop into another shop. It never concerns Mireille—she never refuses. "A town's only as small as its people."

Anyway, he'll only be gone a few minutes. There's a peculiar tug in André's gut. What if that's what Mireille thought?

"Did you see her? When you came in? A woman your height?" He scours the woman's face, but the only thing he finds are her eyes, dark-circled and unblinking, looking back. She gives a slight shake of her head. Should he believe her? That's the thing: either you believe nothing out of a stranger's mouth or everything.

A stench reaches him. He thinks it's cream gone rancid, and is about to check on it, when he identifies the putrefying odour of human excrement. André turns his head so the woman doesn't see the reaction he has no control over.

He could offer her the perfume he bought for Mireille's birthday, but that would be an insult as well, no?

An idea comes to him. He roots around in the armoire. When he emerges, he holds up a light blue flowered dress, the one Mireille wears to the park on Sundays. Her lucky dress.

"You should wash and change. Mireille will insist. You should get out of that before..." He can't bring himself to list the possible consequences. "If you want," he adds, and lays the dress on the bed.

André turns and catches her sliding another biscuit to Frédéric.

"Stay clear of the window." André moves to the stairs and takes the first step, then turns to her again. "I'm André. May I know your name?"

The woman merely stirs the contents of the bowl, so André starts down the stairs again.

"Émilie," she says softly, as though afraid he'll hear. "I'm called Émilie."

André pauses in case she has something else to say, but there's only silence again. He continues on, leaving echoes of his footsteps behind.

In the pâtisserie, he opens the front door. As much as it pains him to lose what little business they have, he turns the sign around to FERMÉ and steps outside.

The broom Mireille was using that morning leans against the building. André's insides tilt towards panic. He scans the street for her, but there are only passersby, none of whom pay him any attention. The two shopkeepers are no longer there.

André puts the broom inside the door and crosses the street.

Émilie is still eating when Frédéric starts to cry again. She tries to ignore him, but he doesn't stop, so she sets down the spoon and stares into the bowl, telling herself over and over it'll end soon enough and his father will be back any time now.

The boy's crying stabs into her head. "Shh. Shh," she says, but with no effect. She tries to collect her thoughts. She has to keep moving. They have to be looking for her.

She stands and wraps her arms around herself, shaking ever so slightly as chills dart down her spine. Only monsters deny comfort to a child. After taking a few deep breaths, she reaches out and touches his hand. He only wails louder.

Émilie looks to the stairs, desperate for the baker's return, and spots the puppet on the floor. She winces when she has to use her injured hand to slip it on, then wiggles it in front of him.

"*Bonjour*. What's your name?" she asks in a high-pitched voice. His crying quiets to sobs as he searches for her face hiding behind the puppet. Émilie manages a cautious smile, sits at the table again, and attempts to eat with her damaged hand.

How long will it be before the baker turns her in?

While he was searching for the dress, out of the corner of her eye Émilie looked at his reflection in the full-length mirror hanging inside the armoire's door. She hadn't really seen him until then, only daring a glance or two. Thick black hair, short on the sides, a bit longer on top, and longer still in front so a lock of it falls over his forehead. Broad shoulders supported by a slim but healthy build, the type she hasn't seen in a long while. He has a kind face, and when he paused to push the lock of hair away, she also saw kind eyes. She'd forgotten how humanity can be reflected in someone's expression. The faces she sees are angry, or terrified, or hate-filled, or defeated.

When Émilie finishes eating, she licks the spoon. Suddenly she can't remember what she was thinking about. Having her mind empty as a shattered bowl panics her for a moment, a tourniquet squeezing her heart.

There's knocking downstairs, and she goes cold. She detests that familiar growl of fear poised to maul her. Will she ever be free from it? She waits motionless, hoping whomever's there goes away.

More knocking. She pulls off the puppet with a stab of pain, scrambles to the window, and peeks out.

A postman is outside, a bag of letters slung over his shoulder, an envelope in his hand. When there's no answer, he glances up at the window.

Émilie steps back against the wall and struggles for breath. In the glass, she notices the yellow badge on her work uniform.

She rips it off.

Across the street, André raps on a door leading to the flats above. Impatient, he knocks again.

"Madame Pelletier? It's André Albert." Nothing. "Madame Pelletier?" Still nothing. He waits a few moments more, but no one comes to the door. Bewilderment edges into concern, but he tamps it down. Nothing bad ever happens to them. Not anymore. There has to be a reasonable explanation.

As he trudges back to the shop, a man his age walking a bicycle bids him "*Bonjour*," but André doesn't respond. His breathing stops with the force of a hammer against an anvil.

He's spotted something.

Oblivious of an oncoming motorcar, André steps into the street—he doesn't even flinch when the vehicle sounds its horn—and picks up a white apron.

FOUR

Émilie perches on the lip of the bathtub and undoes the rag from around her head, exposing her matted hair. She tries to separate the dark strands with little success. A chunk comes out in her hand—now there's even less of her. How's that possible? Her hair used to be so long, it disturbs her to feel the air chill her neck like a finger's running across it. Bumps rise on her trembling body.

With her good hand, she scoops water out of a bucket and pours it over her arm, its simplicity a forgotten sensation that's new again. She undresses, and washes quickly as though such luxury will be ripped from her at any moment.

She puts on the dress and stares at herself in the armoire's mirror with a mix of anxiety and surprise, not recognizing the figure before her. A woman who owns such a dress must've danced at many happy occasions.

Émilie sits beside Frédéric on the small bed while he naps. Her face contorts slightly, trying to comprehend the concept of a child sleeping peacefully. She reaches out to touch his forehead, but stops herself, and her hand hangs in the air like an unanswered question. The boy stirs. She pulls her hand away.

The shop bell rings and heavy footsteps crash up the stairs. Émilie staggers to her feet, arms raised, ready to defend herself, when André walks in.

The baker ignores her as he takes the ledger from the table and puts it in one of the buffet's drawers. He shuffles to the stove, removes the pot's cover, and peers in.

"Have you had enough to eat?"

"Yes, Monsieur."

"Where will you go? Your home? Your family? Where are they?"

Émilie looks down and smooths a wrinkle from the dress. There's the distinct scent of lilacs. "This is lovely. I can't take such a nice garment, Monsieur." She expects him to change his mind about having given away his wife's clothes, but he continues staring into the pot.

"Thank you," she whispers. She's stayed too long. There's no reason to postpone the inevitable.

Émilie descends the stairs as though sleepwalking, the fingers of her good hand rubbing along the banister.

At the front door, she stops when she sees the activity on the street—passing silhouettes in the dusk. She walks to the alley door instead, about to slip out, when footsteps drum nearer from behind her.

"Do you have food? Money? Of course not." André takes some coins from a solid brass cash register beside the display case, puts pastries in a box he pulls from the bottom of the display, and holds them out to her. "It's not much."

Émilie sees his brow furrow as he examines her unkempt hair. When he looks down, his eyes widen as if only noticing his wife's dress on her.

"It suits you." His mouth tightens like he regrets saying it, probably an attempt to make amends for how he treated her when he discovered she's Jewish.

André looks around and spots a kerchief on the worktable and adds it to the items. "Here." He offers them to her again and nods reassuringly. After a moment's more hesitation, Émilie takes them.

She glances at the door and the grey figures passing by outside. It's not that she doesn't want to go, she just doesn't know where to go. If there was a map, she'd drop her finger on it and be on her way.

André follows her gaze out the window. "At least you can blend in dressed like that." He sounds less convinced when he adds, "It might be helpful if you also wear Mireille's coat and hat."

Émilie waits, but when he doesn't go for them, she still doesn't move to leave. North, south, east, west. None of them lead anywhere she wants to be.

"Maybe after curfew would be better?" André asks tentatively. Then in a flood he says, "There must be people who can help you. We can wait for Mireille, she knows everyone, she'll know what to do. She won't stand for this, Jew or not."

Émilie feels herself go light-headed as she weighs her decision. She's long since passed trusting her own judgment. Only one thing keeps repeating in her head: Flee. Get out of here and go far away as possible.

Above them, Frédéric starts crying. André gives her a sympathetic smile. "*Bon retour.*"

At the stairs, he pauses, but doesn't turn around. "Madame Pelletier... No one was there. I don't— She's a shut-in. The woman never goes out, not since her husband died. Mireille calls her a lonely caged bird."

He pulls out an apron from his jacket. "It's my wife's. I found it in the street. This was in the pocket." He takes out the sardine can and stares at both items.

Without another word, André treks back up the stairs.

André watches Frédéric eat. It's past the time when the boy's mother should've been back from wherever she is. This thought sinks him, driving him through the floor, and the floor below that, into the ground.

Émilie walks in and sets the things he gave her before him. Why did he suggest she wait until night to leave? He motions to a chair and slides a bowl of ragoût over.

"I must go to the police before curfew." When Émilie twitches, he hastily adds, "I won't mention you, of course." Not looking reassured, she dips a spoon in the bowl but doesn't eat.

He's been postponing going to the police, hoping Mireille will walk in any moment and tease him for needlessly worrying. But that no longer seems likely. He has no choice but to risk involving the authorities and all they might bring. He should've gone first thing.

"I'll keep the shop closed. Will you mind Frédéric?" André turns to his son and says with as much lightness as he can, "Eat up, *mon fils*. Maman will be pleased you've been such a good boy."

The child waves his spoon like they're playing.

André waits for one of the policemen going about his duties to come over and speak with him. The room reeks of Gitanes and underarms. He clears his throat, causing a lanky, red-faced gendarme to begrudgingly heave himself up from a desk and make his way to the counter.

"I want to report someone missing."

"Missing, Monsieur?" the man asks, already tired of their conversation. "Who? Nowadays, people go missing all the time."

"Mireille Albert. My wife. She works in our shop—the Pâtisserie Saint-Léry—and when I returned from buying ingredients, she was gone."

"Gone, Monsieur? Or ran away?"

André's face screws up.

"It's not unheard of." The gendarme's eyes narrow. "How long have you been married?"

"Almost seven years."

"There are cases when one week is enough," the policeman says with growing impatience. He stands straighter so he looms over André even more.

"I— No. We've never passed a cross word between us."

"That's often worse. An anger that simmers."

André's blood thickens at the implication, but before he can protest, behind them a muffled voice with a distinct German accent interjects. "Is there a problem?"

A short, pale, slob of a man a decade older than André walks over. He's not wearing a jacket, and he holds his black cap between his teeth while he tucks in his shirttails.

"A wife has run away," the gendarme tells him, taking out a large ledger.

"Not Mireille!" André never heard something so ridiculous.

The German removes the cap from his mouth and puts it on. He stands at attention before speaking again. "I'm sure. I'm sure. But we must investigate to be certain, *ja*? I'm quite adept at that—I've received commendations." He looks to the gendarme for a reaction. The man glances up from consulting scribbled entries and dutifully feigns being impressed.

The Nazi extends a hand to André, and they shake. "Hauptsturmführer Egger. Where did you say this was? Pâtisserie..."

"Saint-Léry."

The gendarme shuts the ledger. "She hasn't been arrested."

Egger gives a smug grin. "Well, then," he says.

He waits for André to leave, but André keeps standing there. It takes a second for Egger to realize what he's after. "Oh! No, this is a dreary little town. There have been no reports of anyone being detained by us yesterday. Definitely not a woman." Egger pauses and the corners of his mouth droop. "She hasn't done something she shouldn't have, has she?"

"Impossible! My wife is honest as a mirror."

"So it's off to Pâtisserie Saint-Léry then. I must confess to having a sweet tooth myself. We'll start there."

"Pardon?"

"The pâtisserie. You say your wife is missing under mysterious circumstances, *ja*? She hasn't run off with a man, for instance? No offense."

"I don't—" A man? That depraved suggestion wrings André's heart. Is this German making these wild accusations to provoke him?

"It's natural we begin a search. Perhaps there's been foul play of some sort." Egger gives the policeman a look showing how much he relishes toying with André. "But that's a very different matter. Very different."

The three men find themselves in a standoff waiting for one of them to yield. But André won't give in. It's Mireille they're talking about.

Finally, the gendarme shrugs. "Or she has run off, Monsieur."

Egger nods in agreement. "It happens. Much too often. Especially when there are soldiers about. German soldiers. We're known for our virility."

A phone rings on the gendarme's desk, shrill and insistent, but the policeman doesn't so much as register having heard it. "I know it's difficult to accept of one's wife." A lewd grin spreads across his long face.

"Or oneself. A man has his pride, after all." Egger raises an eyebrow.

André clenches his fists at his side and the tendons in his legs strain as he readies himself to lunge at the Nazi. One more vile insinuation. Just one more.

The bloody phone continues to ring, and it takes all André has to focus his anger on how much he hates that noise.

Egger's voice sheds its friendly tone. "Maybe you would prefer some time to think before—"

André scoffs. "She's a mother! This is her home. She wouldn't abandon us." The muscles in his face go rigid. "Certainly not for a German—"

Any good humour Egger has bursts. He seizes André by the shirt. Instinctively, André grabs hold of the man's arm, ready to fight back if he has to.

"Surely you are not defaming the German Reich?" Egger spits the words at the tip of André's nose.

André glares at the man, fire blazing in his eyes. Then out of nowhere, Egger releases him. All the German offers is a patronizing smile and "We shall investigate."

André takes the apron from his pocket as proof of the urgency of what he's telling them. "It was in the street." He shows them the torn neck strap—sickening him again at what it means.

"We shall look into it," Egger announces with finality.

The matter closed, the gendarme returns to his desk and, at last, answers the phone.

André searches for something more to say, something to convince the Nazi to take his wife's disappearance seriously, but words elude him. All he can get out is a wheeze from deep in his lungs.

Egger makes a show of consulting his watch. "You have very little time. Very little." But André can't move. "The curfew," Egger cautions him, saying each word deliberately and with some heat.

"But it's at least an hour until—"

"You French should be early to bed. Perhaps then your women wouldn't stray." The German speaks with the exaggerated slowness of someone who's sure they're talking to an imbecile. When André remains there, stubborn as a fact, Egger scowls at him, daring him to push the matter further.

The gendarme puts down the phone and strides back to them, excited to see the argument continuing.

André's body sags. It was idiotic to assume he'd find any help here. He shoves the apron back in his jacket and leaves, the two men's laughter hounding him out the door.

He stumbles into an alley and vomits. Mireille's gone. He has to get her back. But where to begin? André wipes his mouth, pulls out the apron again, and looks at it in torment.

When André comes home from the police station, he finds an anxious Émilie waiting at the table. He checks on Frédéric asleep in his and Mireille's bed, and barely hears Émilie say, "He stayed up as long as he could."

André watches his son's face that's calm as a stone. Doesn't he realize his mother's not here? One of the boy's hands is curled near his head, the thumb extended towards his mouth. Mireille had recently coaxed him away from the habit by making a game out of it. She has a knack for transforming tears into delight. The rare times Frédéric laughs, it's a loud noise out of such a quiet boy, hearty and full as any child can produce. There's no sound more amazing.

He kisses his son on the forehead and drags the folding screen from next to the bathtub to between the two beds, for solitude and propriety's sake. He undresses, lies down beside Frédéric, and stares at the ceiling, but finds no answers there.

The rest of the night, André imagines scenarios where Mireille could leave them, willingly or not, and even more where she returns.

FIVE

Wednesday, October 20, 1943

André stares out the window at passersby and shopkeepers carrying on like it's just another day. By the time he got out of bed, all the other businesses on the street had opened, the first time that's happened for as long as he and Mireille have had the pâtisserie. He didn't bother to wake Frédéric and Émilie. Better they not face what today's going to hold.

He couldn't sleep. He went over and over in his mind possible explanations for why his wife wasn't here to wake up beside him. Any reasons he came up with felt equally cruel. Since their wedding, they've never spent a night apart.

Across the street, the butcher teases a stray dog with a bone, while nearby a woman pouts, no doubt disappointed the bone wasn't already in a pot of her soup at home. The florist pulls dead petals from the flowers in the bucket outside his shop and lets them fall to the ground where the breeze tumbles them away. The bread baker stands in his doorway gnawing on a brioche, watching with unmasked lust a shapely woman on a bicycle pedalling past. God knows where the man found flour or the money to buy it.

But for André, everything is flat. Out of habit, he turns around the sign to OUVERT, even though there's nothing to sell since he hasn't baked. How can he? Without Mireille, what's the point? That question keeps exploding behind his eyes.

When he's about to turn the sign back, Monsieur Durand

appears in the window waving a wrapped packet and a book. André looks blankly at him as his brain catches up.

"My ration." Monsieur Durand mouths the words. André opens the door and the bookseller passes him the packet. "Sugar for your magnificent—"

"No, Monsieur." While it's a valuable find, the old man likely got it on the black market. André always scolds him for such illegal dealings, but Mireille makes him take the ingredients anyway. Now he doesn't have to be so obliging.

He tries to give the packet back, but Monsieur Durand waves a hand. "Please. I insist. What would an old man do with such luxuries?" He shows André the cover of the book, a colourful drawing of zoo animals. "It's the one Mireille wanted for Frédéric. Indeed, it's a wild tale of—"

"Have you seen her?" André's words flow out in a rush. "Mireille. Did she come to you?" He hopes to hear Monsieur Durand tell him some welcome news, but the old man's mouth gapes then snaps shut. André recognizes his own pain in his friend's expression—he's just as lost.

"Forgive me, Monsieur." André closes the door to the bookseller's surprise.

Monsieur Durand remains there, his perplexed face framed in the door's window, as André turns the sign to FERMÉ.

André climbs the stairs and finds Émilie kneeling by the bathtub washing Frédéric while the boy splashes. The woman is being so tender with him, it suddenly angers André.

He pulls his son from the tub and holds him tightly to his chest. Perhaps too tightly—the child struggles to be let down. The boy's hair is shiny clean and his skin's bright as a cherub's—a major achievement given how much Frédéric hates baths.

"I-I was..." Émilie tries to explain. "He made a mess. I just thought..." She glances up at him, but he looks away. "It's good for a father to be protective of his child."

"He needs his mother." He gives Frédéric back to her and sits down at the table. "I finally spoke to Madame Pelletier," André mutters, more to himself than Émilie. "She doesn't know anything. Or so she says."

Émilie wraps Frédéric in a towel and carries him to his bed. She helps him into his pajamas and entertains him with the puppet. She wiggles the Guignol in front of the boy, but his expression only brightens a shade in response. André looks away.

"She wouldn't leave me. Us. She lives for that boy. It's not..." He pauses to check if Frédéric is listening and lowers his voice to ask, "Was she talking to someone? Was she with a man?"

Émilie lays the puppet in her lap and pulls a loose thread on its little red coat. She starts to break it off, but stops, and slowly shakes her head.

He slams his fist on the table and thunders over to her. "You had to've seen her. Did she let you in?" He raises his fist.

Émilie looks at him, not flinching at his intimidation. Her defiance surprises him. Compared to yesterday, she's not so meek. And it aggravates him even more.

"So help me God," André spits. "I will turn you in to them if you don't—"

She grabs his wrist and pulls his fist close to her face. "Go ahead. If that will be punishment enough for me being here."

Frédéric's lower lip trembles and he starts to blubber. He's scaring him. André breaks loose from her hold and slinks back to the table, his legs unsteady. He's scaring himself. What is he doing? This isn't him.

Émilie gently rubs Frédéric's back in circles to calm him. "Shh. Shh." The child clambers onto her lap and burrows into her shoulder.

"The door was open," she says softly. "The one from the alley." André stops breathing to better hear what's next. "No one was here."

He waits for Émilie to say more, but she looks down at the puppet, and with a yank, snaps the stray thread. Seeing she's no help, he thuds down the stairs.

André crosses to the front door and scrutinizes the street. It's infuriatingly no different from any other day. How can people carry on with their lives when there's only confusion?

He throws open the door and steams out. Who should he ask that he hasn't already? Coming back from the gendarmerie yesterday, André knocked on every door on the street, but no one knew where his wife was. He'll knock on every door on the street again, in the entire town, if he has to. He scours the buildings opposite, desperate for a sign. A clue. An omen even.

The sky over the roofs hold nothing but the harsh absence of clouds mirroring the piercing emptiness inside him.

Émilie waits until noon for the baker to return so she can thank him before she leaves, but when he doesn't come back, she plods downstairs. Frédéric follows her into the pâtisserie. Should she leave him alone? He seems to read her mind, and starts to mewl and stretch out his arms, opening and closing his fingers. He must be hungry. She carries him back up and finds him some bread and cheese he eats with the emotions of a mannequin.

She sits next to him on the bed as he amuses himself with the puppet. She probes her damaged hand with her fingers, winces, but doesn't stop. When she was bathing him, she realized Frédéric hadn't said anything. Except for crying, he's a quiet child. She's the last person to fault him for that. Sometimes silence is the deep breath your soul takes. But not a word? She had wanted to ask André about it, but didn't know how to broach the subject, particularly not with the mood he was in. She can always ask how old the boy is. She guesses three, but something in his eyes makes her think he's older—he looks like he has the wherewithal to find his way out of tall grass, a thing adults used to say about her when she was younger. The boy could just be small for his age and lacking proper food like so many children are these days.

Any possible discussion about Frédéric ended when André slammed his fist. He's so different from yesterday. His threat to turn her in may not be an idle one. She could be in jeopardy; she needs to move on. Her deliberations about Frédéric not speaking are only distracting her from having to figure out where she'll go.

When André asked her if there was someone who could help, Émilie thought of the Brihah in Poland and Hungary who organize the escape of Jews to Palestine, but she's never heard of them in France. How can she even begin to find them?

There's knocking from below. She freezes and her breath knots.

More knocking, insistent now. It echoes up the stairs, deepening as it travels, until it booms through the room.

Émilie creeps down to the shop. On the last step, she peeks out and sees an old man peering in through the window in the front door.

She jumps back.

Monsieur Durand shields his eyes, trying again to glimpse the unfamiliar woman he's just spotted inside. Despite the sign saying FERMÉ, he reaches for the handle to let himself in when he's startled by a voice behind him saying his name. He spins around, sees André and reddens, embarrassed at being caught.

"My apologies. I was worried. You're shut on a Wednesday. Has something happened? Is it Frédéric? Is Mireille—"

"She's gone away for a while."

"But just now—"

"If you don't mind, Monsieur." Any passion the baker had in his tone that morning has dried up.

"I saw a strange woman on the stairs."

André unlocks the door and goes in. "You were mistaken." He starts to close the door.

Monsieur Durand puts his hand out to stop him. This doesn't make sense. He's never known André to be untruthful. If asked, Monsieur Durand would wager his own reputation on the younger man's impeachable one. But he knows what he just saw: a woman on the stairs who isn't Mireille.

"What's going on, André?" Monsieur Durand's hand stays rooted on the door. The baker looks at it as if willing it to disintegrate.

Small feet scamper above them, and both men look to the ceiling. André tries to shut the door again, but Durand says, "Would a mother leave her child behind? Would Mireille leave Frédéric?"

André weighs the situation.

His face drops, then he opens the door wider.

Monsieur Durand moves his feet out of the way of the route Frédéric is traveling on the floor with a woodblock truck. He sits across from Émilie at the table, André between them at its head. Anyone not acquainted with the circumstance would be forgiven in presuming they're about to play a dire *jeu de cartes*. Fittingly, their expressions give nothing away.

"A strange affair indeed," Monsieur Durand says as his opening bid.

André's jaw clenches. "I've asked everyone, but no one will tell me anything."

"That's not surprising. It's difficult to answer when intentions are unclear. Who knows the reason why you're asking? Or for whom?" Monsieur Durand refrains from adding that the wrong word uttered to the wrong person has caused tongues to be excised. But surely his dear friend knows this. If he didn't before, he does now.

André disappears behind the folding screen. When he reappears, he places a ball before them on the table: Mireille's apron. "It was on the street."

"The street?" Monsieur Durand spreads it on the table, waiting for an explanation, but André turns away. "Maybe there's been an accident? Have you been to the—"

"No! She's not— She can't be!"

"She may be hurt."

All at once such a possibility appears to crush André. His eyes dart wildly and his face blanches in horror. "What if she's..." The question dries up in his mouth. He cannot say out loud what must be his worst fear. "What do I do without her? What will the boy..." André shakes his head. "No! I have to find her."

He looks over at Frédéric who's watching, his face growing concerned. Seeing his father give him a tight-lipped nod, the boy resumes pushing his truck to its destination. The child's innocence cuts Monsieur Durand to the marrow.

"I'll make enquiries. Someone must know something and is willing to tell." Monsieur Durand turns to Émilie. "And you? Ending up here out of nowhere?" He tries to decipher her, and she quickly looks away. He feels his brow wrinkle. "You're Jewish," he says cautiously.

Émilie gauges him with suspicion. And rightly so. A stranger is of no more consequence than a fly flitting past.

André gives her a small nod, and she answers, "Yes."

"So you're what he's been hiding." Monsieur Durand huffs with frustration at their predicament. A dear friend is missing, and a Jewish woman turns up here. While he's a firm believer in the existence of balance in nature, this is absurd.

Émilie lifts her head, waiting for his verdict, looking resigned to whatever it is.

Monsieur Durand looks at the bruise below her eye, but thinks better of asking about it. He's not unaware of the hate targeting these people, convinced it prospers in failed societies where lies go undisputed. It's women like her who bear the brunt of it.

"She has no one," André tells him, more apology than explanation.

"No one? What a distressing condition to be the sole word on a page." Monsieur Durand leans towards her in his chair. "Then we must whisk you away from here. That won't be an easy matter." He leans back. "No family? Hmm."

"I have a family." Émilie takes a long swallow of air. "A mother. A father." She flinches almost imperceptibly. She's regretting telling them. Who are they to hear of her loved ones?

How can they understand? They're not Jewish; they're not seen as enemies.

Silence overtakes them. Monsieur Durand hopes she sees his and André's empathy. Too often people's compassion sits below the surface, profoundly felt but seldom acted upon.

Then, with a sigh, Émilie starts again. "We were taken together to Drancy." She lowers her eyes, and repositioning herself in her chair, traces the table's woodgrain with her index finger.

"And you ran off? So I see." Monsieur Durand looks at André who blinks, his forehead creasing just above the bridge of his nose.

"I was healthy and had a skill. They made me work in a factory sewing uniforms, flags, banners, dresses for their women."

"Ah, you're a seamstress."

"Yes, Monsieur." She looks up at them, a tiny light dances in her eyes. "Before the war I worked in an *atelier* in Paris, but the couturière closed her shop. It was no longer a time for fashion. They were taking me to the trains with the others who were no longer of use."

"And back to Drancy?" Monsieur Durand prompts. Looking at her face, he can tell something ghastly must have happened.

"Perhaps."

"A detention centre for undesirables," he explains to André. Realizing the insult, he turns back to her. "Apologies, Mademoiselle. I meant no offense."

"There are worse places than Drancy." The spark in her eyes goes out. She looks about to speak again when André interrupts.

"Your hand. I didn't realize you were hurt."

Émilie follows their gaze to her damaged hand, now on the table. "I got too close to a machine weaving the material they need, and my hand was caught in its belt." She hides it under the table. "I was feeling faint. I was careless. They told me I was lucky my arm wasn't torn from its socket, as though I'd won a prize. I assured them over and over I could go on working, but they still sent me away."

"May I?" Monsieur Durand reaches for her hand, but Émilie covers it protectively. After a moment, she reluctantly allows him to take it, barely suppressing a wince when he touches it. Monsieur Durand tuts. "It might be broken. It should be seen to. And your eye..." Her eyebrows arch as if not knowing what he's talking about.

"We must send for the doctor." André springs to his feet, ready to go for help.

"No!"

Émilie's plea stops them. Monsieur Durand is about to argue her hand needs to be attended to, when he remembers there are realities of the times they can't ignore. Too many doctors have been called who, when they left, slithered to the Germans to secrete what they've seen or heard. That kind of scum are even commended for providing the medical attention that ensures their patient is well enough to meet a firing squad.

"We can wrap it and hope for the best."

André sits down again, more defeated than before.

Monsieur Durand looks from Émilie to André and back again.

"Two lost souls."

At the front door, André speaks quietly with Monsieur Durand. It's dark and the street's empty, the bells of Saint-Joachim having rung moments before announcing the nine o'clock curfew, tolling the end of their existence for another day.

"Be strong, *mon ami*." The bookseller rests a hand on André's shoulder. "Mireille will be back soon, of this I'm certain. Will you open tomorrow?"

"I-I don't——" Finding answers to questions like this will only clutter his mind.

"Open. Force yourself if you must. Keep this the place you want to welcome her home to." The old man gives André's shoulder a squeeze and scans the street. With a slight tip of his hat as his goodbye, he heads home.

André watches him unlock the bookstore and slip inside. Monsieur Durand's friendship has been one of the greatest blessings André has known since he came to Saint-Léry d'Espoir—a welcome steadying influence. If someone had asked, André would have said he didn't know why he hadn't gone to his friend straight away. But that's not true. He was going to go to Monsieur Durand for help, but that decision was carved away by a razor-edge of doubt whispering Mireille had left him on her own, just like the gendarme and that Nazi had insinuated. Maybe not alone. The humiliation of even thinking that was overwhelming. He was terrified his all-knowing friend would tell him it was true.

Mireille will be back soon, but for now he needs the steadiness his friend offers, if not for him, then for Frédéric.

Shutting the door, André glimpses a sliver of light from the window above the *boucherie*. A curtain's been pushed aside, and he can make out the silhouette of someone peering at him.

André continues looking until the light disappears.

SIX

Thursday, October 21, 1943

Another morning where André reaches deep in the bag of flour with a scoop and tips its contents into a bowl. But today he pauses, and seconds melt into minutes.

"Monsieur?" Émilie is at the stairs, her hair hidden by Mireille's work kerchief. She looks warily towards the windows.

"Can I be of help?"

"It isn't necessary," André snaps, and returns to his task.

"But I must repay your kindness."

"You're hurt." It's an excuse. It's better if he carries on with preparations on his own, difficult as he's finding it. By now, Mireille would be next to him, and together they'd be baking. André is not sure he'll be able to finish the last touches alone, he hasn't the heart for it.

When he doesn't hear Émilie go back up, he glances over. She holds up her freshly bandaged hand and shrugs.

"Yes, okay," he says with a sigh.

Again, Émilie looks to the windows as two schoolgirls skip by.

"Never mind them. No one will guess you're a Jew, not dressed like that. People will assume you're someone we hired." André couldn't be less worried about her now—he's busy trying to contain the turmoil churning within him. But so what if his emotions run amok? Who is he sparing by keeping them in check?

Émilie walks over, quickening her pace as she crosses by the windows.

"The old man knew."

"He's not easily fooled." André passes her an apron and places a large bowl in front of her. "Just stay back here and don't speak to anyone."

He instructs her how to make madeleines in an even but vacant tone. It takes every crumb of his self-control not to scream out in frustration. André passes Émilie a wooden spoon and watches her vigourously fold the mixtures with her bandaged hand while using her good one to hold the bowl secure on the table. She winces with every stroke.

"Not so rough. It's done you no harm." He takes the spoon and demonstrates. "Gentle. Show it you care." He hands back the spoon. "Two more minutes."

He remembers how pleased Mireille was when she persuaded her father to teach André all his tricks of the trade. Once she was the one at her father's side learning. It was only a week ago when Mireille, in an uncharacteristically maudlin mood after climbing into bed, told André how appreciative she was they were keeping her father's spirit alive. So moved by that sentiment, André could only grunt in reply.

The bell rings when Monsieur Durand walks in. André hastens over to meet his friend by the empty display case. Right away, André asks, "Have you heard anything?"

"How are you, Mademoiselle?" the old bookseller calls over to Émilie. She nods, not missing a beat in her rhythm. He turns back to André. "I see you have her working. Good. And will there be pastries today?"

"It's the last of the flour." Impatient for an answer to his question, André cracks his knuckles. It sounds like dry twigs breaking.

"Then I'll have to find more in my travels. There's a widow on the next street who's taken to me." Monsieur Durand chuckles. "See? There's always hope." He glances over at Émilie again. She swipes her brow with an arm and carries on working.

André tugs at his foulard like it's strangling him. "Monsieur, have you heard?"

The old man hesitates before saying, "Not a thing."

André deflates like a soufflé.

Monsieur Durand gives André's shoulder a pat, and André averts his eyes, unable to stand even this simple act of intimacy. He doesn't need sympathy. Mireille will be back.

"André, there may be certain truths you must—"

"No! I'm going to find her."

"Of course. We mustn't give up, but we must be careful whom we ask." The bookseller lowers his voice. "I believe the busy-body across the way—Madame Bujold—has seen something. She has said as much. While her declaration was more a cipher than a confession, I could tell she was keeping something back, something was weighing heavily on her."

André's muscles tense so tightly, he might as well be in a straightjacket. Yesterday, when he went to the neighbours asking about Mireille, no one was home at the woman's flat. "Then I have to speak to her." He rips off his apron and hurries to the front door and yanks it open. A passing woman, pushing a pram without a baby in it, startles at the abruptness and quickly trundles away.

"André! Wait." Monsieur Durand grasps his arm before he can run out. André stares up at Madame Bujold's apartment, willing the window to fly apart and the old hag to float out and cackle what she knows.

"She's afraid." His friend's voice becomes louder. "She won't breathe a word, not a word. But I have her confidence. She'll tell me soon enough."

André turns to him. "Soon?" He moves his mouth as though there's something acrid on his tongue. He wants to growl back that any lapse of time, no matter how short, is torture. Forget soon. He aches to hear now.

Monsieur Durand attempts to lead him back to the display, but André wrenches away and bolts out of the shop. If Bujold knows, she'll have to tell. Surely she can be reasoned with.

Monsieur Durand dashes out after him. "André! André!

Listen. Don't be rash. You must think these things—"

In a second, André is across the street and taking the stairs in twos to the flats above.

The old man follows him into the building and struggles to keep up. "Don't make trouble," he shouts. "There are other ways to contend with such matters."

Already at the landing, André rattles the door with his fist. "Madame Bujold!" There's movement in the flat. "Madame Bujold! It's me. André Albert. From the pâtisserie."

A woman's thin voice hisses, "Go away. Leave us alone."

André knocks on the door again and tries the handle.

Monsieur Durand reaches him and tugs on his sleeve. "Come away. They'll call the gendarmes."

André ignores him and bellows, "Madame, if you know where Mireille is—"

The door flings open and from her wheelchair Madame Bujold scowls at him, so old and frail she's folding into herself. The smell of damp and stale sweat hits André, then the over-powering medicinal odour of balms and ointments. His nose creases in disgust. The sewers give off a more bearable aroma.

Before André can say anything, the woman's son, all muscles and rage, flies out. He grabs hold of André, and they grapple on the narrow landing. Their bodies lurch one way, then the other.

The woman's son crashes into Monsieur Durand, who only just keeps from tumbling down the stairs. The old man presses his back against the wall and raises a hand in a futile attempt to stop the fight.

André fends off two quick jabs to the face, but the third smacks him squarely in the cheek. It rattles him, but barely hurts. Adrenaline courses through his veins. He swings hard and hits the man in the nose, knocking him into the wall next to Monsieur Durand. The bookseller's eyebrows shoot up when Bujold's son wipes blood away with his hand, smearing it to his ear.

André's fists hang there, his lips curled back, his teeth bared. With a roar, the man charges him, pushing him down the stairs.

"Here we mind our own business," the old woman's son says triumphantly. "You'll get us killed."

André bounds up the steps, still full of fight, but Bujold's son retreats into the flat and slams the door with a finality even André with all his determination can't doubt.

Anger still burns around André's pupils, and he breathes in quick gasps. He steels his shoulders to cave in the door, but Monsieur Durand blocks his way. He takes André's head in his hands and turns it towards him.

"What are you doing? This isn't what Mireille would want." The bookseller's touch is warm and comforting.

"What would she want then? To do nothing?"

Monsieur Durand keeps his palms firmly planted on André's cheeks, and reason returns to him like he's been miraculously healed of a fever.

André pushes past his old friend. What's the use? No amount of punches will make that ratface Bujold talk. He bursts out of the building into the path of a workman carrying a tool bag. The man gawks at André as he staggers to the middle of the street, disheveled and bloody, and glares up at the Bujolds' window. With a shake of his head at the insanity of it all, the workman carries on.

Monsieur Durand battles to regain his breath as André frantically searches the street.

"You know," André yells. His nostrils dilate and blood hammers in his brain. A type of madness takes hold of him—a combination of grief and anger and self-pity. He's fierce and helpless in quick succession. Nothing can restrain him, nothing can stand in his way, yet he's lost and without direction. "You have to know." His voice rises hysterically. "Why won't you tell me?"

He yells again, something nearer to a roar than anything intelligible.

By now, the street's almost deserted; the last few people take off in opposite directions. Monsieur Durand tries to pull André away, but he doesn't budge.

"Where is she?" André screams at no one other than the

world.

His words rumble along the street and reverberate through the alley beside the pâtisserie.

As the sun sets, red and yellow like rose petals thrown in the air, shops close, lights snap off, and blackout curtains are drawn.

André watches from the front door, his arms hanging at his sides, as shadows lengthen, blurring the features of the buildings across the street. Only then does he turn the sign to FERMÉ and lock the door. Another day wasted. All he can smell is the vinegar Mireille uses to clean the windows. His face aches, the bruise on his cheek throbs, and pain pierces him like fishhooks. Not all because of Bujold's son.

He only wanted to ask a question. True as that is, it feels hollow now in light of how he acted. He shouldn't have been so aggressive—the man was just protecting his mother. André's heartbeat slows to a tick. But he won't apologize for what he has to do to find Mireille.

In the preparation area, Émilie cleans the worktable, and Frédéric sits on a chair eating one of the unsold pastries she baked. André wasn't much help—he spouted some more instructions, threw out a few choice swear words when Émilie made a mistake, and stormed upstairs in frustration. A few hours later when he came back down, less agitated mostly because time had passed, there were a dozen madeleines waiting. He tested one, and while it wasn't perfect—it lacked that crucial taste of almonds, but that wasn't her fault if they had none—it was better than nothing. Mireille would be ashamed of him for holding that out as the standard.

There's a loud knock at the door. André squints, but whoever's there has stepped back into the dark. He eases the door open a little: it's Egger in his black SS uniform.

"How are you this evening, Herr..." the German says with as affable a grin as anyone has mustered. He pauses, expecting André to complete his sentence.

"Albert." André crosses his arms, barring the man from entering. After this morning, is now the wisest time to start another fight? He uncrosses them and wipes his hands on his hips.

"Herr Albert," Egger repeats with a precise formality, as though he's announcing an arrival at a social event. "*Ach nein,*" he corrects himself. "*Monsieur* Albert." With a sweep of his hand, he motions to the door and the shop beyond. "May I?"

"We're closed." André starts to shut the door.

"It's about the investigation." Egger raises an eyebrow and purses his lips with amusement, signalling to André that he can't refuse. Or shouldn't.

André edges the door open a bit more, and Egger seeps in like water through a crack.

When Émilie sees the German, she kneels on the floor, ostensibly to play with Frédéric. She adjusts her kerchief to cover her hair and faces the wall. Frédéric stares at the visitor, and she tries to distract the boy by waving a whisk, but he doesn't look away from the Nazi.

"First, I must apologize for my behaviour the other day," Egger tells André. "Rule number one: Do not antagonize the locals. We Germans are looking for allies, *ja?*" He turns to the display case. "Oh, *pâtisseries françaises.* Not as much a delight as my mother's *Schwarzwälder Kirschtorte*, but a passable substitute while abroad."

Egger examines the meager offerings. "War. Tsk. Tsk. An artisan without his materials." He looks down to scratch at a stain on his shirt. When he lifts his face again, he spots Émilie and Frédéric.

"Oh. I'm sorry." The German straightens and calls over to her. "I didn't see you there. *Guten Abend*, Frau Albert." He tilts his head to André. "You didn't say your wife has returned." Then to Émilie again: "Back from your travels?"

Without taking his eyes off her, Egger moves nearer to André. "I trust you've resolved your marital woes." When André doesn't respond, Egger adds, "So no investigation," and looks disappointed.

André keeps mum, he certainly doesn't correct him. Let him think what he wants and go. But it nags at him that an official investigation might find Mireille, especially if he can't. But how to explain a Jewess being here, let alone hiding one?

Despite the German's scrutiny, Émilie flies the whisk like a plane by Frédéric's nose. Still, the boy gawps at Egger.

The Nazi gives him a smile, and when Frédéric doesn't do likewise, Egger's pitch twists higher. "Are you enjoying your playtime?" He pauses long past when the question has faded in the room. He shifts where he's standing. "Well? Is it fun?" His tone is too jovial to be genuine, but Frédéric's only response is a line on his brow.

André clears his throat in an attempt to distract the man. He won't let him take a step towards his son, that's for sure. Finally, Frédéric nods without seeming to understand.

Egger says, "Excellent," to no one in particular.

He moves to the door, and André is quick to open it, but then the German no longer seems interested in leaving. "Although wasting my time on such trifling—"

"Monsieur," André interrupts, "if you don't mind." He jerks his head to the door, but Egger unexpectedly points at the windows.

"And no blackout curtains?" His face shows suitable disappointment, seemingly more for dramatic effect than anything else. "That is an offense, you understand? I should order you to paint the windows. Our royal enemies across the Channel will spot us from above and you know what that means..." Again Egger waits for André to finish. When he doesn't, the Nazi says, "Well," with a condescending sigh.

André glowers at the man with an animosity in danger of boiling over. The street's had infestations of rats that were easier to rout.

"We shut at sunset. We don't open the lights down here."

"And upstairs? That's where you live, *ja*? I trust you have curtains there."

"Of course." André opens the door wider.

"I'll take your word. But I know what you French are like. You readily cover your windows, as required, but when you hear a Lysander overhead looking to pick up a spy or two, you just as willingly throw open your doors to help them navigate."

"I know nothing of that, Monsieur."

Egger sniggers. He takes off his cap and mops sweat from his forehead with the back of his hand, then turns to inspect the display case again. "Your treats, Herr Albert. After a long day, they must come dangerously close to going stale."

"Monsieur?" André can no longer keep impatience from his tone.

Putting his cap back on, Egger runs a glove along the display, tender as a hand along a naked leg. His lips tighten, then slacken like a shot of pleasure just coursed through him. André grimaces at the thought. Egger stops and rolls his fingers in one direction, then back again, as though performing on a piano he doesn't know how to play. He looks directly at André and waits.

André stomps over to the display, takes out a box from the compartment below, and roughly drops pastries into it. It's a small price to pay to be rid of this son of a bitch.

"No! No!" Egger feigns objecting. "I couldn't accept—"

André shoves the open box at the man. Egger stiffens. No doubt other men have regretted showing him less disrespect. André scolds himself. Be careful. Don't push him any further.

Frédéric watches with eyes thick with fear, all the more heartbreaking to see in a child who has never really been frightened. He gives out a brief, but loud shriek.

Egger reacts with an exaggerated look of surprise and a lift of his shoulders. He places the box of pastries on the display case and closes the top. "*Merci*, Herr Albert. *Danke*," he says quietly. Then he laughs boisterously and says to Émilie, "*Bonsoir*, Frau Albert."

Émilie gives a quick nod in return.

"A lovely family." A smile crosses the German's face that only seems an excuse to show off his salt-white teeth. The man lingers a moment more, looking from André to Émilie and

Frédéric—his smile evaporates and an ugly curl reappears on his lips. Just when it seems he's about to say something else, something contemptible, something dangerous, he saunters to the door.

With a hint of a bow, Egger leaves.

André locks it, and his body stops winding tighter.

He remains watching through the window as the Nazi crosses the street, already cramming a pastry in his mouth.

Émilie paces while André sits at the table running his hands through his hair.

"The old man says—"

"Monsieur Durand," André corrects her, talking on top of her.

"—he's heard of someone in the next town who helps Jews find passage to—"

"But he doesn't know who yet." André's tone is measured in counterbalance to the panic in hers. How can he be so calm?

"I'll go there. I'll ask around." Émilie stands over him, even though she's unsure why she's trying to convince him of anything. Why does she need permission? She should just go.

When the Nazi walked in, fear shot through her—there was screaming in the back of her brain, and her neck and fingers went numb. She was just beginning to think she could stay longer—the baker hasn't told her to leave. It's as good a place as any to be. To hide. How naïve! Everywhere's a good place to hide until it isn't.

André scoffs. "Who will you ask? Who will you trust? No. You can't go until things are arranged. Mireille would never forgive me." He throws back his head and exhales. When he said his wife's name, his mouth snapped shut like he wants to lock it away.

There are footsteps on the stairs, and Monsieur Durand carries Frédéric in. As soon as Egger left, André slipped out to ask him to come over—he told her he needed the bookseller's counsel. But when Monsieur Durand came back with him, André's old friend said he preferred to keep his opinions to himself for the time being, and suggested he occupy Frédéric in the shop while she and André discussed the matter on their own. But they're only going around in circles.

"I'm sorry, but the Petit Prince demands a biscuit." Monsieur Durand puts Frédéric down, and the boy toddles over to André and tries to climb up on his lap. André picks him up and sits him on a chair.

"Mireille calls him that," he tells Émilie. "Petit Prince." He asks Monsieur Durand to find some biscuits and stops himself. He pokes a finger at the buffet and a plate covered with a cloth, and the old man brings it over. He pulls away the cloth to reveal the marzipan tableau.

Frédéric grabs one of the figures, the fox, and stuffs it in his mouth.

"Today's his birthday." André's voice catches. "His mother wanted to make a fuss over him."

SEVEN

Friday, October 22, 1943

André is woken in the night by the muted drumming of rain on the roof. It brings back summer nights in bed with Mireille when they were first married, the window pushed wide open, their bodies entwined under the covers, lips almost touching, softly singing to each other made-up songs to the rhythm of the raindrops. A surge of bliss races through him, and just like that is gone. The void it leaves emphasizes with great power his stark reality: Without her, he's nothing more than a corpse.

He catalogues what he's done so far and decides his attempts have been useless. Everyone André spoke to claimed they saw nothing or were too afraid to say if they did. He's asked everyone on the street, everyone he could think of in the town. They remain quiet as the moon.

The only person who seemed to know anything was Gilles Lussier. But when André went to him, the butcher's son dismissively waved a hand and said he didn't want to be involved. "I have things to do," he said, even though André never saw him lift an eyebrow to help out in his father's butcher shop. Yet André could see in his face there was more he wanted to say. Why didn't he press for answers right then?

André thinks back to every detail and chastises himself for being so ineffectual. He supposes it was because, at first, he didn't believe his wife was gone, at least not gone forever. He knows now that's not how the world works—it rapidly dims even the brightest of hopes. Those who see clearly and without distraction already understand that. Why couldn't he have been one of them?

He lies on his back, eyes shut, listening to the rain for the longest time, before easing himself out of bed, quietly so not to disturb Frédéric. He pulls on his trousers, steps into his shoes, grabs his shirt, and stealthily makes his way to the stairs.

In the shop, André slips on his shirt as he crosses to the side door and unlocks it. He sprints up the alley, stopping when he reaches the cobblestones black with rain. He scans from one end to the other, listening for footsteps or approaching vehicles, but sees and hears nothing but the downpour.

André darts over to the door leading to the flat above the *boucherie* and knocks.

No answer. Wake up, you louse. He knocks again, this time more loudly. Come on. The dead can hear this.

A minute passes, then the door opens a sliver and an eye blinks at him.

"We need to talk." When there's hesitation, André adds, "About Mireille."

The door opens to let him in.

The butcher's son brings over a glass and a bottle, and placing them on the table before André, sits sideways opposite him and neatly crosses his legs and lights a cigarette. André pulls the cork from the bottle and pours himself a drink. He downs it in one swallow and begins coughing.

"My father would drink petrol if it reminded him of the way things used to be," Gilles says.

Soon as he can speak, André gets to the point. "Do you know where she is?" He fixes his eyes on the man, believing he'll be able to detect any lies, as though the last week has bestowed on him that power.

Gilles takes a draw on his cigarette and slowly exhales. In this stagnant room, the smoke thickens above them and mixes with the stale, rotten-egg smell of boiled turnips.

"You speak to her. I've seen you." André's voice cracks getting the words out. There's no disgrace in showing fervour given the reason.

Gilles uncrosses his legs and crosses them again the other way. "And what of it?" He takes another drag on the cigarette, then taps it so the ash drops to the floor. He glares at André, not in anger but with puzzlement, as if asking: What sort of man shows up in the middle of the night, sweating such desperation?

André knows he's being looked down at, but he couldn't care less about losing anyone's respect. Especially not his. He continues looking Gilles straight in the eye and shamelessly starts to plead, "You're my last—"

Gilles cuts him off. "We've been through this already." He stubs out the cigarette on a plate and gets to his feet. "Now leave."

André won't be sent away so easily this time. Why did Gilles let him in if he won't talk?

"Then your father. Nothing on the street escapes his truffling nose." André doesn't realize until he's spoken how resentful he sounds. "If I have to, I'll yank your father out of his pit and make him tell me." He jumps up and moves towards the hallway leading to the bedrooms. Just as quickly, Gilles blocks the way.

André steels himself, ready to fend off blows, ready to start the fight if necessary. But immediately his body unfolds. His fists didn't get him far at Madame Bujold's.

"My father's not well. You should go," Gilles tells him. Instead of growling with the expected menace, he speaks softly, patiently, even.

"I'm not leaving until you tell me where she is."

Gilles squares his shoulders and takes in a sharp breath. "If I knew, I'd tell you. I wouldn't keep something like that from you."

André doesn't believe him, but he catches pity in the man's eyes. He's seen hints of it in Monsieur Durand, and even Émilie, although they try not to show it. It's difficult enough to see it in them.

Gilles goes to the door. "I'm sorry." He motions for André to leave.

André lingers a moment more, trying to find something to say so the butcher's son reveals what he knows, but fails at this, too. What chance does Mireille have with André as her only hope?

He bounds down the stairs and out into the street. His thoughts are sudden, like knocking over a pot of ink, and just as dark. Now's when he stops running from them.

Gilles is close behind. "André!" he calls. André stops, but can't bring himself to turn. "Maybe she doesn't want to be found." His voice is tinny as it elbows through the pounding rain. "My advice to you is to get on with your life."

What life is he talking about? He no longer lives, he exists, and little else.

André twists to face him. "You're asking me to give up on her."

"Not give up. But what good is searching under pebbles when you're looking for a mountain?"

With that, Gilles returns inside.

Head drenched, clothes dripping off him, André's brain spins with questions, some too dire to contemplate for more than the second it takes to banish them.

But one confounding question amongst a forest of them stands out.

What does he do now?

Just before sunrise, Frédéric wakes up, crying convulsively. Émilie hears André trying to comfort him, but his son is inconsolable as a newborn.

She rolls onto her side and faces the wall, her hands over her ears. Once you dry a child's tears, your love for that child will never end. The boy's wailing reaches her distorted like she's underwater. She feels lighter and begins to float up—it's all at once wonderful and frightening.

A bright flash of light behind her eyes jolts her, and they blink open. An outline of a man is standing over her. Her heart stops. Oh, God, no!

"Mireille's the only one who can calm him when he gets this way." André's voice is plaintive and distant, the cry of an injured seagull.

Émilie's heart creaks to a start again. She goes to the other side of the folding screen and sits next to Frédéric. His face deforms in terror. He moves away and draws himself into a ball.

"It's okay. Everything's going to be alright." Her tone's soothing as a harp, but it has no effect. Why would it? Her words are vapid. How does lying to a child make anything better?

As a last-ditch attempt, Émilie tries to take the boy in her arms, but he screeches, his tear-washed cheeks plum purple, and pushes her away. It's as though he's seen a hideous creature.

Perhaps he has.

André stands there helpless, looking ready to cry, too, but Émilie can't bring herself to tell him the obvious. He shuts his eyes and exhales loudly, and she doesn't have to.

Frédéric's realized his mother's gone, and he's devastated.

Émilie combs Frédéric's hair. Exhausted from crying, he finally fell asleep. When he woke, she went to him, and it was like nothing had happened. He wanted her to lift him up.

When André came to check on his son, the boy made a funny face and stuck out his tongue the way a toad does. André gave him a kiss on the head and told him to get dressed. Émilie helped Frédéric when he struggled with the buttons. A sentimental pang kicks violently inside her. What is she like? More grateful for the memories she no longer has than the ones she does.

André hasn't moved from the table since, staring at remnants of the marzipan tableau, anguish pouring from him like blood from an open vein. He stopped speaking to her, and didn't eat when they did or go down and start baking for the day. Émilie wants to do something to help him, but she's seen enough misery to know there's nothing anyone can say to lighten its burden. Not a word.

All of a sudden, André grabs his jacket and leaves. Seconds later, the front door opens then slams shut, causing the crucifix to rattle on the wall.

Émilie goes to the window and watches the baker hurrying along the street. He pushes through a group of men talking in front of the *boulangerie*, and they yell and wave their arms at him, but he ignores them and goes around the corner and out of sight.

She turns back to Frédéric, still sitting there, his expression empty as though he's storing his emotions for when there might be a famine of them.

Now that his mother is gone and his father is consumed with finding her, the child is disappearing.

The lobby of Hôpital Saint-Léry d'Espoir is cramped and claustrophobic, despite having walls stretching up to ceilings so high they trap the noise from below and ricochet it to the floor. Walking in is like entering a large drum.

André looks around—doctors, nurses, patients, and their families mill about in a daze. The reek of antiseptics fights with the stench of blood, vomit, urine, and unwashed flesh. His nose starts to run in complaint, and he has no choice but to dry it with his coat sleeve.

He stops a passing nurse, a short, young woman with the slumped shoulders of someone who's already put in a month of work that morning alone.

"I'm looking for Mireille Albert." André hesitates a moment before forcing himself to add, "She could be hurt."

The woman yawns, her open mouth tilted up towards him like a baby bird, and points to a long line of people at a window, before sleepwalking away.

André joins the queue and concentrates on the back of the head of the person in front of him, trusting that emotions can't overrun a distracted mind. He focuses on the pattern of the woman's flowered kerchief, trying to commit it to memory: the number of stems, the number of leaves, the number of petals. Anything is better than looking at the faces of the people around him—the walking wounded whose afflictions he envies. They're only physical.

He hangs his head. He's here now. He can't avoid the inevitable, whatever that is. If Mireille is here, it's only for one of two reasons. He prays it's to receive medical attention. No matter how serious it is, they'll manage and it'll be alright. Life can return to normal despite what form it might take—he'll make sure it does. He resolves right then to dedicate the rest of his days to caring for Mireille regardless of how ill or injured she may be. He shakes out his hands, his fingers flapping loosely. She'd do the same for him without a second's thought.

André repeats his prayer until it's a rush of words in his head, more a rub on a genie's lamp than anything pious. For the first time in the last few days, he breathes freely again.

When it's his turn, a woman at the window with eyes shiny as marbles tells him Mireille isn't a patient. She shrugs and says, "The only other place your wife might be is downstairs." She expels her words with such a rotting odour, André recoils like it's mustard gas. He turns around, and a girl with a white ribbon in her hair, standing behind him in the queue with her coughing father, gives him a smile radiating kindness. Or condolence.

André's insides roil, punishing him for his negativity. If he loses faith in Mireille, who'll have faith in him? How could Frédéric have any?

Outside a room marked MORGUE, André steels himself to enter.

He slips in and finds himself alone with a half-dozen tables, a body under a white sheet on each of them. This is the point he should turn around and leave—a man with any sense wouldn't have come. He's supposed to be looking for her; being here's an admission of defeat, that he's given up searching. More than that, it feels disloyal. To believe in Mireille is to believe she's alive and can survive anything.

But André doesn't leave. He wills himself to approach a corpse, choosing a smaller one, although he has no idea why. Then it hits him: it's the nearest to Mireille's size. He shudders. He can't count the amount of times he's seen her sleeping—just as he wakes, but before she does—when he thinks what a blessing it is that a woman so loving is with him. How could he have predicted those moments were also in preparation for this?

The smell of charcoal reaches him, then the heavy stench of meat. The pit of his stomach freezes to ice and he can hear his breath rasp in his throat. He lowers his eyes to the sheet. Someone has taken care to smooth it out so there are no wrinkles. He whispers a quick prayer for forgiveness and lifts it.

It isn't her—it's a man with a horribly burnt face. André stares at the gaping eyes and bared teeth, white islands in a sea of charcoal. What he sees sickens him, yet he can't stop looking.

André's relief it's not Mireille is tempered knowing the loss of this man is being mourned by someone. And there's still all the other bodies to check.

An orderly walks in. "Can I— You aren't supposed to—"

"My wife," André mumbles. "They said she might be here."

"There are no women here, Monsieur. A factory was firebombed."

"What?" It comes out as a bark. André rubs his neck with a focused intensity, trying to break free words gripped by shock. So Mireille's not here. Thank, God!

He pulls the sheet back over the dead man, and brushing past the perplexed worker, stumbles out.

Outside the pâtisserie's front door, André is putting a key in the lock when he hears someone approaching behind him. He spins around and sees the postman, a dour man whom André has never seen be pleasant in all the years he's been delivering their mail.

"At last," the man grumbles. He thrusts a letter at André and clomps away, his disposition burdening him far more than the cumbersome bag hanging on his shoulder.

André recognizes his mother's handwriting on the envelope. He tears it open, slides out the letter, and reads. He sits down on the stoop, not caring about the funny looks passersby give him.

His parents will be arriving tomorrow from Nantes.

He pulls out the key and walks away.

Émilie lets the blackout curtain fall back into place. She's about to tell Monsieur Durand at the table reading to Frédéric that she just saw André heading up the street, but stops herself. She can't think of a way to say it that won't sound disparaging.

Towards her more than anyone.

Despite having climbed the stairs in the dark so many times before, André stumbles. There's not a step he doesn't know by memory: the one that squeaks if you put both feet on it at the same time, the one that shifts ever so slightly, lying in wait to throw you backwards. And the one where Mireille sat, tears in her eyes, when she was certain she was losing the unborn baby that was to be their son because of a pain inside her that was excruciating and sudden. But tonight, André can't recognize any of them. Where they lead, he hasn't a clue.

He makes it to the top and walks over to his bed and undresses. He sits beside a sleeping Frédéric, then goes to his knees and folds his hands. O Heavenly Father, he silently begins. Then he softly says out loud, "Please."

On the other side of the folding screen, Émilie lies facing the wall, listening. She identifies the sounds of clothes being removed, the moan of bedsprings as André lies down, and then him standing again. The floorboards creak, but she has no idea what he's doing. Then she hears André make his despondent plea.

Émilie slips out of bed and into the broken shoes she placed side-by-side minutes before. She hadn't bothered undressing—she's that exhausted. The emotions of the day drag on her like chains, yet she can't sleep. Her feelings are a throbbing toothache that, even when they go away for a moment, only return with a vengeance.

She peeks around the folding screen and finds André on his knees praying. He gets to his feet and is about to speak—his lips move as if he's still talking to God—but instead charges to the stairs. Rash as a blind bull. Émilie listens to his footsteps fading into silence, then glances at Frédéric.

As if sensing eyes on him, the child turns towards her, still sleeping, his face screwed tight, and like his father, forms words he's not able to say. Émilie can't imagine what nightmares he's having.

The boy settles again, so Émilie goes to check on André. She finds him at the worktable with Mireille's apron spread before him. Émilie stops at the foot of the stairs, wary of moving any closer. Unpredictability in men too often manifests itself in violence.

"I was on my way to Paris." André's shoulders square, but he doesn't turn. "That's how we met. I'd left home—I wasn't going to spend my life working in the vineyards like...like my father. Be like...my father." André folds the apron again. "I never went back, not even to visit." He holds the apron against his chest. "A father should want more for his son. A son is a father's hope for a better future."

Émilie sits on a step and waits for him to go on, apprehensive he's about to divulge something she's not sure she wants to hear. Sharing personal secrets only mire you deeper in each other's quicksand. How will either of them extract themself then?

André lets out a small chuckle. "I fell asleep on the train. I was that excited, I exhausted myself. When I woke, the train was stopped, so I grabbed my case and ran out. Paris!"

He puts the apron on a shelf, comes over, and sits next to her. The scent of cinnamon mixes with his reminiscences.

"It wasn't Paris. I had arrived here in Saint-Léry. By the time I realized my mistake, the train was gone. That's how I met her. She was delivering pastries to the café near the station." His voice lightens and his eyes crinkle in the corners. "I'm sure I looked confused, and she gave me a smile, mostly out of pity, I know, but her face lit up like sunlight on water. Mireille was the most breath-taking woman I'd ever..." He swallows hard. Then his expression darkens as though a cloud is passing over.

"She's not coming back."

"Monsieur, you can't think that way."

"I feel it. In my gut. She's gone and she won't—"

"Monsieur!"

"—be back."

Émilie wraps her arms around him, and he buries his face in her and weeps. For a moment, she's able to shove aside her own pain and feel his misery in her bones, while fighting falling apart with him.

EIGHT

Saturday, October 23, 1943

André's parents, Edouard and Cécile, dressed in their finest clothes, traipse in. André trails in behind them, lumbered with their luggage like a pack animal, half-listening to his father prattle on with a torrent of opinions and commentary that hasn't stopped since the station.

"The trains are slower and more crowded now the Germans are running everything. Commandeered most of the carriages, I expect. Why do we put up with it? Oh, but we do. Of course we do. We sit back and complain, and no one does a thing about it."

André makes a non-committal noise and puts down the bags. His patience tested in the walk from the station, he warned himself to do his best to get along, and found himself taking frequent gulps of air. It isn't easy—his jaw is already aching. His father repeated three times how their being able to travel under the occupation "is a minor miracle." It takes all André has to hold back from remarking the "miracle" is more likely the result of bribing high-ranking officials than any divine intervention.

Edouard takes a deep breath, rattling his substantial frame, and declares with unflinching certainty, "Chocolate," even though André hasn't been able to find it for weeks. His father removes his hat and wipes sweat from his forehead with his arm.

Cécile looks around eagerly. "Where's my grandson?" There's a slight vibrato to her voice. "You should've brought him to the station to meet us."

André expels a puff of air. Although his brow remains unwrinkled solely by force of will, the worry of what's lying in wait now his parents are here eats at him like root rot.

Edouard examines the contents of the display case and shakes his head. A strand of his grey hair falls over his close-set eyes, and he swats it away like it's a bothersome fly.

"You know, there's always work at the *vignoble*. It's been a good year, a good vintage at last, and the Germans are buying. You can move back and—"

"We're doing fine, Papa." André dreads resuming the push and pull of his relationship with his father—constantly grappling without either of them gaining advantage. Just the thought of it squeezes energy from him like the last icing in a piping syringe. Once those battles seemed so important and fateful, now they're the least of his concerns.

The patter of footsteps approaches, and André's parents turn expectantly to the stairs. They break into generous smiles when Frédéric pads into the shop.

Émilie follows the boy, but stays on the last step, pressed against the wall.

"There he is!" Edouard waves his hat as if signaling a plane to land.

"My God, how he's grown!" Cécile moves towards her grandson, but he turns and runs back to Émilie and buries his face in the folds of the dress she has on. André's mother raises a hand to her mouth when she realizes it's not Mireille, although she's in Mireille's clothes.

A startling fatigue invades André. Here we go.

Edouard glowers out from under his heavy eyebrows. "Who's this?"

"Émilie. She helps us out." André strains to keep argument from his tone. It was a mistake letting them come to stay. He should've turned them back at the station.

Edouard's leathery face remains closed as their suitcases. The man is set in his ways, not unlike an old sailor who's plied the same route for years without ever seeing a storm. At least his mother has the manners to nod to the woman.

André's father takes his watch from his waistcoat pocket and opens it. Growing up, André saw him do this repeatedly. Only after André moved away did he realize it has nothing to do with the hour, but is the way his father distracts himself when he's about to be angry. It seldom works.

"Come along," André tells Frédéric, "give your grandparents a kiss." When he doesn't move, André puts out his hand and his voice deepens. "Frédéric. Come here. They've travelled a long way to see you." The boy keeps his face hidden.

André turns back to his parents. "It's been a while. He doesn't remember—"

"You're coddling him." Edouard clicks his watch shut and tucks it back in his pocket. "Here." He stumps over to Frédéric to show André how to discipline a child.

André bars his father's path. He hasn't forgotten how little it took for the man to lift a hand to him. Although André doesn't think his father would dare hit Frédéric, he won't let him have an opportunity to try.

"Give him time," André warns him.

"You'll raise him to be weak."

"Edouard. Please." Cécile shoots him a look of disapproval, then asks brightly, "And where is my daughter-in-law? We've brought some things I'm sure she's had trouble finding."

She shuffles to the luggage and starts searching through them. She's more gaunt than the last time André saw her. She hasn't been well, but in her letters she always assures him she's fine and only needs more sun. It doesn't ring true. What does a vineyard have but grapes and sun?

André crouches down and stretches his arms out to Frédéric. The boy peeks out from behind Émilie, and scurries over to his father's arms.

"We should get you settled," André tells his parents. Without waiting for a reply, he carries his son to the stairs.

Edouard and Cécile exchange looks, puzzled at what's

transpired, but follow him anyway.

As Edouard passes Émilie, he sneers at her, and she averts her eyes.

"What do you mean, 'She's gone'?" Edouard's eyes narrow. They're the same golden brown as André's, but couldn't be more different. André can't remember his father's eyes holding a drop of compassion.

Sitting at the table with his parents, André hangs his head, a prisoner being interrogated. Over on Frédéric's bed, Émilie watches, her face wracked with fear the situation's about to combust.

"Just that," André mumbles. "She's...gone." What else is there to say? If only there was more to tell.

Edouard sways to his feet, and in frustration, takes off his suit jacket and drapes it over the back of the chair as though he's about to negotiate the price of a dozen crates of wine.

Cécile leans in and rests a thin hand on André's—her touch is weak and glassy, and she smells of lilies. "Dear, we don't understand what you're telling—"

"Is she on holiday?" Edouard snarls. "Gone mountaineering in the Alps? Horse riding in..." He searches for another location as fanciful. His sarcasm isn't lost on André, but he chooses not to rise to it, even though any tolerance he has left for his father's anger is leaking away.

"Edouard! Manners! Please!" Cécile's expression is that of a woman chastising a routinely naughty child, part irritation, part resignation.

Her husband ignores her and continues his questioning. "It doesn't make sense. Speak up. What's going on here?"

When André remains quiet, his father takes two steps towards the stairs, then turns around. "Ah!" he exhales. "Knowing exactly what Mireille's like, I bet she's run off with the Resistance, because that's where fanatical ideas like hers lead."

André scoffs. "That's nonsense." Mireille may express her

political views from time to time, mostly when she sees injustice, but she's hardly going to storm the Bastille. But of course his father would jump to that conclusion. He and Mireille are different as molasses and vinegar, but André always felt their quarrels were harmless. More hobby than vocation.

Edouard can't stop himself from driving home his point. "To the Resistance, then to the gallows!"

"Enough!" André yells. His father is pecking at him like a magpie hoping to find a shiny nugget inside. He's in for a disappointment.

They're silent for a while, each of them deliberating their next move. André can't think of what to say that won't make things worse, so he resigns himself to the fall of the axe. Get it over with and they'll leave, and he'll be able to go back to searching.

His father starts pacing. André's mother touches her son's arm and asks in a faltering voice, "Then what has happened to—"

"She left me." André winces. He hasn't a clue if that's what Mireille has done—she would never leave them, she took nothing with her—but maybe that'll shut them up.

His parents are stunned. Edouard sits beside him and plunks a hand on his shoulder, its weight heavier than a cast iron stockpot.

"You must go after her, *mon fils*." His father sounds calmer now, caring even, although his cold eyes are unchanged. "You can't let her abandon your family."

"I don't know where she is." André doesn't see the point in recounting where he's gone and who he's asked. Nothing he's done will be enough for them. He knows that even if he does it all over a hundred times again, it still wouldn't be enough for him.

Edouard turns to Cécile, who gives her head a shake in confusion.

Frédéric makes a low whirring noise in his throat. Everyone looks over at him, and he stops. André's mother motions to Émilie, asking if she can join them. Émilie nods.

Cécile goes over and sits next to her grandson. At first the boy holds on to Émilie, but she passes Cécile the puppet. When she puts a hand inside and entertains Frédéric with it, he gives out a tickle of a laugh.

Edouard leans towards André and hisses, "Who is that woman?" He smells of the styptic he uses when he nicks himself shaving, slightly sweet and medicinal.

"No one. She's good with him."

"But she isn't his mother. Isn't it time for her to leave?" He calls over to Émilie, "Mademoiselle. Isn't it time for you to go home?"

Émilie doesn't respond; she smooths a tuft of hair sticking up on Frédéric's head.

"Edouard!" Cécile admonishes again, still with no effect. He frowns at Émilie for a moment more, his face bunching with disgust.

He twists back to André. "Is this why your wife left?"

"No." André raises a hand to his temple, fending off memories. He's bombarded by all those times when he was on his knees in the mud between rows of grapevines after being knocked down by his father, forced to listen to a list of his failings. Later, André would find him kneeling at his prie-dieu, praying for what, André still can't imagine. Most likely for a good harvest than forgiveness.

When Mireille is here, André never mulls over those things—he feels bitter he's doing so now. It's enough they revisit him in dreams, painful and disgusting. But what does it matter? Aren't all childhoods little more than a series of bruising experiences?

Edouard's voice rises again. "You've brought another woman into your home. And with the boy here? A *putain*! We raised you in the Church. You won't bring up our grandchild in a godless—" He's that repulsed, he doesn't bother finishing. "I have no idea what you're doing, but I've had enough of this—*bordel*."

He stands and calls, "Cécile!"

With laboured breath, André says, "It's not like that. Émilie helps—"

"Yes. I'm sure she—"

André hits the table with his fist. "Listen, you stupid old man!" He leans in, and his father's eyes widen. "I have no choice— I'm hiding her. There's nowhere for her to go. If I don't, she'll end up dead. I'll be damned if I know what God would say, but I don't want that on my conscience."

His father gapes at him, his mouth uselessly opening and closing as he searches for what to say. "Hiding her?" he sputters. "Why would..."

He turns to Émilie, who doesn't look up from nervously rubbing her hands on her dress. André has seen Mireille do the same thing hundreds of times.

Cécile holds Frédéric awkwardly on her lap, a stricken expression marring her soft features.

"Is she a..." André's father begins, but breaks off.

André nods. The truth's the only thing left when you no longer have the strength to lie.

Astounded, Edouard stares at Émilie while still speaking to André. "Do you realize what will happen when—"

Before the man finishes his awful thought, André interrupts. "Émilie, go close the shop. Take Frédéric with you." If André and his father are going to have it out, a stranger and a child don't need to be here.

Edouard pulls out his watch again. Instead of opening it to consult the time, he idly taps it on the table and shuts his eyes like he's concentrating on the rhythmic sound. It's another of his ploys. He's waiting for an explanation, but making it clear what little patience he has is ticking down fast.

Émilie moves to take the boy from his grandmother. Cécile holds onto him for a second more, hugging his little head against her pale cheek, then walks him to the stairs, holding his hand gingerly as though it's a paw.

Picking up Frédéric, Émilie continues on down to the pâtisserie.

André's parents look at him, anxiously waiting for answers, but he doesn't offer them anything in return. Where to start?

Edouard whispers, "Are you mad?" as though someone is

eavesdropping. "A Jew!"

At first, André shrugs, unable to argue against that. Then he says matter-of-factly, "What else could I do?"

"How is it your concern?" Edouard angles his head back in exasperation, exposing his Adam's apple like he's waiting for the last touches of a shave.

André traces the table's woodgrain with a finger, squeaking it along the surface. His fingertips have been burnt enough from pulling pans and sheets out of the oven, mainly from when he first began baking, he no longer feels anything. One of the perks of the job. While what his father is saying isn't untrue, André's already made up his mind about Émilie. It's what's right. But then, out of nowhere, doubt tugs at him.

Edouard carries on relentlessly. "How are these people— these Jews—any of our concern? It's between them and the Germans. Do you understand?"

He's sure his father would be happy to know he's questioning himself. André's finger keeps squeaking along the table, louder and more adamant now.

"Stop that."

His eyes snap up to his father and see anger hard as the tabletop.

As if given license by this minor transgression, the man starts making vile comments about Émilie's "people." He accuses them of all manner of atrocities, speaking with the authority of someone who's certain he can peer into the souls of every Jew, while not even knowing a single one of them.

André clamps his teeth so hard it hurts, and his hands form into white-knuckled fists. His father's voice diminishes until it's no louder than the buzz of an insect flying around André's ear. It's one thing to disagree with a father's opinion, but entirely another to loathe him for its ugliness.

Edouard wags an index finger and stands. "Such selfishness. We won't stay here. Not with *that* here." He jabs his finger at the floor twice, before snatching his jacket and hat, and marching to the stairs.

Cécile hesitates, then rises to her feet and follows her husband, her eyes down as she passes her son.

André can't read her. His mother always sided with his father while making feeble obligatory noises to the contrary. But when his father was gone and she was alone with André, she'd speak out against the man.

Once, when he was a boy, André asked her if she loved him—he was her son, after all—and he never heard someone say that to someone else before, not even between her and his father. She told him not to be silly. That's when André learned expecting to be loved was silly, too. It was years later when at long last he heard it, from Mireille right before they married. She said it without hesitation and with a conviction even André couldn't doubt. The way she's always said it to him since.

It seems to him his mother's affection for children, only developed after Frédéric was born, is an attempt at penance for the lack of it she showed André when he was young.

On the first step down to the shop, Edouard turns back. "One woman—your wife—disappears, and another woman—a Jewess—has taken her place. How will you explain that?"

He shakes his head again, and tramps down the stairs with André's mother close behind.

Émilie tries to imagine the argument upstairs as the distant muttering of thunder, as impossible to stop. She distracts Frédéric by showing him what baking utensils are for by making the motion when using them. With the whisk, she performs a few circles and passes it to him. Frédéric makes a tentative wave with it, so she takes his hand in hers and guides him. He does an awkward oval shape, then a circle, then another.

"Just like your papa." She puts an arm around the boy's shoulder and gives it a squeeze. Every child's as smart as he's allowed to be.

Frédéric brings the whisk to his mouth and his tongue darts out. Émilie's about to stop him, but realizes what he's doing.

"That's right. That's what you do when you're finished."

She was surprised when André told his parents his wife had left him. Does he really believe that? It's very easy for lies you tell yourself to become truths.

She finds André's father to be loathsome. When he was speaking, panic hit her like a thrown rock. She has no doubt he's the exact type who turns people in. And André's mother? If pathos was a perfume, she'd be drenched in it.

The impulse to run rises within her, but Émilie can't move. She's come so far, through so much, only to feel besieged again, trapped in a room without walls, or a floor, or ceiling, so she can't even claw her way out.

Émilie hears them move around above her, the floorboards creaking like the hull of an old sailing ship. Then there's a calm before André's father barrels down the stairs and into the room. His wife follows, but she waits at the bottom step while her husband stamps over to their luggage. André comes down a moment later.

"You can't tell anyone." André is insistent, almost pleading. "You can't say anything. Think of—"

"We should take him with us." Edouard clenches his teeth and reddens. "This is no place for a child."

"You can't take my—"

"A home is where a boy's raised with morals. What does he find here?"

"Edouard," Cécile begins, "don't say such—"

"They'll come for her. They'll come for the Jewess and they'll take both of you with her." Edouard blatantly scowls at Émilie.

Frédéric tilts his head as though trying to understand his grandfather's anger towards her.

André scrambles for the words to convince his father how wrong he is, as Edouard yells.

"Don't you care about your son's safety? Or have you already chosen her over your own flesh and blood?"

André glances at Frédéric, who's motioning with the whisk with a genuine finesse. André's heart jumps. His fondest dream for his son is one day he'll take over the shop. It's something André seldom allows himself to hope.

They almost lost Frédéric at birth. Mireille says she has no more than a shadow of a memory of that time, distraught and medicated as she was, but André can detail what happened as though it were last night. The baby was breech. André can still taste the dusty grit in his mouth when the doctor warned him they "might" be able to save one life, "and one alone, God willing."

When André was asked for a decision, without hesitation he said, "Mireille."

A priest was sent for to perform the last rites, someone André never met before or has seen since. It intrigued him to learn later he was *Jésuite*. They were taught in school Jesuits were driven out of the country centuries before. How this one came to be there, André never found out.

Whenever he recalls the night Mireille gave birth to their beautiful boy and what could have happened to them, no matter how fleeting the thought, he goes cold and his saliva turns to paste.

"No! Don't let them take your child!" Émilie moves towards him, torment raw in her face. "Don't do it!"

André's father glares at her as if she's tied him to a chair and is cutting away strips of his skin. André recognizes that look from his past, as excessive then as it is now. The agony the man has caused—forcing André to live in fear—is it any wonder André won't go back to living behind his hands, only catching glimpses? He has Mireille to thank for that.

André decisively scoops up Frédéric and turns away.

Edouard smirks. He takes out his watch and scowls at the time, transparently giving André a chance to reconsider. A full minute passes before his father shuts the watch and hides it away.

He puts on his jacket, then his hat, adjusting it with practiced care until it sits just right on his head.

Still André doesn't stop him.

His father storms over to the suitcases and struggles to pick up all of them himself, clearly needing help, but doesn't ask for it. He'd never ask. Asking for help is something weak men do.

Edouard humps to the door and steps out into the sun. He walks past the window in the direction of the railway station.

André grinds his teeth, rebuking himself for allowing his father to anger him one more time. He has no one to blame for letting the man into their home to destroy the spirit of everyone around him with his indiscriminate cruelty, then to retreat to his vineyard. Why did he think his father would break a habit of a lifetime?

Cécile straggles to the door where she stops to look back at André holding Frédéric to him. She grimaces, and her eyes soften to tears.

André knows what she wants to say: Why such needless conflict between a father and a son when all either of you want is the other's heart?

Well, to hell with the both of them.

Cécile gives Émilie a parting nod and slips out.

When André hears the door close, he turns to see his mother reel past the window to catch up to his father.

"They're your family," Émilie gently reminds him.

"No. My wife and son are my family."

Monsieur Durand has his ear to the wireless when there's a knock at the door. He was fretting over whether to tell André how Madame Bujold had misstepped and called whatever had happened to Mireille, "a wicked affair."

It surprises him to see André at such an hour. He snaps off the radio, tired anyway of reports filled with the ambiguities of war, and adjusts in his chair, ready to listen to his friend.

When André finishes his account of his parent's visit, Monsieur Durand pours more cognac into their glasses and jokes,

"One should only imbibe the drink of the gods to heal a heart," but he sees André is not listening, his face turned away.

They down their drinks and sit for a few minutes, staring at the top of the desk, looking for answers.

André finally raises his head, waiting for Monsieur Durand to offer whatever wisdom he's found to questions most likely having none, not much different from what someone would expect a father to do for a son.

Monsieur Durand doesn't know what to tell him. To be honest, he has no ability to discern the motives behind human behaviour, stolen from him by experiences he hoped would make him more astute, but rendered him an idiot. It's as though the calibration of the compass he always relied on has been thrown off, and he can't even determine by how much.

But he has to tell André something—his friend needs comforting, even if it means he has to mouth meaningless noises. Monsieur Durand mines what he can from inside him and endeavours to dispense it as sage counsel. Anyway, such things usually end up taking the shape of what it's poured into.

"I doubt your parents will report her," he tells André, cautiously at first. "There's Frédéric to consider." He sees from André's face how little this alleviates his worry.

Monsieur Durand rubs the back of his neck and says, louder and with certainty, as much to reassure himself as André, "There are fathers who do not love their sons, but show me a grandfather who doesn't adore his grandson."

NINE

Sunday, October 24, 1943

Émilie has a firm hold on Frédéric's waist as he balances on a chair at the open window and watches a pigeon strut along a roof on the other side of the street. To the boy's delight, the church bells clang, calling parishioners to mass. Without warning, he tilts forward, but Émilie yanks him back. He gives out a squeaky giggle and her heart starts beating again. He tries to lean out once more, but she draws him in just in time.

She examines his face and finds something in his bright eyes she hasn't noticed before, like he wants to say something. Or is she imagining it, another of hope's optical illusions?

"What's my name?" She lowers her voice so over at the table André won't hear. "I'm Émilie. Can you say 'Émilie'?"

Frédéric stays silent. He presses his palms against her cheeks, then pulls them away with a little squeal. She turns to ask André about it, but he's hunched over drinking wine straight from the bottle, glaring at who knows what in the centre of the room.

Frédéric squeals again. André shuts his eyes as if the sound cuts through him. He takes another swig of alcohol as remedy, and Émilie stiffens her spine. Drinking tends to cure everything except for why you needed a drink.

"It would be nice for Frédéric to go out today."

"You take him then." André's words are coated in bile—he's resigned himself to wallow in anguish. Émilie doesn't fault him for that. She has no right to criticize what despair does to a person. Let him take it out on her if it helps.

She lifts Frédéric to the floor. "Go play, *mon petit loup*." He races over to a toy train as she joins his father. André pushes the wine bottle towards her, but Émilie ignores the offer. Alcohol never appealed to her. Loss of control is her worst fear. Yet what does it mean that she's again in a situation where she's powerless?

"A walk, maybe," she says. "Perhaps Monsieur can—"

"You bring him." André jumps up and opens a cupboard. He rummages around, brusquely pushing items aside. Returning to the table, he slams down Mireille's birth certificate and identity card.

"Here! You wear her clothes. You mother her child. You might as well take it all." He plops back down in the chair and takes another drink.

With an audible breath, Émilie picks up the identification card and examines it. The picture shows a woman with thick, dark hair with a healthy shine even a photograph can capture. The woman's eyes gaze out, warm and carefree. Émilie lays the card back on the table. What good is it to her? She doesn't look anything like his wife. Maybe her hair had lustre a long time ago, but that's it.

"You can use the birth certificate," André says, as though hearing her thoughts. He abruptly stands. "Get Frédéric ready."

"Monsieur, never mind." What was she thinking suggesting they go out? Was it for the child's sake or her own? To walk around outside a free woman seems a preposterous fantasy. A shiver travels to the small of her back as she realizes the risk she'd be taking.

"Should we stay cowering in here forever? The sun's out; the park's a street over. We'll look like every other family on a Sunday afternoon." With that, André barges to the stairs and vanishes down them.

Émilie glances over at Frédéric sitting on the floor with the train in his mouth. When the boy sees she's watching, he plucks it out with a popping sound.

She picks up the birth certificate.

André waits outside the front door, shoving his fists deeper into his trouser pockets. A man in a beret walks past and nods, but André doesn't acknowledge him. The man swears under his breath, and clutching the lapels of his jacket, clumps away.

The aroma of fresh bread wafts over. It rankles André how the bread baker opens on Sundays, and he instantly realizes he's only being mean-spirited for the sake of it. The pâtisserie could be open, too, but he and Mireille had made the decision not to for Frédéric's sake. A man without a family can do anything he wants, but he still has no family.

Last night, after André returned from telling Monsieur Durand about his parents' doomed visit, he went straight to bed. He woke in the night, unable to get air, forced to pant as though learning how to breathe again. Despite what his old friend said to him about a grandfather's love, André has no faith in the sanctity of his family's bonds. Every time someone comes into the shop from now on, André knows his eyes will snap up to see if it's the police or the Germans.

Émilie carries Frédéric out to André. She's wearing a light dress, a coat, and a Sunday hat. André found her an old pair of shoes, and even though they no longer have a shine, are still better than the ones Émilie arrived with, only pieces of leather clinging to her feet.

Seeing Émilie in Mireille's best clothes alarms him. The hair bristles on the back of his neck. She's not the same woman he discovered in dirty rags cowering beside the display case.

His scrutiny causes her to avert her eyes. One of Frédéric's shirt buttons is undone, and she bends to fasten it.

The boy peers up at her, and something turns inside André's chest. Anger and sadness battle. Just as both emotions are about to mix in an ugly combination, they're overwhelmed by an incredible longing, painful as if his entire skeleton is shattering.

It's been a week since Mireille disappeared.

André focuses on a passing woman pulling a cart crammed with three young children, their faces streaked black by coal, and he feels empty as the pastry boxes stored under the display. The morning he last saw Mireille, he wasted his chance to kiss her one more time. Now he'd do anything to have that moment back.

"I can't." Émilie tries to pass his son over to him, but André walks away.

In the alley, he struggles to regain his composure. He's never known loss. He's heard Monsieur Durand say that experiencing loss forces you to be an adult. Well, he's already learnt how it erodes your soul.

Parc des Corbeaux sits placidly at the centre of town, a solid chunk of dark green trees and shady paths with thick boughs hanging low overhead. Couples stroll arm-in-arm, while parents caution little ones not to get too close to a pond teeming with ducks and the toy sailboats captained by their siblings.

Émilie sits with André on a bench as Frédéric sporadically licks a melting ice cream—he's more fascinated by the flotilla sailing past. The pond gives off a faint sickly smell of algae, although the water is clear blue, perfectly reflecting the sky.

She wants to bring up André's parents with him, but isn't brazen enough to start. She pulls down the hem of the dress, touching her legs covered in bumps like chicken flesh. She should fear what his father could do to her, but that hate never acts on its own—it slinks into corners and goads others to strike first. Émilie is sure the old bookseller would readily agree with what she's heard many times: goodness often appears in a veil, while evil always wears a disguise.

When André rests a hand on his son's head, Émilie turns to witness their little moment of affection, despite knowing it will only further damage her heart.

She sees two German soldiers walking towards them. Her

breath catches, and she moves nearer to André.

Surprised, he looks at her, then follows her gaze to the Nazis. He puts an arm around her and pulls her rigid body to him. She trembles until her bones ache.

When the soldiers walk past, André quickly withdraws his arm and keeps his eyes fixed on the pond.

Émilie turns to him. It's been a long time since she felt the touch of someone who doesn't mean her harm, someone without acid pooling in their veins. She feels she'll crumble under such gentle kindness.

When was the last time she was shown affection? Or is this another memory she's lost like a tooth, part of her so easily forgotten?

Watching André pour icing over three small squares, Émilie notices he's no longer wearing baker's whites, just brown trousers, a white shirt, and an apron. He needs a shave—stubble is visible around his chin and along his jawline. Instead of making him look older as it often does most men, he appears aloof and untidy. She's taken aback by his expression, less of a man's and more one of a troubled child.

"That was the last of the sugar." He hadn't made anything before going to the park. "It's Sunday, the shop's closed anyway," he told her. But when they came back, he was restless, a man at odds with his thoughts. Émilie suggested baking would calm him—routine often has that effect—but André scoffed at the idea. An hour later, she found him doing it anyway, although he seemed jarringly mechanical, robbed of motivation now his wife is gone, like she took it with her.

"Why do you bother?" It comes out more dismissive than Émilie means it to be, but André doesn't seem to notice.

"Mireille always says, 'Make at least three. Even if no one buys them, there'll be something for us to look forward to at the end of the day.'" He transfers the petits fours to a plate, their bright colour the sole cheerfulness left in the shop. André considers them for a moment as though he can't figure out if he's pleased or disappointed. He takes off his apron and throws it on the worktable.

"Lock the door."

"Where are you—"

"To the next town. And the next. And the one after that. To as many as it takes to bring her home."

André yanks the front door open, and brushes past a startled Monsieur Durand.

"*Bonjour*, André," the bookseller calls after him, but the baker continues walking away.

Monsieur Durand looks questioningly at Émilie.

"He won't stop." Her voice twists in distress, and she winces. It's so subtle, Monsieur Durand doubts that's what it is, then she does it again. He glances down and catches her digging her fingers into her bandaged hand. Such an obvious act of harm to oneself shocks him. How can anyone be so self-loathing?

"Émilie?" he says, but she doesn't hear him. "Émilie?" he repeats and touches her arm. It's hard as slate.

She spins towards him, then to avoid his eyes, moves away. He follows her to the display case.

"I have news how to leave. They require money, but I must be frank, it's doubtful you'll get far. The Germans—the Nazis are everywhere."

Émilie begins wiping the display with a cloth she pulls from her apron. Is she having second thoughts about going?

"It's safer here, I imagine. They aren't going house-to-house, and no one has turned us in. So far."

She gives no indication she's listening. Monsieur Durand clears his throat and takes his hat off. He brushes unseen specks off its rim and holds it against his chest.

"I see you're not convinced of humanity's goodness. With reason, I suppose. We become accustomed to poison drop by drop."

He expects her to at least mutter something in response, but Émilie doesn't even glimpse at him to show she's heard.

"Do you still want me to arrange your passage?" he asks point-blank.

"Yes."

He's about to ask her if she's sure, but her face hardens against everything around her, killing further queries.

Monsieur Durand puts on his hat and tips it to her. "*À bientôt*," he says between his teeth. He strides to the door and departs.

On his way back to the bookstore, he passes Samuel's gutted shop and sees Madame Monchamp and a German soldier in the doorway, their heads together in conversation. Right from the start of the war this fiend of a woman took treachery as her lover.

Monsieur Durand looks away and quickens his pace.

André fumbles with the key, trying to find the lock in the dark. He manages to open the door, stumbles in, and collapses.

Émilie appears, floating above him like an apparition. Seeing his battered face and the blood dripping from his mouth, she steps back.

"Monsieur!" She falls to her knees beside him and holds him.

They remain this way, him breathing in her ear, his lips brushing her cheek, until he goes slack in her arms.

Émilie and Monsieur Durand watch over André while he sleeps, his face cleaned but marred by bruises and cuts. Desperate, she risked being caught defying curfew to bring back the bookseller, fearful André wasn't going to make it through the night—his pulse was that feeble. They washed him and tended to his wounds until dawn. Thankfully he slept through it all.

The lines on Monsieur Durand's forehead deepen. "You're right. He has to stop. It's enough. He does more damage than good looking for her."

Émilie motions for the old man to step away with her. "Let him sleep," she whispers. She's not sure when she became so protective of the baker and his son, but she believes she has a responsibility for them now. The why is much too complicated to untangle.

Monsieur Durand shakes his head, resolute about having his say, and raises his voice, not caring if André hears.

"He's asked the wrong people. Too many questions, and no one will trust you. Next time it may be worse."

TEN

As his son's tiny arms strain to wrap around him, André's not sure he'll survive another slice being cut from his heart. There's been so much turmoil and upset this past week, it doesn't surprise him Frédéric is holding on so tightly. André challenges anyone to question their boy's ability to love.

Monsieur Durand once told him the first thing you think about when you wake up tells you who you are. The first thing André thought that morning wasn't of Mireille, exactly, but of the hole inside him where she's supposed to be.

Émilie brings over a bowl of soup and a spoon to his bed.

"I can get up." He moves to stand, grimaces, stifles a curse, and falls back against the pillow.

"Rest." Émilie starts to feed him, but he puts up a hand to stop her.

"I'm not the one who needs mothering." He tries to get up again. "She's still out there."

"André!"

He's as startled she said his name as with the force she used in saying it. The lioness roars.

"You have Frédéric to care for. He needs all of you, and not just what you have left over from grieving."

André flinches. What nerve she has. But before he can argue, he sees Frédéric looking up at him, his expression made tentative by the tones of their voices, causing him to teeter between giggles and tears. André's not sure he can deal with either right now.

"He's our— He's my life." André strokes the boy's cheek with his thumb, and Frédéric makes a soft guttural noise like a purr.

Émilie offers him the soup again. "Go on," she prompts.

Not wanting an argument, André gives in. He takes the spoon and starts eating, but can barely swallow it. It tastes of skunk soaked in sea water.

Émilie leans over him. She wants to know what happened— who did this. To avoid being asked things he'd rather not confess, André turns away. She doesn't so much as twitch. She won't leave him alone until she knows.

André lowers the spoon, almost knocking the bowl from her hand. "It's like I told you—I've been going to the towns between here and Paris. Yesterday, I went to a church in this one town with the foulest river I've ever seen and spoke with the priest. He was an elderly man, his eyes phlegmy with cataracts, but when I showed him a photograph of Mireille, he shook his head. Then he warned me that wasn't a town to be asking questions in."

Émilie holds the bowl to her, almost hugging it, and André has to lift the spoon until it feebly bobs in the air for her to notice.

"But you didn't listen." She holds out the soup to André as he sips another spoonful. This one's not all that bad. His taste buds must be rotting in his mouth.

"For the rest of the day, I stood in the town square outside a *boulangerie* and shared Mireille's picture with anyone who I could stop long enough to listen. No one had seen her.

"Just before sunset, my heart seized when I saw her walking across the square. I sprinted after her, but froze when a man approached her and kissed her on the lips."

André places the spoon in the bowl. "No more." He lies back on the pillow and looks up at the ceiling, imagining the endless sky above it. Like a road, it can lead anywhere. You just need someone to travel with.

He sighs heavily and sits up again, wanting to finish his tale soon as possible and be left alone with his thoughts.

"Only when they turned, I saw it wasn't Mireille. I was relieved and devastated.

"After the bread baker shut his shop for the day, he came out and offered me a *petit pain*—I guess he mistook me for a beggar. I told him about my search, and he sympathized with me. He was a kind man. He told me he'd given a son to the Great War.

"He hadn't seen Mireille, either, but he said there was a café at the end of the street where, as he described it, 'those with their ears glued to the ground gather before curfew.' I should've taken that as a threat."

André looks around for where his clothes are. He's supposed to be out there.

"That's how this happened?" Émilie waves a hand at his injured face.

André nods. "Quickly as I could, I was in front of these grubby men who were smoking and drinking, and smelled of idleness and pickled eggs. After telling them my story, they made me promises, took my money, and said to follow them out back where they beat me."

He pauses for Émilie's reaction, but she simply stares at him, her face purged of all emotion. He wants to stop speaking—he isn't thinking straight. But she should know one more thing.

"While I lay in the dirt, spitting blood, they stood over me and warned me not to come back. When they were gone, I could've sobbed with self-pity. But I dragged myself to my feet, not giving a damn about what just happened. They could've saved their breaths. I won't let one beating, or a thousand, stop me."

Émilie's expression curdles.

Loud knocking from below interrupts them.

André looks at Émilie and nods, and she hurries downstairs.

Émilie looks to the front door, but there's no one there. Then there's more knocking, softer this time, at the door to the alley.

She cautiously opens it to Monsieur Durand.

"Tonight. It's arranged." He's out-of-breath and his voice is drained of any tone except the weariness of a traveler far from his destination.

Émilie nods. She has no illusions. She has to move on by herself and go far away from here as she can.

She's sure there isn't a single person who'd believe such a fate for someone like her unfair.

Once they've eaten their evening meal, Émilie goes to put clothes in a suitcase, the one André told her he and Mireille used on their honeymoon. He leans against the wall near the stairs watching her, favouring his left side from the beating he took. Émilie is uncomfortable taking Mireille's dress, and now her coat and hat. But what else does she have?

She peeks one last time around the folding screen at Frédéric, who's sleeping in his parents' bed as peacefully as if he were back in the womb. When Émilie picks up the suitcase, the boy says something. It's muddled, but it sounds like, "Maman."

Émilie goes to him—he sits up and blinks. He extends his arms wanting her to pick him up. "Maman," he mumbles again, his little tongue jutting out flat and limp. Pleased as she is Frédéric is talking, she's mortified he's called her that. She doesn't dare look at André, worried he's heard, afraid his face is reflecting an unbearable pain.

"Go back to sleep, *mon petit tresor*," she tells the child. He pushes off the covers—he wants to go with her. Émilie gently lays him down and kisses his forehead. "I'll return. One day. Now go to sleep. That's a good boy."

Émilie's throat closes as she picks up the case again, her fingers feeling asleep. She brushes past André and disappears down the stairs.

Saying goodbye is worthless. They'll meet again or they won't. One word doesn't make either inevitable. Nor a thousand.

She steps out into the alley and sees Monsieur Durand waiting for her.

André appears behind her in the doorway and says to the bookseller, "I can't ask you to do this. Let me——"

Monsieur Durand shrugs. "They're expecting an old man."

André grasps Émilie's upper arm. "Are you sure?"

"I've been enough trouble. Thank you, Monsieur. For the money. The clothes. When I can, I'll repay you. I promise."

"When this is over, I hope you'll come back to see us. *All* of us."

Émilie dutifully echoes his optimism. "When there are no longer wars." More a parting gift than anything she has faith in.

She extends her hand, but André hobbles over and takes her by the shoulders and kisses her on both cheeks. She feels weak as watered-down milk.

André ekes out a smile. "*Bon retour*. Again."

There's the noise of an approaching vehicle.

"We must go," Monsieur Durand says. "Quickly now."

They start down the alley, but Émilie stops and turns back to the baker. "Please forgive me."

Before André can ask what she means, Monsieur Durand hustles Émilie away.

They vanish as headlights from a passing delivery truck drown everything in white.

In a wooded section of the park, Émilie and Monsieur Durand glide like ghosts along a path lit by moonlight. Birds rustle and coo in the branches above as they settle for the night.

Up ahead, a silhouette of a man rocks back and forth on his heels. Émilie assumes this is the contact they're meeting, and starts walking towards him.

There are three low trills of a whistle, and a murky figure crosses their path. The bookseller grabs Émilie's arm and pulls her into the trees.

"But Monsieur——"

The old man shushes her and increases his pace, dragging her along with a surprising burst of energy. They dash away through a minefield of tree roots and fallen branches, careful of where they place their feet so as not to trip.

Émilie and Monsieur Durand round a large trunk and come face-to-face with a German soldier smoking and urinating. Shocked, his features melt.

Her vision clouds, and she feels as though she's dropping to the ground. Don't let this be it. Keeping a tight hold on Monsieur Durand's arm, she runs back with him the way they came.

The soldier fumbles with his buttons and gives chase. "*Halt. Halt.*" He blows his whistle. Its trill, loud and urgent, pierces the quiet, and the park resounds with the drumming of countless running feet.

André pours himself a second cup of wine, then drains it down his throat. He can't deny feeling less anxious now that Émilie is gone. If only for Frédéric's safety. He hopes she'll be okay, although he doubts it. But what more can he be expected to do?

He's about to pour another drink when he senses someone behind him and turns around. No one is there. Then he sees it. He drags his chair over to the stairs and removes the crucifix from the wall.

André hasn't given it much thought until now—it's always been here. From the time of Mireille's parents? Before then? Probably from the days when Saint-Léry d'Espoir was a village and the pâtisserie was the home of a blacksmith who had a passing trade with carriages on the way to the capital. The rare occasion when a pastry went stale, Mireille would kid that their wares were no different than what that man used to shoe horses. God he misses laughing with her.

André twists the crucifix, and it separates into two pieces: the top with the Christ figure, and a bottom that has a cavity. Inside, he finds two candles and two small bottles, one of consecrated oil and another of holy water. Implements of the Last Sacrament. The smell of sandalwood reaches him, and he lifts the crucifix closer to his nose. It reminds him of going to mass with his parents, one of the few brief times his turbulent father looked at peace. Unfortunately, there weren't enough masses in a month of Sundays to cause any permanent change.

André had worked hard as anyone in the fields of the *vignoble*, but his heart wasn't in it. When he told his parents he was leaving, they didn't try to dissuade him. There'd be no point—his mind was made up. André was surprised his father hadn't done more to stop him. It seemed out of character not to.

Just before André set off on his journey, his mother held his hands, hers always stained by grapes, and gave him her blessing. She asked him to pray with her for his protection, and together they got down on their knees. Instead of joining in her plea, André silently asked to be able to hold her hands again one day, not having any idea when that would be.

His mother passed him a vial of water. "It's been blessed," she told him, and squeezed his hand around it. Walking away, André put it in his pocket, more to please her than anything else, and kept it for a couple of years, not thinking much of it. When he realized the vial was missing, either misplaced or accidently thrown away, his shoulders lifted to say, "Oh, well." Now that thought seems as careless as he was with her gift.

In a letter that found him months after he left, André's mother wrote him his father didn't stop André from leaving because he didn't believe André would be gone for good. He read how his father said, "He'll be back, sooner rather than later." But André never went back, more to prove his father wrong than anything else. He was bitter as dandelion greens. Mireille would tell him not to let thoughts like that ferment in his head. He always agreed, but he didn't tell her how difficult he found getting over the past. Hell, sometimes it's difficult even to see beyond it.

André pushes the two pieces of the crucifix back together and bangs over to the buffet. He pulls open a drawer, shoves the crucifix inside, and slides the drawer closed—it protests loudly going in both directions.

He stares at the buffet's wood top, focusing on one scratch, deeper than any other in the myriad of scratches from years of use. André follows its route until it falls off an edge.

The buffet smells of lemon oil, and it cuts through his deteriorating mood. Mireille spent so much time and effort polishing it. Besides the display case, the buffet's the only piece of furniture with any sentimental value, a family heirloom Mireille's parents were given by one of their parents when they married. When the business was first his and Mireille's, André was so proud of the display and the buffet. His chest used to puff out when he walked past them. But now he knows they're only objects.

André is rescued from the past by insistent knocking from below.

He struggles down the stairs fast as his injuries will allow, limps to the alley door, and unlocks it. Émilie and Monsieur Durand push in.

"They were waiting." The bookseller's face is flushed and he's breathing hard.

"But we paid," André says. Again, thanks to the old man's generosity.

"We paid traitors," Monsieur Durand manages to utter before coughing into his fist.

Émilie hastens to the preparation area and returns with a cup of water. The bookseller takes a drink and starts to cough again, spitting most of it down the front of his suit. He blots his mouth with a sleeve and looks away. Despite knowing him for as long as he has, this is the first time André has seen the man make such a coarse gesture, no different from a farmhand after a gobbled meal. He feels strangely embarrassed for him.

"You can't stay here," André tells Émilie, his voice harsh and rising. He's swiftly overtaken by fear. If the consequences of hiding a Jew aren't dire enough, being caught helping one escape is...

He rounds on his bookseller friend. "She can't stay here. They'll come for you now."

Monsieur Durand gapes at André, making no effort to hide

how appalled he is with him. "I didn't give them our real names." He takes another drink of water, and this time keeps it down.

"They know what you look like. They can describe you to the—"

"Only me. I doubt they saw Émilie well enough. And one old man," Monsieur Durand adds with a shrug, "looks much the same as another, no?" He looks from André to Émilie and back again. "It will be alright. We can try again."

André points a finger at Émilie, and although not meaning to, it's menacing enough to prompt Monsieur Durand to say his name in reprimand. André still pushes his face towards her. "Either you leave tonight, or you stay. But if you stay, that's it. I can't put my family—" He stops himself. Better not continue.

"No more taking chances. Stay and we'll just have to hope no one will..." André trails off when Émilie closes her eyes, bracing for something bad to happen. Why does wanting to keep his family safe seem so selfish? He can't save everyone.

Émilie finishes his sentence. "Turn me in?" Her hands go up behind her head and she unpins her hat.

André's face screws at her bluntness. The way she's looking at him accuses him, even though he'd never do something so— But a dark thought interrupts: Not if he didn't have to.

"You must understand my position," he pleads, but with less intensity. He turns to Monsieur Durand for help. Surely he sees the point André is trying to make.

At first, his bookseller friend says nothing. Then his shoulders slope and he gives out a long sigh. He tilts his head to Émilie.

"What André is saying is reasonable. You'll stay. Soon the war will be over. We have to believe in the inevitability this will end. That all evil eventually destroys itself."

ELEVEN

Tuesday, October 26, 1943

André goes through the motions of making pastries, while Émilie polishes the display case. They work in silence, each exhaling puffs of rancor and regret.

A truck rumbles past. André gives the batter another rotation with the spoon before turning to the windows and catching the back of a military truck followed by a motorcar with Nazi flags on each fender. *Merde!* André and Émilie look at each other before hurrying to the front door.

The vehicles stop outside the *librairie*, and a handful of soldiers jump from the truck. The motorcar's door swings open. Egger strides into Monsieur Durand's shop, shadowed by two more soldiers. The remaining soldiers stand guard, glaring menacingly at passersby who promptly scatter. The Germans smirk to each other.

André limps out. Egger must know something. Monsieur Durand shouldn't have to face him alone.

Émilie stands in the doorway and cranes to see what's going on. André motions for her to go back in. Her being seen is all they need.

Almost at once, Egger and the soldiers exit the bookstore and frog-march Monsieur Durand to the truck. André starts towards them, but the bookseller discreetly shakes his head. André stops in his tracks. He's right—better the Germans don't realize they know each other. The soldiers help the old man into the back of the truck and scramble in after him. André feels stranded at the edge of some great expanse, unable to move forward or turn back.

Egger pauses to give André a nod, before getting back in the motorcar and signaling the driver to go.

André steps back into the pâtisserie and starts to close the door, but Émilie stops him.

"We can't let them take him. It's because of me—"

"What can we do?"

Her brow furrows. "Are you telling me you're willing to abandon your friend?"

What does she expect of him? To run over and fight them all single-handedly? Of course he has to do something, but what? Answering that is difficult as making a *croquembouche* blindfolded.

Émilie looks through the open door willing some miraculous intervention. The only response is the erratic idling from the truck outside. When it's clear she doesn't have an idea of what to do any more than he does, André moves to the worktable and stares into the bowl of batter. Durand is an old man. They'll ask him a few questions and let him go. They won't hurt him. These thoughts, forced as they are, do nothing to slow André's galloping pulse.

The truck thunders past the shop again. In a burst, André picks up the bowl and throws it against the wall. It shatters soundlessly, any noise it makes overwhelmed by the vehicles passing on the street. Batter dribbles down the wall.

With one last look at the vehicles driving away, Émilie shuts the door.

Along the street, shops are closing for the evening. André wonders why he bothered opening. Soon as he unlocked the door that morning, Madame Monchamp steamed in, saw how few pastries there were, and went out again without saying a word. She was the only customer who came in all day. As bad an omen as a table set for thirteen.

He watches Émilie remove the three petits fours from the display case. At least Frédéric will have some treats. André drags himself to the front door where he turns the sign to FERMÉ, pulls out a key, and reaches for the lock.

There's a knock. Egger's cake-shaped face fills the door's window. Not again. Doing his best to suppress any signs of contempt, André opens the door. Just seeing the man makes him think of livestock...and their stench.

"Good evening, Herr Albert." The Nazi reacts to André's cuts and bruises with an impressed look. He spots Émilie at the display. "Ah, Frau Albert. A pleasure."

He walks in and waits for André to close the door after him. Seconds snail along as André makes up his mind what to do. Throwing the man out on his ass would be a good start.

Finally, André shuts the door.

Egger shirks his shoulders at the inevitability of André's action, and strolls over to the display case. With each step, the sounds of his boot heels thump against the walls. Émilie braces as if expecting an assault.

The German inspects the meagre offerings for sale, yet his eyes widen as he feigns delight at how wonderful they are. His charade further annoys André, who has to stop himself from grumbling under his breath.

"The remainders of the day? They look delicious." Egger spots the plate Émilie is holding. "Oh! What are they called? Small stoves?"

"Petits fours," André answers and folds his arms like he's knotting rope.

"Ah, yes. Small ovens." The Nazi snickers and reaches out a greedy hand. "May I?"

Émilie thrusts the plate towards him without even a flicker of an eyelid. André frowns at her. How can she be so obvious with her hate? No good will come from it.

"*Merci*, Madame." Egger gives out an amused chuckle, and pulls off the glove of one hand, finger by finger, with slow, deliberate gestures. With his bare hand, he lifts a petit four and takes a dainty bite of a corner. "Mmm. *Magnifique!*" He talks as he chews. "Is that the word? *Magnifique?*"

No one answers. Had André known, he'd have slipped in some arsenic and let the German feast on that.

Egger puts what's left of the pastry back on the plate and turns to André, all of a sudden solemn. "I saw you during that business with Durand, the bookseller. You must know the man given you are neighbours."

"He's a friend of our family." Denying it is probably useless now.

"A friend? There are rewards to being friends, *ja*? Being new to this country, I dearly miss good friends. The gendarmes with whom I work are surprisingly...hostile? No! What am I saying? *Reserved.*"

He gives André a moment to respond, probably expecting him to agree about the dour disposition of his fellow Frenchmen, like two buddies sharing a joke, but André's eyes remain fixed on the man's every move. As if friendship is easy as *bonjour*.

"Sometimes blatantly so," Egger adds quietly. He scratches the bridge of his nose and inspects the shop with a discerning eye like he's measuring its dimensions.

"Now Venice was a very hospitable posting. They complain about the smells, but..." He shrugs and turns back to them. "I took many snapshots. I met this lovely couple—glass blowers. They welcomed me into their home as a long-lost cousin. I acquired quite the collection of their work." He pauses for effect. "It's a shame what happened."

Egger almost seems genuinely forlorn. But then he brightens again. "Next I hope to visit North Africa. Perhaps England. America even." He laughs and looks to André to join in. Not a chance. The Nazi's smile fades to a scowl that hangs limply on his bulbous face. He stamps a foot, and looking down, spots his dirty footprints. "Oh! What have I stepped in now?" Egger scrapes his boots as he carries on talking, seemingly more concerned with that than what he says next. "So, you must be aware of what Herr Doktor Durand was doing last night?"

André watches him scuff the wooden floorboards and fights his revulsion with decreasing success. This German will turn their shop into a feed trough, and he'll be back to root in it every day.

"Then let me tell you, shall I?" Egger stops scraping and looks up. His right eye narrows. "Your friend was helping a Jewess escape." He taps a glove against his wrist.

André gives nothing away, but Émilie stiffens and slowly turns to him. Egger raises an eyebrow.

"I find that difficult to believe, Monsieur." André speaks in a plain tone, although his insides are a tempest. How does the Nazi know? Has Monsieur Durand told him?

Émilie stares at the alley door. André catches a quiver in her lips as though she's counting the steps. She won't get far. He can't remember if the door's unlocked.

"So he says. So he says." The German is perplexed, or pretends to be. "But I have my doubts. He was terminated from his teaching position for his politics, *ja*? And there were—rumours. Sordid rumours I've heard. I won't elaborate on them given there's a lady present."

Egger bows to Émilie, but she's still staring at the door. He gives the top of the display case a solid whack with the palm of his hand as if he's slapping a friend on the back who's just shared good news.

Émilie jumps. André's mouth curls when he sees the man lick his lips like a thirsty mastiff.

All at once, Egger is bright and airy again. "How's trade, Herr Albert? I imagine ingredients are hard to come by."

"Of course."

"I'll have some delivered first thing."

"Pardon, Monsieur?"

"No need to thank me. It's what friends do. I'll expect an occasional treat, but that's understandable, *ja*?"

"No. I mean, yes. But I can't accept..." André's voice peters out as he has the sudden urge to slash the man's throat. Satisfying as this would be, it sickens him such an impulse exists in him.

He's not a violent man. He's not. He knows a desire like this will suffocate him, but even worse, he doesn't care if it does.

Egger pulls on the glove and saunters to the door. Just when they're about to be free of him, he twists back.

"Oh, Madame. I'd like to see your papers, if that doesn't trouble you. You as well, Monsieur."

André drives his hands into his pockets, withdraws his identification card, and stomps up to the German. He knows who André is. Doesn't he have better things to do?

Egger takes the card and examines it. "Fine. Fine. As expected." He hands it back. He turns to Émilie and taps his foot with mock impatience. "Frau Albert?" He sing-songs the name.

Émilie plunges her hand into her apron, pulls out Mireille's birth certificate, and holds it out to him. The Nazi eyes it from where he's standing with a smirk, but doesn't move. Émilie has to bring it to him. Standing so near to him, his face shiny with sweat, she casts her eyes down.

André's throat dries to dust.

Egger reads the document out loud, "Mireille Madeleine Pellegrin, at birth." He hands it back. "An exquisite name. And your identity card?"

"I misplaced it, Monsieur."

"Misplaced it? In here?" Egger sweeps his head from one side of the room to the other searching for it.

"Or upstairs. I'll look again if you'd like?" Émilie moves towards the stairs.

"No, no," Egger says. Émilie stops and remains facing the other way. "But you do appreciate it's an offense to be without one?" He flagrantly leers at her body, then looks to make sure André saw.

André shakes his head. Disgusting pig. Again, terrible thoughts fill his mind. It feels as if everything awful that's happened recently has taken the form of this maggot of a man.

"Yes, Monsieur," Émilie mumbles.

The Nazi ogles her for a moment more, then crisply marches to the door where he glances at them over his shoulder.

"Tomorrow morning expect a delivery," he tells André. Then to Émilie: "And I'll expect you and your card first thing tomorrow at the gendarmerie."

At last Egger departs, shutting the door in his wake with a solid thud.

André lurches over and turns the key. He watches Egger get into the motorcar and drive away. He wants to breathe out in relief, but can't. It's not the last of that arrogant prick. Next time the German won't ask for what he wants.

"I have to leave." Émilie's voice jangles on the edge of panic. She stumbles to the alley door and opens it. It wasn't locked after all.

"You can't now," André tells her with a brusque, almost vindictive tone. If only it were so easy. "If you don't show up, he'll be back. And when he finds you gone..."

What he doesn't finish saying hangs there, its enormous weight poised to crash down on them.

Émilie untangles more of her hair at the armoire as André stands over her watching her in the mirror. She pulls on one large knot with force and doesn't flinch. It hurts, but she's determined not to show it. No one will forgive weakness. It'll be seen as an opportunity.

"Go to a gendarme," André tells her, "not Egger. Avoid him at all costs. A gendarme might not bother to examine the photo closely."

"And if he does?"

André's expression curdles. He can't bear thinking about it either. Émilie is moved. If there are any *gute mentshn* left, he might just be one of them.

She works the comb through again, and a clump of hair comes out in her hand. She glances at André to see if he notices. He does. "They didn't feed us," she explains, and hides it in her pocket. This remnant of vanity bothers her. How can she think herself so important? What a hollow emotion. It causes a twinge of recollection of when she worked in fashion where being vain was a badge of honour.

André draws the blackout curtain, then joins Frédéric at the table and hangs his head. Émilie watches him in the mirror, careful not to let him catch her. When he moves to hand another biscuit to his son, she turns back to her reflection. Witnessing the smallest affection between them will end her.

She examines the bruise under her eye—it's barely noticeable now. What questions will it evoke? She runs the comb through her hair to another knot.

André looks over. "There isn't time. Just keep your head covered."

Émilie pulls the comb out, as André tenderly brushes biscuit crumbs from his son's chin. Her stomach heaves like she's swallowed one of those squalls that come out of nowhere to capsize everything in its path. He has no idea of the possible ramifications.

"Monsieur... Tomorrow... If I don't come back in an hour, you and— You and the boy should leave."

TWELVE

Wednesday, October 27, 1943

A military truck noisily idles while German soldiers unload it. Neighbours are at their doors gawping, each face leaching judgement.

André watches with building resentment as one soldier carries in a large bag of flour and drops it on the floor. On the work-table sit blocks of butter and packets of sugar, even some choc-olate—more ingredients than he's seen in a long while. His thirty pieces of silver.

In the past, when there were plenty of supplies, Mireille had countless ideas of what to bake. They hadn't made a *gâteau opéra* since André's parents visited the first Noël after Frédéric was born. For what that was worth. André remembers his nerves feeling scraped along their lengths when his father proclaiming loudly he preferred a simple *gâteaux renversés*, another one of his rebukes made more stinging since André had just mastered the challenging dessert. Every bite André took of his work tasted more acrid until there was nothing in his mouth but ashes.

Still, maybe it's time to make another one. This thought de-livers an unexpected pang of joy. André pushes it away, prefer-ring the wretched realization each bag and block and packet is a reminder Mireille isn't here to bake anything, and how much he loathes Egger.

The soldier gives a crisp click of his heels.

André slams the door after him.

❖

Émilie walks into the gendarmerie with all the bonhomie of someone mounting stairs to the gallows. She's wearing Mireille's coat, another of her dresses, and one of her flowered kerchiefs tied at the neck. It still holds perfume, mild and sweet.

A miserable-looking gendarme is listening to a woman who's waving her arms wildly. Émilie hopes if there's a scene, they won't pay much attention to her.

The walls start crushing her, but Émilie purses her lips and takes a step forward. She spots Egger at a desk in the back, speaking on the telephone. She quickly leaves.

On the street, she wants to run. Momentarily freed from the clouds, the sun beats down on her, and she covers her eyes with a hand. Breathe. Breathe. After a few long moments straining for air, she braces herself, turns, and looks at the police station.

She starts backing away, stops, snatches at the courage she lacks, and somehow manages to grab hold. With a deep gulp like she's about to wade into frigid water, Émilie goes back in.

The gendarme is alone now—Egger is nowhere in sight. Émilie approaches the policeman so quietly that when she says, "I was told to present my papers," he jumps. There's a jagged edge in her voice giving away how nervous she is about the lies she's about to tell. It's so pronounced, he must hear it, too.

The man scowls at her and puts out a jaded hand. Émilie digs in her coat pocket and produces Mireille's identification card, but hesitates before handing it over. The policeman gives her a look, of impatience or suspicion, she isn't sure. He looks at the card and hands it back. She shoves it into her pocket and turns to leave.

"Remove that," the gendarme tells her.

Émilie looks back and he's wagging a finger at her kerchief. She laments her luck—he's one of those gendarmes who's maddeningly officious. Like everything they say is in triplicate.

Hauptsturmführer Egger enters the room, and seeing Émilie, gives her a plump smile. "Frau Albert!" He practically skips over as her mind goes blank.

"The kerchief," the gendarme repeats.

"Oh! You're here to present your identification. May I see it?" Egger extends a hand.

She stares at his palm for a moment as if it's wrapped in barbed wire before passing the card over, irrevocably surrendering herself to fate, something she had vowed never to do again without a battle. But here she is, flailing like a beached trout.

Egger examines the card with great drama: he holds it close, reading it carefully, then shoves it out to arm's length and squints from Émilie to the card and back again.

"I can attest unequivocally that it's her," the Nazi announces to the gendarme in a pompous manner that would make all the kings of France blush.

"She should remove the kerchief," the gendarme persists. "Rules."

"Now what have we become if we can't trust an upstanding shopkeeper like Madame Albert?" Egger hands back the identification card to Émilie with a flourish. She pockets it and hurries out.

Trembling, Émilie walks briskly along the street, trying to distance herself from that revolting man fast as her feet will allow. Instead of celebrating another escape, she bites her lip to scold herself for having to submit to a despicable lump like Egger. She feels blood draining from every artery, every vein. Just as she thinks she's rising from her knees, she finds herself prostrate in the dirt.

She calms down enough to smell the moist, earthy air of the coming rain, when behind her a voice with a German accent calls, "Frau Albert!"

Émilie pretends she doesn't hear it. She imagines herself a mare with blinkers and stays on her path back to the pâtisserie.

Footsteps overtake her and the voice says, "Mireille!"

Émilie half-turns to see Egger with a whisper of a smile on his pasty face. He impales her with his deep-set green eyes. "Now you're in compliance with the law." His jaw protrudes with moral superiority.

She knows he wants her to say something, most likely for her to lavish him with gratitude. For what? Enforcing their tyrannical laws? All Émilie can manage is a thin smile as she moves to leave. It's imperative she keeps walking.

"But a word..." The German raises his hand. He keeps it there for seconds longer than natural, as if commanding silence, before letting it drift down like a leaf.

Émilie opens her mouth to tell him she has to go, she's late getting back for Frédéric, but Egger manoeuvres in front of her, uncomfortably close. A familiar dankness reaches her—as offensive and aggressive as them. She once thought it was their uniforms, but unfortunately learned that even when they're out of them, the stink clings to their skin like a curse. She squirms and swallows her disgust.

"A woman such as you could make a man quite happy." Egger's tone is awash with insinuation. "Especially someone without friends, family, companionship, so far from the Fatherland." He attempts an ingratiating smile that more resembles a snarl. He steps closer and asks, low and gravely, his rank breath all over her ear, "May I call you Mireille?"

Émilie becomes rigid and she tastes rust. The glint in the Nazi's eyes is both lewd and condemning and only reminds her to some men she's ugly.

"Monsieur?" She throws up her hands to ward him off. She can hear his breathing rumbling like an overworked furnace.

Egger should be insulted, but he's distracted by her bandages. He takes Émilie's hand in his before she can object. His touch is clammy, sticky as the grease used on her sewing machine at the atelier. Sticky as blood.

"Oh, dear! What have you done? Too often the world is unkind, *ja*?" Egger lifts her hand to his face as though trying to see it better. "Much too unkind. And surprisingly so to some of us more than others, even someone as captivating as—"

"Émilie!" Monsieur Durand shuffles towards them, looking exhausted and disheveled, although still holding his head upright.

Just in time.

She pulls her hand away from Egger and resists the urge to wipe it on her coat. When Monsieur Durand reaches them, she hugs him. There's the sour odour on him of the sweat only fear can produce.

The bookseller glares at the Nazi while telling her, "They've released me."

Egger gives out a laugh, jarringly good-humoured. "It seems we may have a case of mistaken identity."

"I must take my friend home." Émilie links arms with Monsieur Durand, and they turn away and continue down the street. The shiver she's been repressing surfaces. If she begins to shake again, she'll be knocked to the ground.

The German doesn't hide his displeasure at Émilie's abrupt departure.

The old man walks with effort; he leans heavily against her so as not to fall. It takes all her strength to keep from toppling over with him. She looks down. Monsieur Durand's shoes and the hems of his trousers are bloody. She could ask what they've done to him, but she has a good idea.

From up the street, André limps towards them carrying Frédéric. Émilie's lips part, pleased to see him. André spots the Nazi behind her, and his mouth squeezes shut.

The baker makes a point of kissing Émilie on the cheek, much to her surprise, though she does her best not to let it show. It's part of the charade. He's only doing what a husband would do when greeting his wife.

Still, she looks away as her face warms.

They head home. André puts Frédéric down, and the boy runs up ahead. André and Émilie walk on, supporting Monsieur Durand, knowing the German is still watching them.

Egger's biding his time. If she turns around, his expression will be openly mocking her for thinking they've got away with deceiving him.

By force of will, she keeps her steps even and her eyes focused straight ahead.

"He said my name," she tells André. She's trembling again. She turns to the bewildered old bookseller.

"You called me 'Émilie.'"

THIRTEEN

Thursday, October 28, 1943

A nun in her flowing habit, beaming like a celestial revelation, floats out from the pâtisserie carrying a box stuffed with *milles feuilles*. The plaintive sound of Josephine Baker gently flows onto the street, and passersby slow their pace to take in the luscious, rich smells wafting out with the music. It's been too long since such scents have filled the shop.

The shelves of the display case overflow with brightly coloured treats, sugar wonders in an assortment of shapes and sizes. One gâteau after another jostles for space on the bottom shelf. Straining the middle shelf are plates of petits fours, straight lines of macarons, and a varied collection of other pastries and biscuits. In its place of honour on the top shelf, an impressive *gâteau opéra* reigns. André succumbed to impulse this morning and made it, although when he was finished his throat filled with longing.

He serves two indecisive girls who giggle at him, probably thinking this makes them coquettish when he only finds such tactics grating. A woman waiting impatiently behind them rolls her eyes. André forces a smile and asks them for their selection.

Madame Monchamp breezes in, her heavy, fox collar coat especially unnecessary this unseasonably warm day. She pushes past the other customers to inspect the contents of the display case. Her eyes widen, then narrow.

"I heard you have plenty of pastries for a change, but I didn't believe it. How is this possible?"

André scratches his neck and looks from the two girls he's serving to Madame Monchamp and back again, grappling as much with the dilemma of whom he should give priority as with how to reprimand the old woman for jumping the queue. His fingers ache with the arthritis of sudden irritation. Every time she walks in, it ages him.

Before he can decide, Madame Monchamp says disagreeably, "I'm sure they won't mind," and offers the girls an insincere smile that evaporates when she turns away. He swears the woman flashed fangs.

Intimidated, the girls don't even squeak.

"So, Monsieur Albert, how did you come by these?" Madame Monchamp eyes the pastries with a greedy desire. She's seconds away from drooling.

"We made them." André keeps his tone plain as bread.

"The ingredients," Madame Monchamp says firmly. "I would like to know your supplier. My daughter and her husband are still at mine. It's her birthday, so I would like to—"

"Madame, may I help you? There are others..." André motions to the waiting customers. No amount of money she might spend is worth this aggravation. What Mireille must have gone through with such customers. She's a saint. An absolute saint.

The exhausting woman's mouth shifts to something nearer to a sneer. "Yes. Very well." She jabs a finger at the display. "Two—no three petits fours. And— No. Never mind. I'll have a selection of *mignardises*."

While André boxes the order, the woman leans towards him and whispers, "Secrets are always discovered."

He stops, unsure how to react to such a provocative statement. Madame Monchamp raises an eyebrow, waiting for— The pastries? His response?

Émilie, leading Frédéric by the hand, tries to slip in through the alley door. But when the boy yelps, everyone turns. André curses the timing. The snooping crone can't help but notice her. Now the woman will have another reason to cause trouble.

"I see you have money for help, too!" Madame Monchamp is loud and indignant. Ignoring Frédéric, as she always does—she once told Mireille she thought of children, except her own, of course, as "tribulations"—she barks at Émilie, "Girl! There are customers waiting."

Émilie brushes past her and joins André. Madame Monchamp strains to hear what they're saying. Nosy as a starving cat. André and Émilie move closer together. In a soft voice, André asks, "Is he okay?"

"The Monsieur insisted on opening the librairie as usual. I'll just get Frédéric settled." Émilie carries the boy upstairs, as André finishes tying the box with string. Given half a chance, he could just as easily bind the old woman's mouth shut.

Madame Monchamp takes out a change purse and doles out money, placing each coin on André's extended palm with an undisguised animosity that's wasted on him. He doesn't care for such pettiness and usually pretends it hasn't taken place.

He hands her the box, and she clomps to the door, leaving it to swing open after her.

The two girls make mousy noises as André rings up the sale. He can't stop thinking about Madame Monchamp's words. What secret? Where they got their supplies? Fear ripples through him. What if she knows what Émilie is? She's eluded Egger's detection—at least it appears that way—the Nazi hasn't returned yet to arrest her.

Or is it something about Mireille?

André holds up a finger to the girls and sprints to the door. They look at each other with disappointment; the woman at the back of the queue rolls her eyes again, now even more annoyed.

Madame Monchamp is peering in the window of an umbrella repair shop down the street when André catches up to her.

"Madame. If you have something to say..."

She turns to him, and seeing his worried expression, barely holds back a smirk. She tugs on the brim of her hat against the sun and is about to speak, when a young man with a long scar down the side of his face passes by. He pulls out a gold watch on a fob, and the caustic look Madame Monchamp gives him is withering in its judgment of him as a simpleton begging to be robbed.

She talks loudly like she wants the passing man to hear, along with anyone else who might be listening. "I have not a *sou* more for your sawdust cakes. Good day, Monsieur."

When the young man continues on out of earshot, she lowers her voice. "I'll come to yours when it's quiet." She rubs her money-grubbing fingers together in André's face, then walks away. Even the truth has a price.

André watches her go, a slight to-and-fro wobble to her gait. Madame Monchamp is a cruel woman; he's certainly not fooled by her. She might not know anything and is only leading him on.

He walks back up the street, warning himself not to hope, yet he grasps it like a candle on a stormy night.

The shop's front door is still open, and the customers are gone. It doesn't matter. There's no time to fret about the state of the business.

With a quick intake of air, he closes the door, and the bell rings, its sound carving into him. Where it once announced people eager to buy their wares, now it scolds him for having to accept Egger's tainted ingredients, for whatever help Madame Monchamp is going to sell him, and for his lapses in searching for Mireille.

He sees a folded piece of paper on the display case. At first, he thinks it's a complaint from one of the customers. He backtracks to the front door and looks out. No one is there except a boy on the opposite end of a leash being pulled along by his dog, a woolly Barbet.

André opens the note and reads the scrawled words. *She was taken.*

Thick drops of rain strafe the window behind the blackout curtain. Monsieur Durand sits with André, lost in their own personal wildernesses, a plate of pastries before them, while Émilie checks on Frédéric who's asleep in bed. The boy shivers, and she pulls the covers up and tucks them around him.

She returns with a tin basin of water and places it on the floor next to Monsieur Durand, shaking him from his thoughts. The entire evening he's felt off-kilter, on the edge of a mantle about to tumble into a fire. Apprehension infuses every part of him. It's like waiting at a trial for the verdict without knowing your crime.

"Such a feast." He looks from André to Émilie, both appear emptied of emotion. They were this way throughout dinner, and Monsieur Durand felt obliged as their guest to carry the conversation. He told them what he hoped were amusing anecdotes about the peculiar customers who frequent his shop, and he chronicled a trip he took as a young man to the Far East where he was held for a week near Nara by criminals demanding a ransom or they'd kill him. One night while his captors were nodding off, he managed to flee with his life and a rudimentary comprehension of Japanese.

André has heard the tale before, but tonight he seemed to have no patience for hearing it again—he sat slumped in his seat, staring glassily at the pastries, seldom glancing up. When he did, it was with a coldness Monsieur Durand had never seen in his friend. What an old fool to be recounting tales no one wants to hear.

Mireille always loved his stories, but he supposes now they must seem trivial. Émilie also didn't look entertained. Perhaps he offended her. In his zeal to bolster their spirits, was he being too cavalier in the way he spoke? He forgot who she is—what she is. He may have described his predicament as too much of an adventure. She might not consider herself fortunate to be able to do likewise with hers.

Monsieur Durand reaches for an éclair and tries again to engage his dining companions. "And these confections, where did you find the ingredients?" He looks from the baker to the stranger again—both avoid eye contact. "They're splendid. Fit for a king." He takes an enthusiastic bite.

"Or a Führer," Émilie says under her breath as she kneels next him.

André shoots her a look. Monsieur Durand blurts out a small laugh, despite his mouth being full. "Pardon?" he mumbles.

"Your shoes, Monsieur," Émilie says.

He protests, but she doesn't budge. With a sigh, he turns in his chair, and she helps him untie his shoes and remove them.

"*Mon Dieu!*" Émilie cries out. The bandages wrapped around his feet are thick with blood.

André looks over and grimaces. "What have they done?" At last a trace of his affection is restored.

"Not to worry, I'll live. Though if I'm honest, I am a bit shaken. But it will take more than a Bavarian fascist to stop me."

Monsieur Durand's done well to ignore his pain, despite how torturous it is at times. It comes in waves, throbbing like a racing heartbeat, often scorching like his feet are being dipped in acid. Showing hurt would betray an upbringing extolling stoicism, inane as that is. Still, it's one of the last, if not tenuous, links to a childhood that seems to only exist in his memory as a daguerreotype, brown and faded.

Émilie starts to roll up her sleeve and abruptly stops, but not before Monsieur Durand sees a tattoo on her left forearm.

"What is that?" His voice rises with concern. "Is it from Drancy? Did they do this to you there?" When she says nothing, he looks to André, who shakes his head and turns away.

"No," Émilie says, not much more than a croak. She begins unwrapping the bandages from Monsieur Durand's left foot. The blood becomes darker as she peels the layers until the black bandage next to his wound is exposed.

The numbers gouged into her skin profoundly disturb him. How could someone do that to another human being? He extends his hand to her arm, but she pulls away. He wants to know their significance, but how Émilie holds her face, closed and expressionless, leaves him to doubt she will provide him with any answers. Everyone keeps parts of themselves hidden in shadows.

"I see," Monsieur Durand says, and apologizes. So she remains an enigma.

The lights flicker and go out.

Monsieur Durand produces a box of matches from his pocket and passes them to his friend. André opens it, extracts one, strikes it against the side of the box, and brings it to a short candle on the table. Then the baker goes to the buffet and searches through one of the drawers.

Speaking quietly so only Monsieur Durand can hear, Émilie says, "Thank you for what you did." When he tilts his head slightly, she adds, "The park. Helping me leave."

"You've thanked me enough. Both of you. But it wasn't successful." He takes a deep breath as she unwinds the last bandage—it's glued to his wounds.

"They do it to inflict the most pain," Émilie tells him. "But the bastards who did this to you were careless. Torture is much more effective on the mind than the body when you have no proof it happened."

She cups her hands, scoops up some water, and pours them over the wounds. Monsieur Durand is about to assure her that their tactics weren't able to touch his mind, but she speaks with an authority he can't argue with. She's correct. The interrogation was unnerving. Where once his ripostes could effectively vanquish any opponent, he had found himself gasping for words. Egger had flustered him, so Monsieur Durand stopped speaking; he didn't want to help them humiliate him. The Nazi couldn't have been more delighted if he had single-handedly won the war.

Then they started on his feet.

When they yanked off his shoes, Monsieur Durand didn't understand what they were doing. With each question, the pain they inflicted increased with knife-hot cuts. Egger asked little about the rendezvous in the park—he mostly wanted to know about his friendship with the Alberts. Monsieur Durand emphatically told the Nazi had he had children, he couldn't envisage anyone more wonderful than André and Mireille to call his own. Egger laughed in such a derisive way, Monsieur Durand felt small as a lone raindrop in the night sky.

He's proud they weren't able to extricate another syllable from him after that. That defiance did well to mask his weakness.

What they did to him was unbearable and unending. He had read nothing is as bad as physical pain, and in that dank room they had him locked, he believed it. He cried out, of course, at times yowling like a chained animal, but still he wouldn't give anything away. He held his tongue by repeating a single thought: This cannot be happening in the country of Descartes, Voltaire, and Hugo.

And then the Nazi let him go, just like that. Monsieur Durand didn't linger to ask why.

But now? It seems suspect to be allowed to leave so readily, even if he paid a price.

Émilie glances up from his feet. "Why didn't you tell us how bad they are?"

He shrugs. He tried to tend to them himself, bandaging them soon as he returned home, and was about to change them, but found it too tiring after his ordeal. Before he knew it, he fell asleep. In his dreams, he laboured over uncovering what Egger is up to and came up with nothing. Corporeal failings are one thing, but when one fears for one's mind...

Monsieur Durand leans forward. "Émilie. Be wary of that German." She gives him a curt nod. He sits back in the chair. That was a meaningless thing to tell her. As if Émilie, or André, for that matter, won't be cautious around a Nazi. Yet, he's compelled to warn them.

André lines four candles in front of him and lights them. He waits a moment to see they don't go out before pushing them to the centre of the table. Monsieur Durand finds their placement almost ceremonial.

"There's hidden beauty in troubled times. It allows for friendship between strangers." He looks to the others. André turns away, but Émilie's entranced by the flames. "The Shabbat, no?

Baruch ata Adonai eloheinu melech ha'olam."

Émilie looks up, surprised, then her face hardens. "I'm no longer religious." She continues washing Monsieur Durand's feet, the water now dark red. Ignoring what should normally be a shocking sight, she carries on without hesitation. She's seen worse. It's in her eyes.

"Nor you, André?" Monsieur Durand asks.

André follows his gaze to the wall, where now there's only an outline of the crucifix that hung there. A holy ghost.

"I pray. Over and over. Who hears?"

"Sorrow is a heavy fruit," Monsieur Durand says in sympathy. "But we have to trust the Almighty doesn't let it grow on branches too weak to bear it." He sits back and folds his arms across his chest, resting his case. Facile as this platitude is, it seems a comfort to many people. Then remorse seeps in. He should be telling them something he actually believes in.

"If God exists, He's at the farthest corner of Heaven." André's voice is nothing but bitter.

"With His back turned to us." Émilie mutters.

Monsieur Durand and André look at her for an explanation, but she doesn't waver from her task.

They retreat into a brooding silence only broken by the wind rattling the window and the soft murmuring coming from Frédéric as though he's talking in his dream.

No one speaks even when a moth flutters into a candle flame, drops to the table, and flaps for a few frenzied moments.

André visibly rouses himself: he sits up straight in the chair and speaks loudly and with purpose. "Monsieur Durand, I have a question for a learnèd man like you."

"Oh!" Monsieur Durand emits a guarded chuckle. "Nothing wine couldn't answer with more wisdom, I suspect."

"If someone were missing, where would she be?"

He's unsure if his younger friend is being serious. He starts to say, "André, how do I..." but he peters out, unable to come up with something to placate André in the battered mood he's nursing. There's limitations to everything, especially words.

Even miracles have their constraints.

André looks pointedly at Émilie, who's drying Monsieur Durand's feet with a towel. "If she were *ripped* from her home?"

Without looking up, Émilie carries the basin to the sink. She's prudent to evade the looming storm of André's rancour.

The splash of bloody water being poured into the sink covers the whack André's fist makes on the table. His eyes bore into Émilie's back. Shoulders slumped, she watches the water drain away.

Monsieur Durand searches for something to say, frantic to intervene. He rubs his aching knuckles, feeling closer to tree burls than vellum. They live in a desperate time when accusations are lobbed like grenades. Nothing good can come from such animus.

"If she was stolen?" André spits the words.

"Like her?" Monsieur Durand turns his head to Émilie, then raises a hand in a plea for André to calm down. But André ignores him. Embarrassed by his friend's behaviour, Monsieur Durand fills his lungs and forms his protest, but nothing comes out his mouth. It's frightening what André's becoming—what he might end up doing. A man who thinks himself abandoned acts selfishly, no longer caring a damn for anyone else.

When there's no answer from Émilie, André scoffs. "At least you save me more lies."

There's a loud crash of breaking glass from below.

André jumps up and hurtles down the stairs. Heart pounding, Monsieur Durand pulls on his shoes fast as he can and follows, wincing as he hobbles down to the pâtisserie.

Where the shop's name was lettered on the window, there's now a hole with sharp, jagged edges. A brick lies among shards of glass.

André unlocks the front door and runs out as Monsieur Durand limps after him.

COLLABOS is scrawled across the other window, the white paint still dripping. The chef-d'œuvre of cowards.

The baker can't disguise his worry, while Monsieur Durand

does his best to keep his own in check, even though he's arguably more alarmed than his friend.

It's a long road back from being denounced, especially if it's as a collaborator with Nazis.

FOURTEEN

Friday, October 29, 1943
Day

André replaces the broken glass with Monsieur Durand's help, while neighbours watch from across the street, faces sombre as clouds. Among them are the butcher, the florist, Madame Bujold's son, and Gilles, of course, smoking with the casualness of someone at the cinema. Even a drunkard like him wouldn't miss this for all the wine in the Rhône.

Once the new pane is in place, André spreads linseed oil putty around its edges with the same finesse he relies on icing a cake. Monsieur Durand makes a point of positioning himself in front of the other window, blocking the malicious accusation painted on it from the onlookers. Grateful, André squares his shoulders and continues working with renewed intensity.

Émilie steps out with a pail of water and a scraper, but André barks at her to go back inside. What is she thinking?

She does as she's told, standing just inside the doorway. Without flinching, she rips off the bandages on her injured hand, and reaching with it, defiantly turns the sign to OUVERT. André admires her grit. Never forget a mouse can terrorize an elephant.

When André is through puttying the window, Durand helps him scrape off the condemning word. André glances over at the owl-eyed mob. Which one of them denounced him? Which one turned on them after all they've done? Many times Mireille had gone out to aid a neighbour in distress while André was left to make the pastries and tend to customers. Neither of them wanted praise, but to be punished? Who have they ever hurt?

Although pastries fill the display case, the shop is empty except for André standing at attention in his baker's whites. He realizes he's grinding his teeth and stops. Soon they'll be nothing more than nubs. He lets out a slow breath

Émilie comes in from the stairs holding up a small garment. "Monsieur, Frédéric has torn his shirt. May I—"

"Yes. Yes," he snaps. Another André would have chastised himself for that. She isn't the target of his anger, at least not the entire brunt of it. But that André is gone now. Good riddance. He'll be useless in the fight ahead.

Émilie stays there for a moment more, chewing on her lower lip. André remains motionless as an old tree. With a sigh, she thumps back upstairs.

Monsieur Durand appears on the other side of the new window. The door opens and the bell rings. André's mouth forms a snarl at the sound. Might as well be tolling for the end of their business.

"So?" The old man's voice is keen with anticipation.

"No one."

"Perhaps tomorrow. They'll realize they're wrong about you. First contrition, then pleas for forgiveness." Monsieur Durand tops this serving of optimism with a smile.

"I'll know soon," André says. The commotion last night must have scared Madame Monchamp off. Surely she'll return tonight.

"Know?"

"What happened to Mireille. I only have to pay."

Monsieur Durand steps in front of him, but André looks past him. "To whom?"

When André says nothing, Monsieur Durand starts to give him a gentle caution. "André, my friend, you must be—"

"Madame Monchamp said she'd help. She said she'd—"

"Monchamp! That cow? She would have taken your money, told you lies, and handed you over to them."

"No. She wouldn't do—"

"Have you not heard? She was found this morning in her bed. Her precious daughter tried to wake her."

André's expression twists. His thoughts stall, then start up again. "She was an old woman." As much as André attempts to rationalize it, his shoulders slump, guilty of being endlessly gullible.

"An old woman with a knife in her neck." The bookseller's voice tightens as he delivers this punch. "That's your fate when you're a viper. Never trust anyone who rejoices in evil more than those who do it. If you'd just—"

"You should go."

"André, I'm only—"

"LEAVE."

Monsieur Durand persists in standing there, his hurt an exposed open fracture, a bone piercing through flesh. He reaches out and touches André's arm, but André stays rigid and unmoving. He doesn't need anyone's sympathy.

With a weak smile as goodbye, the old man leaves, easing the door shut after him.

In a frenzy, André pulls plates out of the display case. In the alley, he dumps the pastries into a garbage can.

Everything he and Mireille have has been destroyed.

Émilie sits beside Frédéric on his bed, showing him the photograph on his mother's identification card. "Do you know the beautiful lady? Maman. It's your maman." The boy is quiet for a long while before his little face empties, and Émilie doubts she's getting through to him. Has he forgotten her so quickly? Or does she exist in his mind as something different from this picture?

Émilie is about to take back the card when Frédéric says, "Maman." It's much more distinguishable than the first time he said it a few days ago—there's only the slightest muddle in the middle, almost imperceptible. She can't wait to tell André. At last there's some good news shining through.

"Yes. Your maman." Émilie wraps an arm around the boy's shoulder and hugs him, and he makes a contented mewling noise. "A maman will always love her child so very much. Will you remember that?"

Frédéric looks pensive, as though he's going to say something else, when André barges in from the stairs. He sees what Émilie is doing, and marches over.

"What are you doing?" He grabs the identification card, glances at it, and shoves it back at her. "You'll confuse him. He'll realize soon enough she's—" He stops himself and scowls at her as if resenting her for almost making him say it out loud. He mustn't see the point of his son remembering a mother who might never come back. What good are all the memories in the world to a motherless child?

André stomps to the table as Émilie helps Frédéric under the covers. "*Fais de beaux rêves.*" She steals a look at André, and when he faces the other way, she tucks the photograph under the boy's pillow. Perhaps his dreams will be better with his mother's image nearby, irrational as that is.

"She was taken." André says to the air.

Émilie holds her breath. A spasm of fear punctures her at what she expects is coming next. When André doesn't say anything else, she tells him with gentle encouragement, "Then she'll return."

The baker looks over at his son. "At least he sleeps. God knows I can't."

Émilie feels his eyes burning into her when he asks, "Why can't you?"

Monsieur Durand waits inside the door of his *librairie*. The blackout curtains are closed, the solitary light coming from a Tiffany banker's lamp on a desk halfway to the back of the shop.

The reflected colours paint the ceiling, and he momentarily looks up and shuts one eye, imagining he's peering through a kaleidoscope. If only life was so effortlessly superb.

There's a soft tapping at the door. When he opens it, Émilie slips in wearing Mireille's coat and kerchief, startling him at how similar she looks and how profoundly he misses his friend. He can't help but think an absence isn't a hole. It's a presence living inside you, eating its way out.

"I apologize for asking you here at this late hour." His voice lowers even further to add, "But there are things André must not hear just yet."

Émilie searches his face, her forehead tense with concern. Before she has a chance to ask why she's here, Monsieur Durand walks away and sits behind his desk. With a languid wave of his hand, he motions to a stool beside him, but Émilie exhales and turns to examine the volumes on one of the many bookcases lining the shop. She takes a book down and starts turning its pages.

"They hold great advice. Having books is an act of faith— beams of light in darkness." Monsieur Durand pauses, but she doesn't respond. "I suppose such philosophies are vain indulgences now."

He straightens in his chair and clears his throat as Émilie closes the book and returns it to its place. Just when he thinks she'll walk over, she approaches the window and cautiously moves the curtain to look out in the pâtisserie's direction.

"He's a good man." Monsieur Durand peers at her over his spectacles. "A good family man."

"He's done so much for me." Émilie presses a palm to the side of her head as though keeping her thoughts firmly in place. "I put them in danger, yet he still hides me."

"As I said, 'A good man.' At a time when virtue is rare, even small acts make one great."

"He's lost his faith."

"Then there's your answer: all he has is his conscience."

Émilie joins him at the desk where she picks up a children's book.

"For Frédéric." Monsieur Durand scrutinizes her, steeling himself to state what he feels obligated to tell her, the reason he asked her here so close to curfew.

"You must understand, Mademoiselle," he begins. "André has a fragile temperament. I don't say this to malign him, just to warn you. I implore you—be careful." He raises an eyebrow, giving her a chance to speak. When she doesn't, he sighs, as much an admission of his distaste for the task ahead as in disappointment Émilie is forcing him to spell it out.

"I know what happened," he says. Émilie continues rifling through the book. "Madame Bujold finally broke—guilt always rusts away silence." He waits for Émilie to react, but she remains intent on the book. One confession usually facilitates another.

"I went to see the old dear on the pretext I had an omnibus that might interest her—she hates reading without the assurance all subsequent volumes are close by. I stayed for tea and was forced to drink it with a squeeze of the dried up brown lemon she insisted we use." He rubs his chin with the heel of his hand at the memory of it. "Her son wasn't home. Gone, she told me, to find fish for their Friday lunch."

Monsieur Durand attempts to imitate the woman's low, quivering voice. "'We're such good Catholics, we haven't eaten meat all week.'" It comes out more of a mockery than he intends. Entirely unnecessary. He wishes her no ill will. Sometimes she's a pleasant enough raconteuse. He justifies his boorish performance on fatigue.

"She went on to divulge, without any inducement on my part, I must add, how the daughter of the woman who cleans Saint-Joachim is having a clandestine relationship with a German officer. She gave her head a funny little roll that told me she didn't need to enumerate the consequences.

"I indulged her until she revealed what I wanted to know, surprisingly difficult to illicit from her in spite of her propensity for gossip."

What a hypocrite! Even though he had no choice but to reveal this confidence, doing so means now he's guilty of the same transgression. In an attempt to appear less harsh in his critique, Monsieur Durand chuckles.

Émilie lays down the book, walks to the window again, and gazes towards the pâtisserie. Barely audible, she says, "I saw nothing."

"Mademoiselle?" He's not sure he heard her correctly. Émilie saw nothing? How is that possible? Madame Bujold told him that on that day she saw Émilie.

Émilie touches the window with the tips of her fingers. "I escaped. The door was open. I went in and hid."

"But you must have heard or surmised—"

"If I did, what could I have done?"

"Mireille is a daughter to me. André needs to know."

Émilie turns back; her eyes fix on him. "Then why haven't you told him?"

"I— Well—" Monsieur Durand stammers and stops. He leans back in his chair. How to answer? He's willing to acknowledge in the past he's stayed silent so not to lose the goodwill of a friend. Regrettably, too often that only postpones even more strife. He almost says, "The less you know, the better you sleep," but that would be flippant. He obviously hasn't listened to those words making inquiries on André's behalf. And every night he's meted out his punishment as he lies awake deliberating whether to tell André what he has learnt.

Monsieur Durand can almost smell looming tragedy. He hangs his head like a sentenced man, but still manages an even tone. "When one sees another carrying such a precarious load, it seems wise to tread nearby with caution. He's fighting for his family."

Émilie reaches to move the curtain again but stops. "You'll torment yourself no matter what you choose. I assure you of that."

She walks back to him, falters, and plants both hands on the desk to steady herself.

Monsieur Durand helps her to a wing chair. He takes a bottle of cognac and a glass from behind a book, pours some out, and offers it to her. Émilie shakes her head, but he insists, predicting the alcohol's sharp smell will do more to revive her than anything. She lifts the glass and has a guarded sip at first, then a proper drink.

He comes back to his chair and sits down heavily. While Émilie's difficult to make sense of, Monsieur Durand sees a vulnerability in her, but also a brittleness, an underlying enmity he should find off-putting, but in her he decides serves as a substitute for strength.

She's a fine young woman, and he doesn't have an inkling of what she's had to withstand. Everyone suffers alone, but when a kindred soul is encountered, they should join hands and suffer alone together.

"When people you love...go," Émilie says, "parts of who you are melt away. Less and less of you remains to continue on." She averts her eyes, but not before Monsieur Durand glimpses her bottomless pain.

Her spell seemingly passed, she stands and peruses the bookcase behind him and removes a book displayed with its cover facing out, separate from the rest.

"Please." Monsieur Durand carefully takes the book from her. "It's old." His abruptness startles her, and he hopes she's not offended. She couldn't have known.

"There are so many old volumes here," she says.

"Most are from when we opened. This is an original edition of Victor Hugo." He indicates the book he's holding.

"It must be valuable."

"In a way," Monsieur Durand says slowly, deliberately. "It was given to me by a dear friend."

Émilie ponders for a moment. "And where is this friend?"

Monsieur Durand feels a choking tightness in his heart. He sits back down and pushes the lamp to a corner of the desk farthest away from him, the light all at once too bright. "We lost touch." There's a finality to the way he says it that unsettles him.

He's never spoken with such forced indifference.

"These are the times we live in," Émilie says. "You said so yourself."

"He was arrested. Jews are not the only ones who suffer this scourge." Monsieur Durand folds his arms, determined not to disclose anything else. Sharing this already feels like he's being unfaithful.

Émilie looks at the bookcase again. Another book attracts her, but she merely touches its spine. "My husband loved books. He worked in the theatre, backstage at the Théâtre des Champs-Élysées. When I returned home from the atelier, I'd always find him reading. A student for life." She snickers at the whimsy of such a notion, a jarring contrast to her previous tone. "Claude thought I should be a designer and make costumes for the performers. He loved to encourage such dreams."

"Dreams give birth to our future. Why not have them?"

Émilie shakes her head again. "Not me. I wasn't good enough. Only he thought I was. He was my *basherter*." When Monsieur Durand's brow furrows, she adds, "My destiny. My soulmate." She plops down on the stool and gazes at the floor. "He came looking for me. Do you have any idea what the Nazis do to people who go there looking for their loved ones?"

"But André is not a Jew."

"Neither was my husband."

The impact of her words slaps him. Monsieur Durand folds his lips into a straight line and looks away. Memories can only remind us of loss. Instead of diminishing with the years, they burrow deeper, relentless and haunting.

"Claude was one of the few who showed up at the gates. How he learned where I was in Poland, I'll never know. I only found out what became of him because of this one guard—a jackal of a woman—who had an 'in' with an Unterstumführer. She revelled in telling me everything Claude did to free me. It choked me to realize my hopes were stitched to her sadism.

"One day, Herta told me the camp had received word Claude applied for my release, paid a bribe, and was waiting for

Gestapo headquarters in Berlin to approve it. A few weeks later, the repulsive woman couldn't wait to tell me that, of course, it was rejected.

"Claude would never leave me like that. I always said he was persistent as remorse. A month after that, Herta smirked at me for an entire day. Just before bedtime, she said someone had asked for me at the gates—'ein *Franzose*.' A Frenchman."

Émilie wraps her arms around herself and leans forward.

"Thousands of times I wished I was near the gates to have warned him. When I begged her to tell me where he was, she laughed and said the guards 'took him to the woods.'"

Émilie leans back and closes her eyes.

Monsieur Durand steeples his hands and brings them to his mouth. For one of the few times in his life, he finds himself floundering. All they can do is share the silence.

She draws a laboured breath and asks, "And your friend... what was his name?"

Monsieur Durand deliberates whether to say it out loud. Suddenly hoarse, he's scarcely able to get the word out, even though he no longer feels agony saying it. "Alexandre." That's the thing about pain—unlike a memory, it eventually fades despite the scars it leaves behind. Another remembrance.

Émilie gives him a tender smile. "And you haven't searched for him, have you?" Her expression darkens. "You do well to fear for your own safety. Only pray it doesn't make you cruel."

Saint-Joachim's bells ring.

"You had better hurry back," Monsieur Durand says coldly, forcing himself to look at her. As a man of words, he appreciates how often talking is fruitless. No one can hear the plaintive hymn someone else's soul sings. He feels that depleting thought throughout his body. He's lonely, the last book on a shelf, made even more so because he's aware of the reasons why.

Émilie walks to the door. She pauses and turns back.

"What would you have me do? I know my fate, Monsieur. I know it too well. And with it, now, all of yours."

FIFTEEN

Friday, October 29, 1943
Night

Émilie makes her way back from Monsieur Durand's past buildings shrouded in grey. How many lifetimes would it take to read every book in his shop? How many of those lifetimes would she be willing to forgo to have avoided what he told her? While she was listening to him, his voice grew distant like he was walking away across a long field. She was overcome as much by the musty odour of books that reminded her of old potatoes as by what he was saying.

When she told the bookseller about her husband, despite the effort it took, she was easily transported back in time: Claude running after her because of some little squabble and taking her in his arms; joy spreading on his face as he tells her he's been offered a position at the *université*; sticking out his bottom lip, pretending to be sad because she is, trying to make her laugh.

How can she remember those things and so little else? She feels dizzy as blood thickens in her veins. His eyes. When he kissed her. All the times he said, "I love you." Where have those memories gone? It's like they've been cut out, and the hole mended with the disbelief they ever existed. Once Émilie held them close, simple as they are, but now they're meaningless. Stolen along with hundreds of her other cherished memories.

As Émilie turned the pages of Monsieur Durand's books, she focused on passing words: *audace, visceral, inconstant, morne*. Each one more rebuking than the last.

She understands why Monsieur Durand was reticent to speak about love. He isn't the first homosexual she's known—she worked in the theatre, after all. She sewed beside Maxime who'd rush home after work to help his mother take care of his three younger siblings, one blind; made patterns with Philippe who designed the costumes and whose lover was a prominent politician; and laughed with Charles every day at lunch, who wanted to do more with his life than paint sets all day.

Where are they now?

She likes to think they're there, hard at work, although she has no idea if the theatre is still open. If it is, at least they have a chance at happiness, if they haven't already been found out and detained. Or worse.

She's known others like them who weren't so lucky. A Czech student named Alfie who told her he was arrested in his last year of high school. The Nazis promised to set him free if he agreed to be castrated to stop his "disease." When he said yes and the deed was done, true to their word, they escorted him to the camp gates and let him walk out to the amazement of Émilie and the other inmates. For a moment, Alfie's eyes lit up and he no longer needed to fight back his tears.

Waiting for him were soldiers who press-ganged him into the army and sent him to the front without a gun as cannon fodder.

There was Claus, a teacher from Bamberg, who even being sickly thin as the soup they were given, never missed teaching the child inmates, many he only saw for a day or two before they were gone. But then the guards decided to use him for target practice, finding the pink triangle pinned to his uniform easier to aim at than the yellow badges on Jews.

And Michel, a pianist from Lyon, a soft-spoken man who was beaten to death by other inmates who didn't want a "deviant" among them. The guards did nothing but watch—Michel's killers were saving them work. Émilie chanced upon his body behind one of the barracks. She railed against those who murdered him and demanded to know who they were, but no one would tell her. Émilie never imagined there was a group of people more hated than her own.

She knew these men, spoke with them when she could, thought of them as friends. Each one of them believed he'd be free soon to carry on with a life filled with wondrous opportunities.

Sometimes Émilie feels them next to her, shadows playing in her peripheral vision, but she's too scared to look less they vanish again. She should have taken the chance to tell Monsieur Durand about them to keep their memories alive.

When the old bookseller slid the lamp across his desk, she saw a troubled man. Despite part of his face being turned from the light, Émilie noticed how age was hollowing his features—just his eyes remain youthful, but even they're dimming. Her compassion strained to its limit at that moment, Émilie had nothing to say to lessen his anguish.

Anything she might have said could've only added to it.

André lies awake beside his son, who's immersed under the waters of whatever dreams a boy with no mother can have. André's mind churns with sour recrimination.

When he can no longer endure his thoughts careening against each other, he gets up and shuffles to the other side of the folding screen to confront Émilie, but she's not there.

He doesn't find her in the shop, and tries the front door. It's unlocked. Has she gone? As André peers out the window wondering where she is, the door to the butcher's flat opens. Gilles steps out and tugs the brim of his cap lower before slinking down the street. André steps back and watches him cross over to the church and out of sight.

Exiting the pâtisserie, André hastens over to Saint-Joachim and looks around. Gilles is nowhere to be seen. André walks up to the main doors and goes in.

The sole light is from a rack of votive candles—the church hasn't gotten around to putting in electricity—almost all of them lit because so many parishioners have stuffed coins in the offering box in memory of departed family. At this rate, the church will be engulfed in an inferno of bereavement.

A door shuts. André glances over at the confessionals. Is that him? He doubts Gilles is the type to own up to his transgressions willingly, but it's a poor Catholic who doesn't have something to confess, even if that means making it up.

André scans the room and spots a man's shadow stretching up a wall to the ceiling. He traces its source to a priest in robes on his knees in prayer at a Station of the Cross: *La deuxième chute de Jésus*—Jesus falls for the second time. André recognizes Père Blais who baptized Frédéric, and who arrived from Québec to take over the *paroisse*, accent and all, not long after Père Le Roux, the priest who married André and Mireille, passed away from consumption. André thinks it best to avoid the praying man. Fewer questions, fewer lies. He can't afford another venial sin, let alone a mortal one.

He makes his way towards the altar up the aisle farthest from the priest. No one. It's as though Gilles has ascended to wherever the self-righteous go after they've shed this life.

Père Blais rises, shuffles to the confessional, and disappears inside to listen to the penitent's sins. If that is Gilles, the priest has a long night ahead of him.

As André moves to leave, he detects the faint murmur of voices edged with anger. He listens with effort until he determines the sound is coming from deep within the darkness to the right of the altar. Here he discovers a doorway and descends stone stairs to the church's catacombs.

André edges down a pitch-black passageway, feeling his way along the coarse stone wall towards the glow of candles. It reminds him of the cellar at the *vignoble* where, as a child, he used to hide from his father's wrath behind the wine casks. He instantly shoves this memory away. Why does he continue to cripple himself with thoughts like that?

At the end of the passageway, André pauses at an archway leading to a chamber and listens, but the voices are lower now and all he catches is the word, "message." He ventures a look. A handful of people are hunched together, talking over each other, their backs to him.

Rallying his courage, André walks in, his steps alerting them to his presence. The talking stops as though a wireless radio has been switched off. A bright light shines in his face, and he holds up a hand to shield his eyes.

"I-I'm looking for Gilles—"

A woman's voice hisses, "No names."

The flashlight is redirected. André does his best to identify the people before him: a middle-aged white-haired woman who scowls at him, a young man with only one arm who averts his eyes, a teenage girl who's smiling sweetly for no apparent reason, and a mechanic in overalls who sizes up André and grimaces like his appendix is about to burst.

"I know you." André smelled engine oil even before he entered. "You repair motors next to—"

"Shut up!" the white-haired woman snaps. "Maybe you know him, maybe he knows you. But it won't do us any good to shout it from rooftops."

"Better you forget faces." The mechanic squares his frame, making sure André understands he's ready for whatever happens next.

Footsteps in the passageway, and the butcher's son walks in, holding a lantern. He shines it at André. "What's he doing here?"

The white-haired woman levels an accusatory finger at Gilles. "He says he's looking for you."

The mechanic's unblinking gaze is back on André. "I say he's looking where he shouldn't."

Something in all their mannerisms, something André can't place, maybe nothing more than the inexplicable hostility of a church group towards him, makes him come to one conclusion. "You're the Resistance," he blurts out.

The woman gives out a contemptuous laugh. "We're here to meet with Père Blais about the feast of Saint François."

André has no idea when that feast is, or any other ones, for that matter—there are so many—but he isn't duped by their feeble explanation. "No, you're the Resistance." When the mechanic opens his mouth to object, André interrupts. "Why would you be here after curfew?"

No one contradicts him. The mechanic extends his arms and his hands curl into fists, as if he's decided to pummel André to death and be done with it. André doesn't care—he's working something out, his mind suddenly made shrewd if by nothing else than desperation. People who skulk about in the night must discover all sorts of things.

Gilles drags André into the passageway and back up its length until they're out of earshot of the others.

"We're patriots. This isn't your—"

"You could find Mireille. You must be able to find out where she—"

"We're given our assignments."

"But if you ask? Whoever you deal with, higher-ups, they must know, or at least they can nudge me closer."

Gilles puts the lantern on the floor, and their faces fall into shadows. He removes his cap and tucks it under his arm before pulling out a cigarette and lighting it. He has a draw and his expression screws up, then he exhales smoke right at him.

André shifts, impatient for an answer.

"We're lucky, you and me," Gilles says. "Countrymen our age are working in factories in Germany as slaves. But not us. The Germans understand the French people will never go without bread, or some meat, or pastries even."

"So you're telling me there's nothing I can—"

"Not until you know where she is. Even then..."

"Let me join you. I'll find out what I need. And I can help your cause." André shrewdly adds, "*Our* cause." He scrambles for the exact measurements of words, reason, and emotion to convince the man.

Gilles takes another drag. The cigarette's amber burn briefly illuminates the passageway and a small alcove in the stone wall beside them with a statuette of a saint André doesn't recognize, holding the baby Jesus and some lilies. Witnesses. But to what? To future miracles or sins?

The butcher's son exhales, tamps the cigarette out on the wall next to the alcove, and picks up the lantern. He puts his cap back on, ready to return to the others, so André takes one last gamble.

"What choice do you have? I know who you are now."

Gilles's face bunches. "Then we should kill you."

"You're welcome to do what you want to me after Mireille is back home."

The two men stand there for a long moment.

The lantern flickers erratically and threatens to go out. Gilles moves to go join the others, and André grabs him by the arm.

"Please." André hopes the man has had a glimpse of someone more determined than he first thought, as much, if not more than some of his fellow fighters. He might even be able to overlook André's self-serving motive.

"Someone left me a note telling me Mireille's been taken."

All André can hear is Gilles breathing through his mouth.

The butcher's son whispers, "Now you know she didn't run out on you." He pulls his arm away. "There are things bigger than all of us."

He swings the lantern in front of André's face like a clock's pendulum, then goes back to the chamber where he tells the others, "Seems we have one more."

André silently thanks God, but quickly dismisses it as just a reflex. To hell with the man's gibberish. André's plan is in motion.

When he walks back in, the others eye him with no less distrust. He holds his spine straight and glares back at them.

"One more would be welcome," the white-haired woman reluctantly admits. "There's no shortage of assignments, certainly no rationing of ways to get killed. But what can he do?"

"He doesn't have the nerve." The mechanic throws up his hands. "Just look at him."

"Are you willing to attack them?" the woman asks André, hostile again. "Cut their supply routes?"

"Blow up their ammunition depots?" the mechanic says.

The teenage girl stops smiling long enough to ask, "Help downed airmen back over enemy lines while half the German Army is searching for them?"

André waits while they finish their list of ways to attack Nazis. They expect more from him than any man could achieve, maybe more than they expect of themselves. When the others have had their say, André turns to the shy man for his, but he looks at his shoes.

Hearing more footsteps, everyone tenses. Père Blais slips in and nods to each of them, one after the other, like he's anointing them with holy water.

They turn back to André for his answer, the look in their eyes as interrogating as tearing off fingernails.

"Just tell me what to do."

"If you're caught," Gilles tells him, "then we're all in danger."

"And our families," the white-haired woman adds.

"I would never reveal your names." André's unyielding stare is the guarantee.

Gilles grunts. "You will. Eventually. You only have to hold out for twenty-four hours while they beat you, place a rope around your neck and gradually tighten it, then submerge you in ice to freeze any courage you have. Twenty-four hours and we'll be gone by then."

"I can if they can." André tilts his head towards the teenage girl. "If she can."

The others laugh.

"*She* worked in a hotel in Vichy," Père Blais tells him, "and she found out more German secrets than a dozen British spies ever could. She was tortured within a hair of her life for it, and never said a thing. She still had the will to break out on her own."

André looks at the girl with a puzzled respect. In return, the girl continues to sparkle her sweet smile.

What an odd bunch, as unlikely a group of Resistance fighters as can be, yet each of them seems willing and able to fight Nazis. They've made their point. It won't be easy, but to be constrained by what's only possible won't bring Mireille home.

In spite of everything they've said, André tells them, "I'll do what I have to."

Their footfalls dully echoing off the cobblestones, André and Gilles walk away from the church, keeping near to buildings, hidden from anyone who might be observing them from the windows above. The air is peppered with the flat smell of road dust.

"You're lucky they let you in. We're a small cell—no one pays us attention."

"I'll find her." Even though André whispers, it doesn't disguise the hope in his voice. "They'll help, I'm sure of it."

"We're not here for one woman. If this is personal, then you're of no use. We can't afford to make mistakes. We're fighting for the greater good."

André is barely listening. Again he clutches hope with both hands. Monsieur Durand told him once optimism is fleeting as desire and as heart-breaking a betrayal in the end. Not this time. Mireille's coming home. André is sure of that.

A bounce returns to his step.

"Mireille understood what we're fighting for." Gilles's voice is louder than it should be, and he falls behind to scan the windows above them. André turns to see the butcher's son put a cigarette in his mouth, so he has to wait until Gilles lights it and catches up before he can ask what that means.

What would Mireille know about that sad group? Look at Gilles. He can't be that savvy an underground fighter if he's out after curfew, practically yelling in the street and waving around a glowing cigarette.

Reaching him, Gilles pecks at André's chest with his index finger trying to drill the meaning into him.

"The truth is, we're only taking you to replace her."

André wants to drink until he passes out. He dreads sleeping—it's fitful and full of rotting dreams where fragments of the day come back to him, grotesque and brutal. Each one scolds him for not doing enough, for not being smart enough to figure out what to do next, for not finding her. He's macerating in the vinegar of his own incompetence.

Throughout the night, he repeatedly woke with a start, unsure where he was. He lay there like a man who's been rescued from drowning but doesn't believe it, too terrified to take a breath. He can hear blood hammering in his head.

When he returned from the church, he found Émilie back in the other bed, asleep, or at least pretending to be. Is everything some sort of ruse? André didn't wake her to ask where she'd been—he had almost convinced himself she was gone for good and didn't want her thinking it made any difference to him. His meeting with the Resistance showed him the only way forward is to be pitiless.

Qui veut la fin veut les moyens. The end justifies the means.

He stumbles over to the bed and climbs in beside Frédéric. As the brown murkiness of partial sleep closes in around him, André hears Mireille's voice, clear and melodious, smooth as *crème Chantilly*. She slips in next to him and has her lips against his ear—he can feel her warmth, tender and soothing.

She whispers, "I'm waiting."

SIXTEEN

Saturday, October 30, 1943

While he waits to hear from the Resistance, André goes about his day with all the purpose of a small gust of wind, and with the same result.

He finishes decorating the three petits fours like he's dragging himself across thorns. When he finally puts the finished pastries in the display, the blood drains from his heart. Why bother? Will this make a difference to Mireille, or is it only tradition? Neither seem enough of a reason when it brings with it emotions that only weaken him.

He tries to fend off the oppressive thoughts at work in his mind. How was Mireille taken? And by who? If at least he knew why, he'd have a clue to where she is. Or is the note a nasty joke?

André starts scraping the inside of the oven, and when he's had enough of that, he paces in front of the windows until his legs ache. He takes a long gulp of air trying to bring life back to hope. The Resistance will bring his first assignment. He'll win their trust and be that closer to finding Mireille. A charge shoots through him and lifts his spirits. Is it optimism or delusion? More likely it's what Monsieur Durand calls "cruel naïveté."

Sitting next to the display case, André crosses and uncrosses his arms until he realizes how futile doing that is, too. It won't make them show up any sooner.

Whenever the bell rings, his head snaps up, his glare piercing through whomever walks in. But the few people who enter are the most loyal of their customers or someone who hasn't heard the rumour about him being a collaborator.

"Nothing today," André tells them. The customers either furrow their brows or give out a tut in mild disappointment. When they leave, they let the door slam after them, exposing their true feelings. Only one customer, the town's optician, a Monsieur Colomb, couldn't hide his surprise. The disapproving look in his eyes said it all. André believed he was doing well to hold his face hollow as a mask, but people see through him and don't have the decency to pretend otherwise.

Still, he waits for word.

They'll come. They have to.

André eats dinner with Émilie and Frédéric accompanied by neutral, if brief, conversation. After their meal, Émilie tucks Frédéric in, and André sits alone at the table contemplating a life that has stopped like an unwound clock.

Frédéric doesn't notice anything amiss, but Émilie is a different matter. She reads his son a story, but when André looks over, her eyes flick up to him, her forehead puckered with worry. He quickly looks away. His nerves twitch. He resents her for her intrusions: of passing silent judgement on him and for being here.

André can't push the swirling thoughts from his brain. Gilles claiming Mireille is in the Resistance is absurd. André goes over the occasions she could've been away long enough to carry out one of their tasks. She said she was visiting neighbours, and there was no reason to doubt it—she'd only be gone for an hour or so. Then he remembers one time she came home just before curfew saying she lost track of time at Madame Pontier's talking about her daughter's impending nuptials.

Then André recalls another time when she was quiet for the entire evening like she was somewhere else. When he asked what was wrong, she kissed him but said nothing. He thought she must be remembering her parents, and not knowing what to say, held her. Even if he didn't have the words, he'd show her he'd always be at her side.

A dozen more instances flood back.

How could he have overlooked them? He never distrusted her, so why would he be concerned or even curious? Now everything seems a deception.

His heart hammers in his chest.

What's Gilles not telling him? Is Mireille on one of their missions now, never to return? Ice water courses through his veins. Maybe it would be better if she had run off if it means she's safe.

André finally goes to his side of the folding screen, and a moment later he hears Émilie lie down, too. She tosses in bed, the springs protesting her every movement. She must be thinking of family she can't be with. Or maybe he's just casting on her what's keeping him awake.

His head hurts as if it's being prodded from both inside and out, but he can't stop his mind from being clogged with negative thoughts and the ensuing emotions. Why's Émilie still here? She should be gone by now. Just as abruptly, he agonizes over whether his father has betrayed them to the authorities. How can André expect anything less from him?

Determined to purge himself of these worries, at least for the night, he plans how he'll organize the supplies in the morning. But that only opens another one. How long before Egger comes back to demand what he wants?

Eventually André falls asleep, his feelings too exhausting to bear for another second.

SEVENTEEN

Sunday, October 31, 1943

When André tells Frédéric they aren't going to the park, the boy starts to cry. Nothing André says stops him. Frédéric garnishes his sobbing with sporadic shrieks, a fork shoved into the blades of a fan. André can feel it in his teeth.

When Émilie asks why not, André can't bring himself to tell her, like he might jinx something. He has to be here when the Resistance comes for him. He makes a promise to himself to bring his son to the park every day for a month when his mother's back.

Frédéric only quiets when Émilie sits next to him on his bed and puts her arms around his quivering shoulders, his eyes closed, his bottom lip peeled in a pout. André sees how the boy might feel it's a reprimand—it feels that way to him, too. His insides become leaden.

He sits on the floor and rolls a ball towards his son, but Frédéric ignores it. Then André has an idea. He goes over to a cupboard near the stove and retrieves a tin basin and places it in the middle of the room. He bounces the ball, and it neatly drops into the vessel with a resounding clunk.

Frédéric opens his eyes a slit. André fetches the ball and bounces it into the basin a couple more times before Frédéric scuttles over, his hands stretched out begging for a turn. It only takes a few attempts before the boy flings the ball and it lands squarely inside. His eyes shine, and his cheeks are bright as the pinkest fondant.

André claps his hands, and Frédéric looks over, baffled at first, then delighted. He bounces the ball again, and again it lands in the basin. The warmth André feels rebukes him for how he hasn't always been as good a father as he vowed to be when his son was born. He could blame the pâtisserie occupying his time or even being pushed out by Mireille's boundless devotion to the child, but both reasons, while partly true, weren't the real obstacle.

When Frédéric didn't sit up, or crawl, or walk when he was supposed to, André and Mireille took him to the doctor, who told them not to worry, children develop at their own pace. But when it was long past the time for Frédéric to talk, the doctor confirmed their fears their son was behind other children, most likely due to the complications at his birth.

Not wanting to believe something was wrong, André convinced Mireille they should seek other opinions. One after another, doctors called Frédéric "stunted," and "backward," and "retarded." Those terms made the Alberts wince, a red-hot spike impaling their hearts. Ultimately, André and Mireille rejected any other name for their son except for their own affectionate "our Frédéric" and "Petit Prince."

The last doctor they saw was adamant—there was only one thing to do with a child like theirs. "He'll always be a burden." André and Mireille hurried out of the office, and before they were even out of the building, they swore to each other they'd never send Frédéric away to some institution.

The diagnosis only made Mireille love Frédéric more—she didn't shed a single tear on hearing it. André suspects she secretly relished the idea that as long as her little boy never grows up, he'll always need his mother. Only once did Mireille express any reservations—she told André she was afraid of what will become of Frédéric when they're gone. "Who'll take care of him? Who'll still love him?"

She asked André if she were able to have more children, would he want them?

"A hundred more," he told her, "if it would make you and Frédéric happy."

Frédéric glances at André to see if he's watching. He bounces the ball harder this time, and it goes straight into the basin. He does it again and again, now aiming with care, each time landing the ball in the basin like a piece of meat tossed into the maw of a lion.

André doesn't love his son any less than Mireille, but he used to be uncomfortable alone with him, largely because he was so intent on scrutinizing Frédéric for any signs the doctors were wrong. What irony. It made him no different from his father and the judgmental glare the man always levelled at him.

The way André's parents took the news surprised him: they didn't love **their grandson** any less or treat him any differently. At least not at first. But bit by bit things crept into what they said or did that made André feel—and Mireille, too, when he pointed it out to her—they saw Frédéric as a beautiful, but broken cup. It angered André, but Mireille thought it amusing, saying that only meant "their little cup could be filled endlessly with love."

André had doubted he'd have much of a relationship with the boy, at least not one like Mireille's, so he sank himself in his work and used it as the excuse for not being more involved. It was easier for Mireille—she saw whatever she wanted in Frédéric, and she only found unlimited potential. She was his mother, after all. What would she make of André being alone now with their son, maybe even having to raise him on his own?

André glances at Émilie, and she gives him an impressed nod.

"I've never known a man to sit on the floor with a child."

He supposes she means it as a compliment, but he's much warier of empty words now. Émilie's expression is open as a field, but her comment only makes André think of his shortcomings. He'd be mortified if anyone suggested he's been ignoring Frédéric since Mireille's disappearance. It would sicken him, but they wouldn't be wrong.

EIGHTEEN

Monday, November 1, 1943

When André's has enough of waiting and feels every muscle is about to turn to dust, he leaves the pâtisserie.

In spite of having every intention to search for Mireille, he ends up wandering the streets, grim thoughts rising and doubling, and doubling again, as though activated by yeast. What if the Resistance never shows? What if they do, and he's still not any nearer to finding her? He feels closer to failure with every footstep.

He scours the faces of those passing by, expecting Mireille to walk towards him luminous as a miracle. Instead, he only finds his pain and loss reflected in strangers' eyes. He scrubs his jaw with his knuckles while his legs drag him towards the edge of town.

André puts a hand in his pocket. His fingers close on Mireille's apron and his lungs constrict. Is he destined to wander the earth looking for her? He makes a goat-like noise reprimanding himself. He can't give up. He has to carry on for as long as necessary, until the Second Coming if need be. Rather than finding this debilitating, André feels his mood lighten. Hope is the one bird in a thousand that soars above the others regardless of the weather.

A cloying smell of rot brings to mind fermenting grapes. To avoid any more emotions, André looks for its source. Under an orchard of trees, Anjou pears lay rotting, brown and covered by wasps. What a waste. Are people too lazy to pick them?

He looks at the nearby house and is chastened to see it's been boarded up. This is life now. Better to pack up your pain and start again somewhere else.

André hops a fence and grabs one of the last pears clinging to a branch. He sits down under the tree and takes a bite. It's especially sweet, the juices dribbling down his chin. Mireille would love these. She'd want to make them into a clafoutis, or a *poire Belle Hélène*, or a galette. André chuckles. Or all three at once.

He tries to detect order in the way the wasps swarm the rotting pears, but all he can make out from the confusion is that each one of them is intent on doing his part. Winter's coming. That must focus them like blinders on a horse.

After an hour sitting under the pear tree, trying to think of nothing more than fruit and insects, André returns to the road. Where to now? He looks in the direction of Paris. A slight thrill darts up his spine at the possibility he doesn't have to stop, he can keep walking. Then his stomach hurts as if it's been punched, bringing water to his eyes.

Life without Mireille is excruciating enough. Life without Frédéric, on top of that, would be unbearable.

He starts back to town. The closer he gets to the pâtisserie, the more he aches. He hates coming back with Mireille still not there.

There's no one in front of the shop, and the sign in the front door window is turned to FERMÉ, just the way he left it. Passersby ignore the pâtisserie like it's a ghost at a feast. They don't even bother to glance at it. Seeing this untethers whatever faith is left in him.

There's a line outside the *fleuriste*. Then André remembers it's La Toussaint and everyone's buying chrysanthemums to take to the cemetery. By now he and Mireille would be tidying up her parents' tomb.

André continues to watch stragglers cross the street to get in line. With a shake of his head, he gives up believing Gilles or his comrades will come for him.

André expects Émilie to be in the preparation area. She said she was going to look for a pan to make a *château* for Frédéric, complete with a moat, but the shop's empty and the side door's wide open.

In the alley, Gilles is holding Émilie by her wrist, speaking close to her, as she struggles to break free.

André seizes the butcher's son by the front of his shirt and pushes him up against the wall, knocking his cap off.

"She's putting us in danger," Gilles rasps. He takes a deep breath that ends with a wheeze. "Questions are being asked."

"Don't listen to him," Émilie pleads. "He's dripping poison. Just like them. He knows I'm Jewish. He'll turn me in." She glares at Gilles, daring him to deny it.

André's lips curl. "I'll deal with him. Go inside. Frédéric needs you."

Reluctantly, Émilie goes in.

André shoves Gilles against the wall again. The man smells of damp wool and ashtrays. How André longs to wipe that arrogant grin off his face. It won't take much for André to forget any restraint he has left. For the last two weeks, he's only just contained the anger burning up his back and across his shoulders. And it's increasing.

"Don't come near her again."

"Hiding them jeopardizes everyone," Gilles says.

"So does the Resistance." André glowers at Gilles with a biting intensity. Everything's a risk. Knowing the wrong person. Saying the wrong thing.

They stand there at an impasse, and it's Gilles who's the first to look away.

"We have our assignment."

André loosens his hold on him and takes a step back. Finally.

Gilles removes a pack of cigarettes from his shirt pocket, takes one out, and lights it.

"We meet at midnight."

With a shake of his head, he picks up his cap, walks to the street, and crosses over to his father's shop.

André feels his body loosen as though the screws holding him together have been untightened half a turn.

For the first time since Mireille disappeared, he's confident it won't be long until he brings her home.

NINETEEN

Tuesday, November 2, 1943

André waits anxiously in the pâtisserie for Gilles until well after midnight. Only once does he leave his post to go upstairs when he catches his reflection in the display case and realizes he hasn't paid any attention to his appearance in a while.

He grabs a mug, fills it with some water from the sink, and takes his shaving brush, soap, and safety razor over to the armoire. Standing in front of the mirror, he dips the brush in the water and rubs it on the soap until there's a lather. His beard is longer than it's ever been, and the blunt blade tugs at it. He considers changing it to a new one, but doesn't want to waste time. He ignores the pain as it rips the bristles from his chin and jaw.

Halfway through, it dawns on him being presentable doesn't make much sense given what they're going to do, but he carries on anyway. It makes him feel better scraping away two weeks of pessimism. He pauses to concentrate on a vibration in his chest, an emerging excitement inside him for what lies ahead that both surprises and pleases him. This must be what Cordon Bleu chefs feel before meal service.

André bounds down the stairs like the beating he took never happened, wiping soap from his face as he goes, and resumes his watch.

Almost at once, there's a rap at the side door, and André finds himself charging down the alley with Gilles.

At the park, they're met by the mechanic in a motorcar. With lights off, they travel cautiously along side streets and little-used back roads.

"Up ahead," Gilles warns.

The mechanic steers their vehicle into a field, and they watch in silence as a German truck passes. André's heart beats quicker. They're lucky. Headlights have to be shielded, and Gilles only saw them at the last minute. So he serves a purpose, after all.

It takes them a good twenty minutes to push the motorcar out of the mud, enough time for André's nerves and bluster to subside. This isn't some great adventure. It's only a means to an end.

At railroad tracks outside town, a figure lit by a crescent moon emerges from the woods—the teenage girl from the Resistance. She moves to the rails and places a bag between the ties, then skips away, carefree as air, for the amusement of her fellow fighters observing her from the dark.

André and Gilles watch from behind a thicket. Gilles takes out a handful of pencil detonators from a knapsack and sorts through them.

André grabs some. "I'll do it." It's ridiculous everyone's involved—he could've finished it by himself and been home by now. But that's another of their rules: they risk together as one. The second part is implied: they take the blame together, too. Then no one can afford to rat anyone else out.

When André picks out a couple of the detonators, Gilles wraps a hand around his wrist and tries to wrest them away. "No, you're only supposed to—"

"Your mechanic said all we have to do is jam it into the explosive." André yanks his arm back. Before Gilles can object, André makes his way to the tracks, staying low to the ground. He rips open the bag of explosives and pushes a detonator into the doughy mound. It's that simple.

He retreats to their hiding place.

"Which one did you use?"

"The five minute. Get it over with."

Gilles checks his watch. "Let's go."

"Not yet."

André lies on the long grass, determined to wait for the explosion, but Gilles remains standing. Even in the dim moonlight, it isn't difficult to see anger spreading on his face.

"Get down before someone sees you," André says, more a taunt than a warning.

"She always said you were hard-headed." Gilles turns his head as if he's heard something.

André scoffs. "Oh, your little talks. So what?" The man's smug superiority is off-putting. Although they're unfailingly cordial to one another, waving whenever they spot each other across the street, they're not friends. Mireille, however, has been every bit a good neighbour to Gilles and his family—it was Mireille who sat with his mother while the woman lay dying until the priest arrived to administer the Last Rites.

When Mireille came home and was back beside André in bed, right when the sun began to bleed in around the blackout curtain, she told him the butcher was distraught beyond all reason by his wife's death, and Gilles was inconsolable.

And this is how he pays her back—making dirty innuendos about her to her husband. André understands Mireille's kindness towards his mother, but any charity she offered this insufferable ass was casting seeds on cracked earth.

It isn't a matter of jealousy, although once André felt it for the briefest of moments when he caught Mireille laughing with Gilles outside the *boucherie*, but he shrugged it off, embarrassed with himself for thinking something so silly.

Sometimes Mireille would tease him by saying how handsome Gilles is, but André doesn't see it. The man is shorter than him, unhealthily thin. What Mireille calls "aquiline" is just a plain, pointy nose. The butcher's son seldom shaves, and looks far more destitute than debonair, but that's nothing André would say out loud. He wouldn't want to be thought of as petty.

Gilles chuckles and checks his watch again.

André's face goes rigid at the sickening insinuation. "You're mad. Maybe she helped you with your cause behind my back from time to time, but that's it." What if Mireille passed a few messages for some small Resistance cell? She certainly wasn't out assassinating Nazis." André looks straight at Gilles. "I'd know."

"Then you know nothing."

André scoffs again, although he's finding the man's confidence unnerving. Gilles should be careful hovering over him—André could topple him like a marble bust on a pedestal in the Louvre.

"She came to me. But she didn't stay." The butcher's son clears his throat of a tobaccoey phlegm, and spits as punctuation. "More fool her."

"Mireille would never—"

"And we knew happiness. We were never happier than when we were together."

André clenches his fists. "You're lying." The man's goading him just for the sake of it.

"I'd give anything to touch her skin again, smell her hair, taste her lips..."

André is about to erupt. Even if there's not a shred of truth to the bastard's words, pushing André right now would be as insane as slitting your wrists at the gates of Heaven.

There's the short, piercing sound of a train whistle. Down the tracks, a locomotive pulling numerous cars heads their way. They'd been told there were no trains until daybreak.

"*Merde!*" Gilles curses above the growing clacking of steel wheels on steel tracks. He moves towards them, but without warning, André tackles him. They grapple as the train speeds nearer. When Gilles manages to break away and stand again, André jumps up, too, and tries to drag him back down.

There's an explosion that shakes everything under their feet, knocks them over, and rings in their ears. They cover their heads as stones, dirt, and wood splinters fly around them.

When it settles, they cautiously look and see a chunk of the track is missing.

The train starts to brake, but it's too late. It careens towards the broken section and derails—the locomotive rockets into the woods, and the wagons jack-knife in all directions with a screeching roar. Still that sound isn't louder than the screaming in André's brain.

When everything comes to rest, the two men stare at the wreckage.

All at once there's a silence quiet as dew.

Then moaning and cries for help.

André searches his pockets for the key to the alley door as Gilles pulls out a cigarette, and with shaking hands, attempts to light it.

"We weren't supposed to kill anyone."

"At this hour, that train could only be German." Despite his stony tone, André fumbles with the lock and doesn't make eye contact.

Gilles throws the smoke away, and grabs André by the sleeve. "And for every dead Nazi, they'll execute fifty of us in revenge."

Those words bore into André's conscience—he hasn't thought of that horrible consequence. He's lost deep in a forest now, trees straight as ship masts, yet he's swaying like a drunkard.

"I knew this was a mistake. You should be passing messages, and that's all."

André musters all the conviction he can. "Do you think there was anyone on that train who didn't deserve to—"

"You stopped me. I could've— You're letting anger make you as heartless as they are." Gilles thrusts his sharp features towards him. "I miss her, too."

André's expression sours even more. "There was nothing left on the detonator. All I did was stop you from blowing yourself up."

He pulls Gilles's hand away. "I shouldn't have bothered."

TWENTY

Wednesday, November 3, 1943

A delivery boy pedals up the empty street carrying the first telegrams of the day. A pedestrian comes into view, then another. Soon a steady stream of people bustle past the Alberts' shop on their way to their lives.

Overnight the weather changed. A wind edged with frost skates along the cobblestones. Leaves strain to fall from trees too obstinate to concede summer is long since over and now's their moment to cloak the ground in red, and yellow, and brown.

Émilie scrubs Frédéric's face with a cloth, and with a frail sigh, plops him down with his red ball. The boy makes a humming sound like a poked beehive. He's in a tetchy mood—he refused to eat his morning meal and persistently motioned at the last biscuit on the buffet, snorting with frustration. It didn't take much for Émilie to relent. When she gave him the biscuit, Frédéric just as sullenly took a bite and threw it down. Somewhere in his imagination nothing will do: the puppet has lost its magic, the toy train has broken down, and the woodblock truck's tires have gone flat.

Émilie despairs for him. A child who loses the ability to imagine will be without a sense no less valuable than sight, or hearing, or smell.

She massages her injured hand while she waits for André to wake up. The state it's in! Once her hands were a source of pride: their shape, their elegant porcelain look, their dexterity.

The other seamstresses at the atelier marvelled at her intricate stitching and were similarly in awe of her lightening pace. But now her hands are gnarled and discoloured, countless blue veins protruding on their backs, her fingernails worn and bitten away. Incessant work and malnutrition have ruined them.

Émilie treads lightly over to the beds and finds André lying on his side facing the wall, an arm draped over his head as though preparing to fend off a volley of punches.

"It's time to open," she says softly. Perhaps too softly—he doesn't move. She's about to nudge him, but decides against it. He won't thank her for waking him.

Crossing to the gramophone, she picks out a Piaf record and puts it on. She adjusts the volume before the music starts and stays a moment, listening for the song to begin to ensure it's not too loud. Still, André doesn't stir.

So that's that: the pâtisserie will remain closed today. While it might not matter to him, it's one more straw of guilt added to all the others piled on her back.

With another look at Frédéric—he rolls the ball away and watches it go without making any effort to go after it—Émilie shuffles down the stairs.

She is sweeping when footsteps stomp across the floor above her and the gramophone needle is ripped from the record. She leans the broom against the display case, about to go back upstairs, when her eye catches someone outside the window. A stocky man, wearing a jacket over work clothes and a hat pulled low, stares into the shop. Apprehension tightens his face, and his mouth is misshapen as if tasting something unpleasant.

Then he walks away.

Relieved, Émilie presses a hand against her stomach, but seconds later, the stocky man returns, steps up to the window, and peers in again.

Émilie wants to flee, but can't move and is at a loss to know why. He's probably just a customer, indecisive about spending scarce funds on something frivolous as dessert. Her pulse is a drum booming louder every second. Or he could be someone willing to give her up to the Germans for the price of a croissant.

When he sees her looking back at him, the stocky man moves away again, but immediately reappears and knocks at the door with determination. Émilie hesitates to answer. Who knocks before entering a shop? She spots the sign still turned to FERMÉ, and suddenly it makes sense. She pushes herself to the door and cautiously opens it.

"Monsieur Albert?" The man speaks so rapidly it comes out in one barely intelligible clump. Although Émilie isn't that close, the heavy smell of alcohol wafts its way to her.

"He's not— He's upstairs. I'll call him if you—"

The stocky man looks behind him, says, "Here," and shoves a dirty crumpled piece of paper at her. He turns on his heels and bolts down the street past two women queuing outside the *boucherie* and several pigeons pecking at the cobbles, all desperate to find something to eat.

Émilie squints after him until he's out of sight, then unfolds the paper with trembling fingers. It's a scribbled note.

Dearest André, I am a prisoner in a factory in Argenteuil-sur-Lac. I beg you to come for me. Mireille.

Émilie's breath catches. André's wife is alive! She lets herself bask in that sentiment for a bit more. Despite her reassuring words to the baker the day before, there's been this nagging feeling inside her that this won't end well for any of them.

No matter how long she savours that welcome piece of news, it can't stave off one thought: Now she has to tell André where his wife is and how she came to be there. Émilie's head pounds with the repercussions this revelation will cause. If André knows where his wife is and goes for her...

Fighting not to scream so loud it'll roll like a wave through the shop and spill out into the street, she stuffs the note in her pocket and carries on sweeping.

The pâtisserie transforms to the colour of well-used baking tins as the brightness outside dims. At the door, a figure appears and knocks with an urgency more suitable to a warning of fire or impending death. A light comes on at the stairs. André makes out Egger, cap askew and shirt untucked, his jacket missing, struggling to stand up straight.

This is all they need.

André is about to go back up when Egger knocks again, this time more insistently, sounding like he has every intention of continuing until the door crashes in. The German calls out André's name and glares at him from the other side of the glass. Fine! He'll see what the man wants and be done with him.

André walks over, turns the key, and cracks the door open.

"Good evening, Herr Albert," Egger slurs. He slaps the door with his palm as if not understanding why it's in his way. "Let me in." It's an order delivered with the terseness of a whip.

André opens the door a bit more, and Egger pushes in. The Nazi's motorcar is parked across the street outside the *fleuriste* with its engine running. No doubt the neighbours will see it, and André'll be branded a collaborator again because of this fucking *boche*. André clicks the door closed.

Egger staggers to the display case. "Oh, no treats today? You must be doing well."

"No, Monsieur. No one will buy from us."

The German bangs the glass with a fist, and it reverberates through the shop. "Where are my cakes?" he demands like a spoiled child.

"Monsieur, it's late."

"You know, Herr Albert, the Fren—the French are a boring people. No—no joie de vivre. At the gendarmerie, they won't come drinking with me. Is this right? My friends should— They should drink with me." The light captures his attention. "Oh, is that wife of yours up there?"

He moves towards it, and André quickly blocks his path. Egger gives André's shoulder a playful push, but he doesn't budge, so the Nazi slips past him with a chuckle and stomps up the stairs. André follows right behind, his limbs weighed down with leaden foreboding.

Egger stumbles at the top step and looks around. Émilie is sitting on Frédéric's bed, the frightened boy almost completely hidden under a blanket.

"Frau Albert." Egger gallantly clicks his heels and bows, nearly falling over.

Émilie grudgingly returns half a smile. "Perhaps Monsieur would like coffee." She hurries to the stove.

André feels his expression fold with annoyance. What's she doing? Offer him any hospitality and he'll never go.

"Coffee?" Egger asks. "You have coffee?"

Before she can answer, André says, "Barley and chicory." To get shut of this *tête de noeud* faster, he should've said "piss and manure."

"Oh? I'll have to see about this. It's amazing what feats I can perform." The corners of Egger's mouth sag with mock sadness. "Berlin leaves us all alone in these god—god-forsaken places to do what we—" He notices Frédéric peeking out from under the blanket and brightens. "Oh! Hello, *Männlein*."

The lights flicker, and everyone looks to them.

"The Resistance playing their little games again," Egger sing-songs. "Just last night they blew up a train outside a town not far from here." He shakes his head as if deeply affected by the incident, and searches André's face.

André finds it difficult to maintain the right expression. There's no reason Egger would know something unless one of the others squealed.

The German sniffs loudly. "The ugly, vulgar things we're forced to do to teach these criminals a lesson. But thankfully your shop is a sanctuary from such turmoil. Isn't this so, *Männlein*?"

He moves towards Frédéric, but André steps in his way again. He won't get past this time.

Frédéric cowers under the covers, shocking Egger by his reaction. The Nazi turns to André for answers.

"It's late. My son needs his sleep."

Egger gives him the smile of someone about to be cured of a

toothache. "Then maybe she'll entertain me."

He lurches towards Émilie, but André seizes his arm. "Leave her alone." His tone dares Egger to defy him. Tempering anger is useless—it only encourages men as loathsome as him.

The German's eyebrows lift, re-evaluating André with a steely gaze. André glares back with naked contempt. That's right. He's not as unassuming as people think.

Slowly, as though speaking to a simpleton, the Nazi says, "It's not your concern, Herr Albert."

"She's my wife. I'm asking you to go." André keeps hold of the man's arm. For a fat man, it's unusually wiry and twitches like an eel, and under his sleeve is probably just as slimy.

Egger chuckles. "Your wife? Her? I should be demanding money for—for my silence. But no. I offer my hand in— I let your educated friend off, didn't I?" He yanks his arm away and his face twists into a revolting mask. "This *Jewess* is your wife?"

Before anyone can react, Egger has a coughing jag. Émilie uses it as cover to return to Frédéric, taking the shaking boy in her arms. Her face is ashen and her lips are squeezed together like they've been glued shut.

André knows he has to watch out—it's a trap. Even mentioning Jews betrays them.

Egger dabs his mouth with a thumb. "What have you been telling people? You're a fool, Herr Albert. For a very little price, they talk. Not that I need their tittle-tattle. I've been fully trained by the Gestapo's physi—physiognom—physiognomy brigade." His voice deepens and becomes bloated with pride. "I received a commendation for it. Many might not be able to, but I can spot a Jew. Still, I thought: What's one Jew between friends?"

He looks from André to Émilie and back again as if he's allowing them the chance to argue him out of the inevitable.

André burns with the heat of a furnace. They're done for.

Egger lets out a long sigh. "You—you people, you French— will never appreciate how I've come in good faith with an open hand, a kind and generous heart. I am compelled to ask myself: Has this all been wasted effort?" With another sigh, he says,

"*Perlen vor die Säue werfen.* Pearls before swine."

With an explosive burst, Egger reaches for his sidearm and levels it at him. André leaps forward and wrestles the German to the floor. André has the advantage, then, with an unexpected surge of strength, Egger frees an arm.

The Luger drops and slides halfway towards the beds. Émilie scrambles to pick it up, points it at the Nazi and screams, "Stop," but it has no effect.

Egger locks a hand on André's throat.

"Stop," Émilie screams again.

Egger looks up and stares into the weapon's muzzle. With a grunt, he releases André, who rolls over and coughs, trying to catch his breath.

Frédéric scampers to Émilie, wrapping his arms around her as she continues aiming the gun at the German.

André staggers to his feet, and takes the Luger from her. He waves it at Egger. "Get up."

Egger laughs, high-pitched and crazy, a rodent who has a leg in a trap and assumes the rest of him has gotten away. André bristles at the unnerving sound of it.

"GET UP."

Smiling, the Nazi stands and raises his hands, feigning fear. He gives a little shudder for emphasis. Émilie shakes her head in disgust at his antics.

"Downstairs," André says. He wishes Egger'll do something stupid, lunge at him or move towards Frédéric again, anything to justify squeezing his finger against the trigger until the Nazi is no longer here. One sniff will be enough.

"*Ja, mein Kommandant.*" Egger sways his hands from side to side, making a point of showing they're still up, and starts down the stairs. André's on his tail, muscles twitching on the brink of rage.

Émilie gives the top of Frédéric's forehead a quick kiss. The boy sits still, emotionless as an unloved doll.

In the shop, André motions with the gun towards the alley door. Egger sighs and crosses to it, each of his steps pronounced as though wading through a shallow stream.

"Open it," André says. Egger starts to lower his hands, so André barks, "One's plenty."

The German keeps his left hand in the air and uses the right to open the door. André shifts from one foot to the other. Should he let him go free? What's the alternative? Kill him? André tastes acid in his throat. All it takes is a bullet in the back of the head.

Egger grins as if he's amused with everything. The French. The war. André.

"Get out."

The German shrugs and leaves.

Émilie bursts in from the stairs. "What are you doing?"

André follows Egger into the alley. He jabs the gun towards the street. "Start walking."

Egger sets off up the alley, arms still raised.

"You can't let him go." Panic sharpens Émilie's tone. "He'll be back for me. And you. And Frédéric." She turns to Egger. "STOP."

André fights the urge to put a hand over her mouth—she's more of a threat to them right now than the Nazi. Thankfully none of the neighbours' windows overlook the alley.

Émilie storms over to Egger. "Who knows you're here? Who knows about us?"

"Everyone. I told them I was—"

"LIAR!"

She dashes back to André, and in her manic state stands in his line of fire. He lowers the gun.

"The son of a bitch is lying." A fleck of spit flies from her mouth. "He wouldn't tell anyone about his little arrangement. But he will now."

André looks past her and sees Egger walking away. He raises the Luger again. Émilie spins around. "Stop— STOP." The German complies, hands still up, still facing away from them.

Émilie races up to the Nazi and stands behind him, her lips next to his ear. "Get on your knees and beg for your life. That's how you do it, isn't it? Toy with those you're about to kill?"

André has seen enough. She's crazed with hate. Seeing it so raw before him, the granite of his own revulsion erodes. He moves next to her, and is about to tell her to go back inside when Egger starts up the alley again. Émilie screeches again for the Nazi to stop. The word erupts from her like a knife thrusting through flesh until it hits bone.

Émilie snatches the gun, runs up to Egger, and presses the muzzle against his temple. He begins to turn, his smirk finally gone.

"You're perilously close to becoming bor—"

BANG!

A flash of gunfire, a wisp of smoke, and the German slumps to the ground with a nauseating thud. His eyes search desperately for something that's not there while blood trickles from the side of his head. His face contorts in pain and disbelief.

Letting out a wheeze, Egger dies.

André takes a step back. A loud ringing beats against his eardrums, blocking out other sounds. The smell of gunpowder burns inside his nostrils. All he can see is the bloody hole burrowed into the Nazi's brain. No loss. If André had given into his wickedest angels, he'd have done it himself. Then his conscience returns with the force of a bolting horse. God save their souls.

Émilie looms over the body, steeling herself to shoot again. André tries to pry the Luger from her, but she grasps it in a white-knuckled grip.

BANG! Another flash as a bullet hurtles towards the street.

André wrenches the gun away and frantically scans the alley from one end to the other. His mind stalls. He looks back at Émilie staring down at the lifeless Nazi without a drop of remorse.

Émilie sits with Monsieur Durand, rocking Frédéric back and forth, a bottle of the old man's cognac and two glasses before them on the table.

"He shouldn't have gone for you." Her voice is low and hollow. Barely a look has passed between them since the bookseller arrived. Which is fine. She doesn't need his opinion, to be either admonished or praised. She's her own judge and jury.

Her fists are wedged in her pockets, Mireille's note crushed against her skin, as accusing as a pointed finger. What's one more crime?

Monsieur Durand pours more cognac into her glass. "Here. Drink. You must be—"

Émilie carries Frédéric over to his bed, laying him on the covers. His eyelids close slowly as flower petals.

She rushes to the window and pushes aside the blackout curtain. He's been gone too long. The Nazis have him.

Monsieur Durand eases himself out of the chair to join her, as she asks, "Where is he?"

Across the street, Madame Bujold appears at her window and brazenly stares at them. Émilie lets the curtain fall back in place.

"Will they come?" She doesn't turn to ask the question, knowing any sign of sympathy from the old man will cause her to deteriorate into madness.

"Yes. But they'll go again if no one says anything."

"The neighbours heard. Her!" Émilie lifts a hand to the curtain. "How can she ignore two shots?"

Monsieur Durand thinks for a long moment. Émilie turns to him, but already has her answer. Secrets never stay unspoken for long.

The bookseller looks at her point-blank and says with as much certainty as she's ever heard in him, "To avoid a bullet, you can't hear gunfire."

Émilie tilts her face towards the ceiling. His aphorisms make her brain spin like dried leaves in a gust. She's about to ask what she should do, when there are sounds from below: the alley door opening and closing, and footsteps on the stairs.

Soon as André walks in, Émilie goes to him and places a palm on his chest to stop him, but he brushes past her.

"The car's in the lake," he mumbles. He grabs the cognac and pours some sloppily into a glass and drinks it down.

"And the gun? Did you get rid of his gun?" Her voice rises again. Anything belonging to that Nazi will incriminate them as surely as a bloody handprint. She doesn't ask about the body. The fish can choke on it.

"Did you clean the alley?" André snaps back. He pours another drink and empties it.

"Yes." It's more a croak than an answer.

Monsieur Durand looks about to interject something, hopefully to caution his friend about becoming intoxicated at a time like this, but instead, presses his lips together as if taking a vow. She wills the old man to speak up. André needs telling. Alcohol has provoked too many confessions and quarrels, one often leading to the other.

"Are you sure?" André grills her.

"Yes. See for your—"

He slams the glass on the table and looks at her with a venom Émilie hasn't seen in him. She turns away from it, inundated by the flood of destiny roaring towards them. What has she done? She's all nerves, loose and twitching, scraped raw by fear. What could she do? Surely André must understand they were doomed either way.

"They'll look for him." André's voice becomes distant. "They'll show up here." He swipes the heel of his hand across his forehead and glances at the cognac bottle.

Émilie wants to go to him, but her feet are a hundred times heavier than normal, her heart even more. She looks to Monsieur Durand. Surely someone so educated, so wise, so experienced in the world can come up with a way out of this. Overwhelmed and drained of thoughts, still self-recrimination leaks around the edges of her mind. A Nazi is dead—she killed him. But this isn't the time to exacerbate guilt. Continuing to fight is how she'll survive and see to it André and Monsieur Durand, two of the most righteous souls she's ever met, and Frédéric, above all, can too.

The bookseller puts a caring hand on the baker's shoulder.

Émilie hungers to be comforted, but it would be pointless. She won't let compassion blind her again.

"When they find nothing, they'll go," Monsieur Durand says. "Without a body, he's just another German deserter."

TWENTY-ONE

Thursday, November 4, 1943

The sun rises like it does every morning, and like every morning, the street prepares for the day ahead. Shops open, customers dash in, ration books in hand, only to appear again clutching packets scarcely containing enough for the evening meal.

A little freckled girl strolls by with a tray filled with brown paper bags of roasted chestnuts, begging passersby to part with their money. Few do. In front of the town's pawnshop, her father warms himself next to a blackened wood-fire roaster, listening to the chestnuts hiss like vipers.

Then the Nazis arrive.

Pedestrians scatter, racing to escape as soldiers jump from motorcars and trucks and knock furiously at doors. Anyone too slow is apprehended and dragged to the waiting vehicles, much to their shock and confusion.

When no one opens up at the *librairie*, a baby-faced soldier with a wisp of a mustache kicks in the door. Other shops and homes are broken into, including the *boucherie* and the *fleuriste*.

An officer, flanked by a handful of soldiers, strides over to the pâtisserie. He knocks loudly at the front door and waits. When there's no answer, he tries the handle. Finding it locked, he signals for the soldiers to force their way in. The door collapses under the impact of their shoulders, and the Germans troop in.

At the church, two dozen people wait at a side door, mostly Resistance fighters and their families, having been warned just before dawn of the raid. Père Blais opens the door and ushers them in.

He looks to the street as men, women, and children are being led away. One woman with hair the colour of plums, going willingly as a bride to the altar, is lifted by a bear of a soldier and tossed in the back of a truck. She screams out in pain. Already another truck packed with those not lucky enough to have gotten away rumbles up the street.

The priest says a prayer to himself, and the heavens respond with a thunderclap in the distance. He looks up at clouds unrolling like a rug and a sky becoming dark and closed. As he turns to go in, four souls walk towards him from around the back of the church. He motions for them to hurry, and they follow him inside.

André chews on a fingernail. The room is filled with the diffused light of the cloudy day filtering through the stained glass. Instead of bursts of colour, everything's dappled in greys. The smell of damp stone seals his sinuses. Holy Mother Church, as oppressive as a boulder.

Émilie steps inside followed by Monsieur Durand holding Frédéric's hand. The bookseller nods to the priest and takes in his surroundings. André sees his body relax. For having a place to hide from the Nazis or for finding his faith again?

Taking a seat in a pew, André waits for Père Blais to lead them where they're going. The catacombs come to mind. Good. They're already halfway buried.

Émilie sits beside André and looks up at the windows high on the walls. Her eyebrows rise. Why's she impressed? It's just a building, heavy with the smells of candle wax and incense. Anything of value lies in the people around them. Next she'll be reciting the entire *catéchisme* in Latin from memory. What have all the houses of worship ever done to move humanity towards good? They only exist so anyone who claims to be religious has shelter from the weather.

The Resistance fighters mill about at the altar, but André doesn't approach them, sticking to his part of their pact not to know each other in public. Gilles isn't here. He's probably long gone, devious enough to have sneaked away, likely told about the raid before anyone else.

No one needed to tell André to be out of the pâtisserie. It wasn't his gut roiling all night that tipped him off. How could it not be upset after what he saw and what his part was? It was another word spoken from somewhere in the dark, a voice clear as a sparrow's trill.

"Leave."

So he woke Émilie and Frédéric, and they slipped to the bookstore just before dawn. Once he made Monsieur Durand understand the urgency, they took an indirect path by the alleys behind buildings to end up at Saint-Joachim.

André picks up Frédéric, the boy's thumb stuck in his mouth seemingly for good, and he lays his head in the crook of André's neck. He's back to being his mother's baby again. Who could blame him?

Père Blais lights a lantern with a wooden taper put to the flame of a nearby candle, and leads them on noiseless feet to the stone steps beside the altar. They file past the chamber where André met the Resistance, and then right to another, even narrower, passageway. Handing André the lantern, Père Blais pries loose a stone in the floor with his fingers, and manages to lift an edge and push the stone aside. André raises the light. The top rungs of a ladder appear leading into a black hole.

He passes Frédéric to Émilie, unable to make eye contact. It's her fault they're here. And his for not turning her in before it came to this.

The boy squirms in her arms and makes grumbling sounds, wanting to be put down so he can leave the dank darkness, but she holds him tighter. His weak, ineffectual fists beat on her shoulder, as if blaming her, too.

André kneels beside Père Blais, and they begin helping the women and children down the ladder. When it's the white-haired woman's turn, she asks, "Where's Gilles?" André keeps his face blank. How would he know?

With a shake of her head, the woman disappears into the hole. If she has no idea where he is, he must've gotten away. André reaches to help the next person and stops. But then, he wouldn't have had an easy time leaving in the middle of the night with his ailing father. With each passing day, the butcher grows frailer than a cobweb.

Émilie looks at Monsieur Durand with horror as André suddenly tears up the passageway.

"André!" she cries out. He can't go out there. Better he stays here with them. The church door's good as marked with lamb's blood.

She passes Frédéric to the bookseller and moves to follow, but the old man grabs her arm and tells her no. After one last attempt to make out André beyond the shadows, Émilie reluctantly starts down the ladder. He's deluded if he believes there's something he can do to Nazis. Tragedy appears swiftly enough, why run to it? It doesn't need help. Despite this harsh judgement, she can't deny her growing feelings for the man, as much as she hopelessly tries.

Monsieur Durand passes Frédéric down to Émilie and follows them into the hole.

Père Blais replaces the stone and blesses those below by making the sign of the cross, before picking up the lantern and gliding back up the passageway.

André bursts out of the side door and runs up the pebble path beside the church. A burst of machine gun stops him. He presses his back against the wall and carefully edges along to the front of Saint-Joachim and looks out.

Bodies lie in the street. Soldiers lead the last of the living to a truck, the butcher among them. He shuffles beside the Germans like he's already in chains.

André's insides are tugged on by a giant hand about to tear

them out, and his frame quakes almost with the force of a seizure.

Two soldiers march Gilles out his door, an ever-present cigarette between his lips. He's arguing with them and gesturing angrily. Breaking free, he starts running, but only makes it past the flower shop before the soldiers are on him. Gilles fights back, giving it everything he has. His fists land blow after blow with the fierceness of a prizefighter. A soldier, seeing his comrades losing, goes over to help, and when the three of them still can't gain control of the butcher's son, a fourth German joins the fray.

André's mouth goes sour as though it's filled with vinegar. No matter what the man's relationship was with Mireille, André can't stand by watching this happen. He starts walking towards them and freezes. Move, or be a coward forever. Yet he can't take another step or turn away, fated to watch Gilles relentlessly battle on.

Finally outmatched, Gilles is subdued by the Germans. They push him up against a wall.

A soldier raises his rifle.

BANG!

Gilles falls to the ground.

The butcher tries to go to his son, but the soldiers beat him to his knees.

All André can do is shut his eyes.

TWENTY-TWO

Friday, November 5, 1943

Émilie huddles with Frédéric under the catacombs in the dark and cold, along with the Resistance fighters and their families, with nothing to eat and drink—they'd departed from their homes that abruptly. Yet no one complains. At first, little is said as they sit in what turns out to be a cave. The hours drip by before someone finally speaks—a man with a low bass tone— and everyone begins talking at once, wanting to listen to something other than silence and their own thoughts. Frédéric mutters like he aches to join in.

They whisper to the person next to them, although it's doubtful anyone can hear them beyond the rock walls. Still, nothing of themselves is revealed as though they've made a pact to only speak of happier times to come: shops to visit in Paris, and trips they want to take to the beaches of the Côte d'Azur or the snowy Alps. One day.

Émilie luxuriates in the conversations, no different from a flower in the noon sun on an August afternoon, tingling at how effortless it is to listen to them. Even though there's caution in some of the voices, trepidation in others, it's a relief not to have to detect hidden meaning in what's being said.

On the hour, a young man who hasn't spoken yet, lights a lantern, and everyone walks around or change places to talk with someone else. When the light flickers, the young man, who Émilie notices is missing an arm, turns the lantern off, just as the kerosene starts to give off a terrible smell and make their eyes water. He does this more than a dozen times like clockwork. Émilie estimates it to be past midnight. The worst time to be reflecting on anything.

Émilie hears people move in the dark. They pass around cubes of meat stock, and a woman with a clear contralto voice goes from one side of the cave to the other offering lumps of boiled candy. While the adults try to hold it in, sooner or later everyone ends up at the wooden bucket in the far corner.

A girl speaks to Émilie about a book she's reading. Even in the darkness, Émilie knows at once she's a child, or at least a young woman, even though she's trying to sound older by using big words, frequently mispronouncing them. It's charming. Émilie is jealous there are still people untouched by the events around them to be able to read for pleasure.

The girl affably chatters on, but what to do about Mireille's note continuously kicks at the back of Émilie's mind, as impending a threat hanging above her as the slipping blade of a guillotine. If she tells André about it, what'll stop him from turning her in to the Germans? He'd trade the world for his wife, why not a Jew? She should tear up the blasted thing and be done with it.

When Monsieur Durand sits beside her, he tells her he's been speaking with a mechanic, someone he couldn't be more different from. "Yet, we've been able to stumble on a shared interest in the Wizard of the Renaissance. He's taken with da Vinci's drawings of machines as I am with his art." Émilie is pleased for him. Friendship's a jewel, scarce and beautiful.

Besides the young man without an arm, the only other person who Émilie never hears say anything is André. He frightened them when he returned and pushed aside the stone above them, momentarily letting in light from the candle he was holding. They feared they'd been discovered. He climbed down the ladder, pausing to jostle the stone back in place, then sat by himself separate from the others, even after Émilie called over to him.

That rejection makes the sting of disappointment burn in her chest, surprising her—being disappointed means having hope. But for what? When has she ever seen a miracle?

Eager as Émilie is to talk to him, she uses the dark as her excuse not to. If she can't see André while he speaks, she's afraid she'll disclose things about herself better left alone. For her self-preservation. To keep her whole. The timbre of André's voice is so remarkably similar to her beloved Claude's, she recognizes it in her bones.

She should tell André about Mireille. She tries to go to him, but her body won't listen. It's not that she can't move, but each of her limbs seems intent on going in an opposite direction, and her lungs stubbornly refuse to take in air.

Anyway, this isn't the time or place to say something, even if his wife's note is a lead albatross. Émilie spends the rest of the night with thoughts as scalding as boiling water, and twice as painful.

Finally, Père Blais comes back to push aside the stone and help them climb out. They blink in the sudden brightness of his lantern as though not sure it's real.

The woman with the whitest hair Émilie has ever seen asks, "Did they come?"

"The Nazis searched, but left without venturing into the catacombs." The priest is more smug than a man of the cloth should be. "They were skittish as cows at the prospect of descending the stairs without a light."

Émilie suppresses a snicker.

Too much like Hell for them.

Émilie and André exit through the church's side door. She's carrying Frédéric, and the boy covers and uncovers his eyes with both hands against the glare of the late morning sun as if playing *coucou* with it like a silent clock. Monsieur Durand and the others trail out after them. Hiding together for more than twenty-four hours has left most of them, if not exactly friends, at least believing themselves more human for having been with each other.

Without an *adieu* or an *à la prochaine*, everyone scatters, and Émilie and Monsieur Durand watch them go before turning to André. His face gives nothing away—a swatch of bare satin. Émilie moves to hand his son to him, but he's staring intently in the direction of the shops.

She looks at the bookseller, and before either of them can react, André starts towards the street. Monsieur Durand hurries after him. Émilie tries to keep up, but quickly falls behind, impeded by the child in her arms.

The men are outside the *librairie* when she reaches them. Although it's almost noon, there's no one else out. She doesn't need to ask where everyone is or what happened. The real question is: How many of them will want to return? Or how many of them will be able to?

The very air has changed. Heavy and stale. There's the smell of iron. Death's been here.

She looks to André for confirmation, but he's lost somewhere under the surface of an ice-covered lake. Whatever took place seems distant to him as the planets. A calloused heart or one too fragile?

They quietly survey the damage: the bookstore's window is intact, but the door hangs askew by a hinge. Books are strewn on the ground, many ripped apart, others marred with the tire marks from some vehicle. A dozen books sit in a pile, charred, but not completely burnt, by a fire the barbarians must've started then left to go out on its own.

Monsieur Durand's expression clouds. "Anyone who burns books, will burn anything." His shoulders harden as though willing himself to go inside.

Émilie turns away. Her arms and legs are ready to fly off, while the rest of her feels about to drop to the ground. They have no idea what people are capable of. There's been worse done, and even far worse being done this very second.

Monsieur Durand gingerly steps over the books to enter his shop. André moves one of them with his foot to look at its cover, then follows.

Émilie picks up a children's book and shows the cover to Frédéric, but he looks away and stares at the bookstore's door, waiting for his father to reappear. Does he do the same for his mother? What does he stare at, hoping she'll come back? Émilie flinches thinking something so glib.

Out of nowhere, she goes cold, but fights turning around. Someone's watching. She decides she's better off inside with the others. When she walks in carrying Frédéric, Monsieur Durand and André are surveying the overturned bookcases and their contents splayed on the floor three and four deep.

"All replaceable if need be," the bookseller says. He moves forward, but his footing is unsure on the carpet of books, and he almost topples over. André guides him to the chair behind his desk.

"Perhaps it's time to leave." Monsieur Durand closes his eyes as if wishing to be somewhere else. "Life has to be better by the sea. That's where old men go to end their days, no?" He opens his eyes and blinks as though disappointed nothing has changed.

Émilie recognizes part of a book's cover in the mound beside her. She pulls out the first edition Victor Hugo and hands it to Monsieur Durand. He holds it against his chest for a moment before putting it back in its place of honour on the only book-case still upright.

The edges of Émilie's mouth bend. Now they've been reduced to cherishing the tiniest second of happiness as a blessing.

André makes his way out the door. Monsieur Durand shoots Émilie a look. Although André hasn't said anything specific to worry them, she knows Monsieur Durand would agree André shouldn't be on his own. A desperate man does desperately ir-revocable things.

She perches Frédéric on the desk, and the bookseller pulls open a drawer and finds a bonbon. The boy squeezes it, but doesn't eat it. When Émilie goes after André, Frédéric watches her, starved of any concern.

André's shoulders fill the pâtisserie's doorway. Émilie waits for him to go inside, but he just remains there, looking into the shop. Baking utensils are scattered and crushed from being stomped on, and ingredients have been thrown around coating everything in white and brown. The cash register is in pieces on the floor.

The glass front of the display case is cracked like the sugar top of a crème brûlée.

She wants to tell André not to grieve for his shop, but the words rising in her throat are gossamer and die on her lips. How many people's passion has been extinguished as irrevocably as lives? The world they're living in destroys everything in its way. It's what the pâtisserie stands for that matters: his wife and son. André must feel helpless as a cadaver being carried to a cemetery.

"We should leave," Émilie cautions in a guilty whisper. "All of us. It isn't safe here now."

André turns, emotion distorting his features, looking about to say something ugly or even attack her. Then he looks past her at the dazed butcher who walks out of his shop, sits on the stoop, and stares at a dried bloodstain on the cobblestones.

"Let them show up again." André's voice is distant, as though echoing from a memory. "Who's left who hasn't already lost everything?"

As if in reply, the butcher cries out in anguish.

André walks over and sits beside him. When the butcher breaks down, André holds him, and the man wraps his arms tightly around him as if afraid of slipping away.

Something awful must have happened to his son. Blame plants itself like a weed in Émilie's heart. She watches the shared act of bereavement, and it reaffirms for her that one pain is indistinguishable from another.

Only the most devoted intimacy with suffering can teach that lesson.

Part II

The Return

TWENTY-THREE

Thursday, November 18, 1943

Two weeks have passed since the deaths of Egger and Gilles, a month since Mireille disappeared. The display case, with a large fissure across its glass front, sits empty. Where once it was a muscular bull dominating the pâtisserie, it's now diminished, less formidable, not defeated, but in retreat, licking its wounds.

It had its beginning in 1916 at the hands of a cabinetmaker in a small workshop beside the Loire. The man crafted the display's frame from cherry trees he harvested from a nearby forest. He milled it, cut it, chiselled and carved its mortise and tendon joints, assembled it, stained it, and waxed and polished it until the wood gleamed a deep red.

Mireille's parents had heard of the man's work from a customer. Soon as they saw how magnificent the display case was, they knew they had to have it for the shop. They handed over the asking price without haggling. Until then, their pastries had been displayed on plates perched on pedestals on a table covered with a lace cloth, looking rather pathetic, Mireille's mother admitted. They needed something more befitting to showcase their wares.

Delivering the display case wasn't as simple as their decision to purchase it. Mireille's father found a man with a cart and two oxen who brought the piece of furniture to the shop in exchange for—once he heard they baked pastries—a year of desserts for his family.

When the display case arrived, it proved too big for either of the shop's doors, so they had to remove a window temporarily. The fathers of the butcher, the florist, and the bread baker—and even Monsieur Pépin of the *charcuterie* down the street who was a young man then—helped carry in the heavy object. Monsieur Samuel, the shoemaker from next door, only a boy, and his father, fashioned straps from bolts of leather to help lift it.

His job done, the man who delivered the display case would wait at the pâtisserie's door every Saturday before opening, ready to make his selection. Fond of regiment in all aspects of his life, and believing, as only a reformed reprobate could, that routine was the only way to avoid temptation, the man always chose two *mille feuilles*, four éclairs, two petits fours, and six macarons, one for each of his children.

The display case excited the town. People came in to the pâtisserie just to look at it, spurring them to buy, not only out of obligation for having viewed such a work of art, but from being genuinely attracted by the sight and smells of the desserts on offer. Every day for weeks, Mireille's parents were sold out. Business had never been so good in the pastry shop that had been in the family since Marie Antoinette. "*Qu'ils mangent de la brioche.*" Let them eat cake.

One evening, two months after they had bought the display, Mireille's father locked the front door and joined his wife as she was removing the only things left from the day's commerce: three petits fours. When he remarked they'd have something sweet for their own meal, at last, she said, "Yes, one for each of us." He laughed, and taking her in his arms, kidded her she must be tired and no longer remembered how to count. His smile magnified when he saw her amused look, mischievous and earnest at the same time. She was pregnant.

The couple were ecstatic—everything they had wished for was coming true. Mireille was born a healthy and cheerful baby who grew into a thoughtful and caring child, and then a compassionate and hard-working woman.

Monsieur and Madame Pellegrin spent the rest of their short

lives grateful happiness always came to them as easily as sleep after a day's hard work.

André keeps glancing at Émilie sweeping on the other side of the window. Anger rises inside him, ready to defeat him with a quick ferocity. But how would she know? He never told her what Mireille was doing when she went missing. André tries to concentrate on something else.

Across the street, the florist's shop has been abandoned and the *boucherie* is boarded up. A few days after the Germans killed Gilles, André helped the butcher nail pieces of wood across his shop's window and door before the man departed for Paris, swearing he'd never return. No one knows what became of the florist and his family. One morning the shop was empty, its door wide open, not a dry leaf or a petal left behind.

The street has changed. Townspeople avoid it as though every cobblestone teems with plague. Most of those who were arrested in the raid were released, but remain tight-lipped about what happened to them, only sharing it in hushed tones. Those who were killed or never let go are not spoken of as if they never existed. It's nothing short of superstition to not mention them, as though doing so will cause Nazis to appear like insects on rotting food.

Monsieur Durand was right: the Germans didn't show up again. Egger proved himself to be an insignificant grain of salt fallen between the floorboards. What sort of legacy is that? Did he have a family? A wife? Children? Who are you if there's no one to miss you when you're gone?

Émilie steps in. She blows on her hands to warm them, changes the sign to OUVERT, and gazes out the window. "It's snowing."

André looks. Where falling snow used to give him a jolt of delight, now all he feels is a strange, flat melancholy, not unlike recalling a friend he hadn't heard from for years.

He turns away and folds the empty flour sack. "That's the last of it." André doesn't relish the prospect of going out for more ingredients. Even if he can find them, what will he pay with? He could sell the gramophone—he sold the wireless back in spring, another time when they hadn't a *sou*. Only Mireille listened to it—André doesn't have any interest in knowing about world events and the misery they bring. But the gramophone? Mireille always said she could never live without it.

So few customers come in, it isn't worth keeping the pâtisserie open. It's nothing but an irritation now—there are more important matters to see to.

Émilie hastens over to the preparation area. She spots a plate of petits fours on the worktable, all there is to sell. "Why don't you use your rations?"

"I already have," André mumbles. He hates when she reminds him of the simplest things—he doesn't need to be told he's distracted. On the days he decides to open, he bakes with a lethargy he knows she finds maddening. Too often he forgets an ingredient and his work is ruined. She encourages him to start over, but why bother? He plods back upstairs, leaving everything there. Some mornings, he doesn't get out of bed until noon, far too late to begin baking. On those days, he tells himself he'll try again tomorrow.

"But it's not the end of the month." Émilie's mouth twists when she realizes what André is not saying. "You've been feeding me. I didn't—" She gingerly suggests, "What about...her ration book?"

"You need identification. It doesn't matter. Something will come up. Monsieur Durand mentioned me to one of his customers who's repairing the Pont Laberge."

It would be manual labour that's very different from the light touch needed to make marzipan figures or pipe rosettes, but André welcomes losing himself in hard work. How many hours did he toil in the vineyard, pruning, picking, and doing other backbreaking, mindless tasks? Seems a lifetime's worth. As much as he despised it then, he'd welcome it now, if only to forget for a little while. He's trying to push away thoughts of

Mireille, even though it hurts nearly the same as thinking about her. Oddly, it's summoning up the steps involved in picking grapes, that calms him.

"What good fortune for the bridge to be blown up one day, and you get paid to build it again the next." Émilie's sarcasm is obvious, but the second it leaves her lips, she looks away.

Upstairs, Frédéric starts to cry. Émilie moves to go to him when André takes off his apron, throws it on the worktable, and slogs past her.

She's disappointed as she watches him head upstairs. There are things she wants to say to him—now's a good time as any—foremost among them is he's putting himself and his son in danger by associating with the Resistance. Unnerved by what happened to Gilles, André admitted his involvement to her. She pressed him to renounce working with them, but he wouldn't make that promise.

"I'll do what I have to," is all he kept repeating.

And she still has to tell him about his wife. How does she broach that? It would be easier to fit a wedding dress on a spider.

With a sigh, Émilie brings the plate with the last three petits fours to the display and places it inside. She takes out a cloth from her pocket and starts cleaning the glass, but stops to examine the crack. How indiscriminately things of beauty are destroyed.

She traces a finger along the fracture's path, and abruptly pulls her hand away when it cuts her.

Squeezing her finger, a bead of blood falls to the floor.

They eat a watery soup without talking. Émilie glances over at André, and he gives her a quick grimace, and goes back to half-heartedly slurping.

Not long after, Frédéric nods off, and André carries him over to his bed. Émilie agreed he'll sleep there with her after André told her he cries when he doesn't get his way. What choice did she have? Despite how anxious it makes her, she said it was alright. Watching André put his son to bed, she feels herself sinking as though filling with water, and she's afraid to stand. She's not his mother. Pretending otherwise will be devastating.

André goes to his side of the folding screen and crawls into bed, still wearing his clothes. Émilie sits at the table until well after she should be asleep. Another night, and her mind won't calm—a frightening thought keeps bombarding her: she killed a man; she took a life. Until now, she couldn't allow herself to feel anything but hate for a Nazi.

She should welcome feeling guilty, if only to reaffirm her humanity after being made to doubt it for so long. Regardless of how abominable Egger was, *shefikhut damim* is forbidden. Yet she shed blood. But in this world they find themselves, *shefikhut damim* is nothing more than a noble idea only suitable for the ruminations of rabbis and philosophers. She did something horrible, but isn't that what war is? What part her desire for revenge played in the German's death is another question. So is whether that need was there long before she even laid eyes on him. But what is revenge other than justice taken into your own hands?

She should ask for forgiveness. But from whom, and what good would it do? Asking to be forgiven when you don't regret what you've done is writing a confession in water.

Émilie knows at her core, even when she's long gone from the pâtisserie, she'll still find herself in that alley again and again. That's the difference between them and her.

She climbs into bed beside Frédéric, knowing sleep won't be easy. Every night for the past two weeks, when she shuts her eyes, it isn't the face of her victim she sees, as the guilty are said to do. It's the gun, floating, the handle towards her, waiting for her to reach out and use it again.

But the real gun rests at the bottom of the lake with the car and that abhorrent Nazi's corpse. André said as much. If it appears again in her nightmares, she'll only be grabbing at air.

Maybe it's the lack of sleep that's making her surrender to the past, but for the first time, Émilie lets herself think of the camps—she'd submerged those memories in a fast-flowing river, never wanting to fish them out again. She won't allow them to ravage what little is left inside her. When those memories float up, her heart clenches in a vise, and she shoves them down. Why do they feel so much like punishment?

Realizing she's sentenced to not settle, she eases herself out of bed and kneels. She reaches under the mattress, careful not to disturb Frédéric, and pulls out a piece of paper, unfolds it, and reads Mireille's note again. She can't run from it forever. She feels its dank breath on her neck.

As she creeps to the stairs, her veins flush with fear.

The full moon fills the pâtisserie with a pale light, like the room is teeming with candles. Émilie slowly circles the display case, searching for clues. She crouches, and peers around it to see out the windows, trying to recall that day.

There's a ringing in her ears, barely perceptible at first, but growing louder until it shatters into a jumble of shrill noises. Out of the cacophony, one sound rises to the clarity of a scream: a horse and cart.

Émilie stands, but falters, overwhelmed with the images she's tried so hard to suppress, the ones that only visit her in nightmares. Flashes of the past, debilitating in their intensity, sharp and cutting, are now paired to amplify her torment:

Of André's open face when she first saw him, and an emaciated camp inmate staring wide-eyed at her.

Of Frédéric laughing in the park, and a woman wailing over her dead child.

Of her and André while they bake, and an inmate couple holding hands as they're shot, falling to the ground.

Of a German soldier looming over her with a rifle pointed at her as she cowers in the pâtisserie, and a woman she went through primary school with on her knees begging a guard for her life, her family moving away, leaving her alone.

Of Mireille in silhouette in the window when she turns to look at Émilie behind the display case, and a Nazi standing in a pile of bodies using his foot to turn them over one by one, each of them Mireille.

It comes back to Émilie as vivid as if she's living it again. Memories of noises, and smells, and even tastes she thought forgotten, return like an executioner to his duty after pausing to sharpen his axe.

Her body no longer feels like hers, as though she's just walked out of a turbulent sea.

She slides to the floor and weeps uncontrollably.

TWENTY-FOUR

Friday, November 19, 1943

Émilie listens at the stairs as André moves around below in the shop. Frédéric watches her, his face more pale and tense than she ever thought possible. The last few days he's been especially morose, and every sound, no matter how small, scares him. That morning, while she was stirring the porridge, the lid from the pot slipped from her hand and clattered on the floor, and the boy began to tremble, then cried until it was a tremendous whine. It was then she realized she'd never seen him smile. He laughs, he giggles, but he never simply smiles without it accompanying a sound, as though it's only an involuntary side-effect of the noise he's making, an optical illusion.

She tried to speak to André about it, but he cut her off, saying nothing was wrong with his son, looking insulted at the implication there was.

At the armoire, she picks out one of Mireille's dresses, and lays it on the bed next to a coat and hat. Her matted hair is finally untangled and hangs limp in strands. Pulling out Mireille's identification card from her pocket, Émilie compares herself in the mirror—where Mireille's hair is styled in a fashionable bob, hers falls below the ears, withered like old roses.

She takes a comb and tries shaping it to match the photograph.

All night, her brain raced to find a way to lessen her debt to the baker, even if it would only remove a sliver of the obligation she's carrying. Her being free means nothing if she does nothing. It's not the actions of evil people that rob our humanity, it's the inaction of the good.

And now there's something she can do to repay André's charity.

Two women gossip outside the *boucherie*. They look identical: the same cloth coats, the same plain hats, the same scowling faces. Once they've caught up on personal news, they turn their attention to the pastry shop on the other side of the street.

"Gone. Just like that. It's been weeks now," one of them says in a low voice.

"And a new shop girl started so soon after?" says the other one, incredulous and condemning at the same time.

Unseen by them, a middle-aged man sneaks up from behind and attempts to pick their pockets. At first glance, he's dressed quite dapper, elegant in an evening jacket, white shirt, black tie and hat, and carrying a walking stick. But on closer inspection, his clothes are frayed and threadbare.

He pretends to be looking at the boarded-up butcher shop, although there isn't much to see except wood planks, as he extends a stealthy hand towards one of the women's coat pocket.

They're the perfect marks, absorbed in their mundane conversation, and ugly enough not to believe anyone would take an interest in them. The pickpocket likes to proclaim to his drinking buddies, "I've only met one kind of beautiful woman my entire life, but thousands of the hideous kind."

"I knew her parents," the first woman boasts. "Fine people they were. Owned the pâtisserie for years. What would they think? The daughter was a charming girl, a new mother at that."

"Marie?"

"No, Mi—" Her brow furrows when she senses someone behind her. She spins around, much faster than her age might suggest or advise.

The pickpocket snaps back his hand and feigns surprise at her brusqueness. He removes his hat and nods. "Mesdames. A nice day for a stroll, although the weather is a tad brisk for my liking." His expression is unflinchingly pleasant, and he appears years younger than he is, another deception he's mastered along with the tight yelp in his voice to give the impression he's less of a threat than he is.

"Can we help you?" one of the women snorts with exasperation.

"Oh, no, no, no. Well...perhaps you can. I'm newly arrived from Paris. The Seizième Arrondissement, actually." He pauses to gauge the effect of his snobbish statement on them, but it has none. Expertly hiding his disappointment, he forges on. "I'm looking for an old family friend."

Not taken in by his patter, the women hurry away, their identical gaits dripping indignation. The pickpocket humphs; his time-tested belief has been proven true again about women in provincial towns being tedious as a penniless and mute drinking companion.

The man shrugs and focuses on the shops across the street. He dips a hand in his pocket and inspects the contents: a few coins, a ticket stub, lint, and a dirty religious medallion. Rubbing it between his fingers, a cheap silver plating becomes visible. With a smirk, he spits on the piece and rubs some more.

When a passerby approaches, the pickpocket clamps his hand around the medallion, and lifting his walking stick, waves its carved ivory horse head handle to attract the fellow's attention.

"My good man, would you happen to know who owns that establishment?"

He points the horse's bared teeth at the Alberts' pâtisserie.

Hearing the bell, André looks up from organizing baking utensils. When he finally got out of bed, he told himself, "Stay busy," and planned to scrub the floor, perhaps even apply a coat of varnish if he could get some. But then he saw how his efforts pleased Émilie, and changed his mind, ignoring how churlish he was being. His feelings for her now a tide that ebbs and flows, always in extreme.

"We have nothing today, Monsieur," André informs the well-dressed man walking in. "Maybe tomorrow."

At the top of the stairs, Émilie is listening again, but only hears muffled voices.

"Oh, I'm not here to purchase any of your wares, kind sir." The man saunters over to the display case and looks around. "Just as she described it."

André gives out an annoyed little puff and goes over—immediately he's hit with the reek of wine and onions. "As you can see, we have nothing to offer." He swipes an arm towards the display. "We've run out of ingredients."

The man raps the display case with his walking stick. "She said it was the centrepiece of your shop. And impressive it is."

André grits his teeth at the scrape of the man's rusty voice spewing cryptic nonsense. "Who? I don't know what you're—" His patience shot, he's on the verge of throwing the nuisance out.

"Oh! My apologies. Your wife, Monsieur. I bring word from her." The man takes off his hat before adding, "As sad and unbearable as it may be."

André's jaw slackens and his legs go numb.

The stranger gives him a sympathetic smile, then walks to the door and looks out. "I met your wife in Paris a couple of weeks ago."

André hurries over. "You've seen her? Where is she? Is she alright?" Twinges of hope invigorate him, shocking as a plunge into a lake in winter.

"She was very striking, Monsieur, even though she wasn't well." The man turns to André, his eyes brimming with empathy. "Typhus. She knew she didn't have long." He rests a hand on André's shoulder. "She didn't suffer, *mon ami*. At least there's that."

André scrambles to understand. He looks around the shop

feverishly expecting Mireille to be in any one of the places he's seen her before. She can't be dead. André doesn't care what the man says, she's not dead. Not like that. Not without him seeing her one more time.

He staggers back to the preparation area. Every emotion within him fights for control, hacking wretchedness and loss the most dominant among them. His body quakes. Who does this...outsider think he is coming in here saying these horrendous things?

"You have my deepest condolences, Monsieur." The well-dressed man puts on his hat and is opening the door when André yells, "Wait!" The man pauses, then starts towards the back of the shop.

Émilie sneaks down the stairs, but freezes when the stranger walks past the display case to join André. She checks they aren't looking her way before going to the alley door. She slips out as the two men continue talking.

The stranger moves nearer to André, hooking the walking stick in the crook of his elbow. "I could tell she was a very loving woman. She was always speaking of you and the...child."

"Frédéric?"

"Yes. Your son."

"Did she say why—why she left?" André dreads hearing it, but knowing the answer at last to this one question might help calm him, even for a few minutes, so he can figure out this insanity, although it's just as likely to whip up his emotions even more. Surely the man's mistaken.

"Only that she had to go. That she didn't want you and the boy to fall ill as well. She came to Paris for a cure, but..." He touches André gently on the arm. "Again, Monsieur, I'm so sorry."

André doesn't move; he hardly breathes. He sorts through his memories of Mireille, both sad and joyous. They sink him deeper. He's locked, physically and emotionally, somewhere between denial and the past. Each battles to distance him from what he's just been told. But all this is overtaken by the blaring horn of a single thought: How will he make Frédéric understand his mother's gone forever?

André draws back his arm and pushes his face in close to the man. "You haven't said her name. If you know her so well, what's her name? Or mine? Or our son's?"

"Your scepticism's understandable, Monsieur. How must it seem my turning up this way?" The well-dressed man glances at the front door, but then twists back and looks André straight on. "I called her Marie. I realize that's not her name—she told it to me when we first met—it escapes me now. It sounds much like that. But I preferred to call her Marie after the Lord's own mother. It only seemed..." He leaves the rest unsaid.

Again, André doesn't know what to make of this. His gut is screaming it's a lie, a tale only as real as those André reads to his son. Does this stranger take him to be that naïve? For what purpose? How could someone be so unfeeling to tell him something like this?

The man tilts the walking stick to André as adieu and moves to leave again. This time André lets him.

At the door, the man stops. "Oh!" He digs in his pocket. "I completely forgot, Monsieur Albert. André, correct?" He shows him the medallion. "She had me buy this for you. For the boy, actually. She wanted him to have something to remember her by. Something to watch over him."

That doesn't seem like Mireille. She's generous, often to a fault, but a medallion? Nothing makes sense here, but that's the thing: her leaving didn't make sense, and nothing since then has.

The stranger waits, his eyes soft with kindness. André shuffles over, takes the object, and examines it. On one side there's a crest, almost worn away. On the other, a bust in relief of some ancient notable.

"Solid silver," the man assures him.

André passes it back. "Now I know you're lying. She wasn't religious. Her parents were, but not Mireille."

"People often change at the end." The man's hand stays

extended, presenting the medallion a little too much like it was plucked from a tree in the Garden of Eden. Yes, people change, but never for the better.

André takes the medallion and scrutinizes it again.

The stranger clears his throat and says with pronounced reverence, "Saint Honoré, the patron of bakers."

André's eyes shoot up. "I don't recognize this—"

"If you don't want it, I'll take it back and return the money she gave me for it."

"The money?" André says absently, looking down at the saint's profile again.

"Yes. All she had. Of course it wasn't enough for such a fine piece, but when I came back with it... Well... I'm only pleased it's brought some solace, no matter what the cost."

André looks hard at the man and pictures Mireille lying on her deathbed like morning dew, more concerned for him and Frédéric with every last gasp.

He can't leave her like that.

"How much was it?" André moves to the till, grabs what's there, and thrusts it at the stranger.

"No, Monsieur. It isn't necessary..."

But André insists, and the man shrugs and takes the money.

With an elegant bow and a crisp flick of his cane, he leaves.

André's attention fixes on the medallion, his wife's last gift to their son. He mourns with the emotions of a lone survivor of a sunken ship—sorrow for a loved one is made worse by the question: Why wasn't it me instead?

On the street, the pickpocket walks along, counting the coins as he goes.

He stops and looks back at the pâtisserie. Where this might be an opportunity for remorse, for salvation even, instead the man merely grins and pockets the money. With the walking stick swinging like a metronome in time to his pace, he strolls away, his conscience remarkably untarnished.

He'll eat and drink well tonight. Only those who keep fighting, regardless of what they have to resort to, deserve to survive.

❖

Lost in the dwindling light, André gulps wine straight from the bottle and turns the medallion over and over. Once the well-dressed man left, André shut the shop and started drinking. It's the last of the wine, but why should it be any different? Everything in the shop is down to the last: the last handful, the last pinch, the last drop. The last hope.

He still can't decide if he should trust the man who brought Mireille's gift. Which is more loyal to her: to believe it or reject it?

Bells signal curfew. Blasted Church! A saver of souls, but not of lives. André raises the bottle. "*À votre santé!*" He takes another swallow of wine. If Mireille is dead, he'd take her place in the grave in an instant, if it would free her.

Émilie lets herself in through the alley door. She carries a bag over to the worktable. With her back turned to him, she's the image of his wife. André looks away. He shouldn't be thinking this.

"Where were you?" he growls.

She turns towards his voice, squinting to make him out in the dark.

André storms over and bangs the wine bottle down. He snatches the bag from her and rifles through it. Packets of meat, sugar, flour, and butter. There's cod for the evening meal, it being Friday. He gives out a bitter little laugh. This Jew's trying to make him an observant Catholic again.

"They gave me her ration book," Émilie explains. "We have enough now to—"

Blood drums in his ears. He throws the packet of sugar at the wall above the worktable—it bursts open and rains down. When he does the same to the flour, it explodes into a cloud, coating everything.

André rounds on her. "Who said you could—" He looks down. "Take that off. The coat. The dress. Take them off."

"I-I only wanted— I thought you'd be pleased. Now you can

keep the pâtisserie going. Surely that's a good thing."

Her words mean nothing to him; he barely hears them. His feelings harden to stone.

"André..." she begins again.

He snatches his wife's hat from Émilie's head and flings it aside. "Don't touch her things again. Take them off."

Émilie removes the coat and hands it to him. She moves to go upstairs, but he's in her way and doesn't shift.

"Now!"

She defiantly stares at him. He grabs her collar, and she raises her arms to protect herself. The dress rips. That sound is all it takes to dissolve André's rage.

A military truck passes on the street, filling the shop with light. They both look to the window. When André turns back, Émilie's hair is illuminated. The way she has it is so like... Is she mocking him?

"What did you do?" He hears the pain in his voice, raw and exposed. Still, it's nowhere near the agony that's sitting at the base of his skull, ready to howl because his heart is breaking one more time.

Again, Émilie moves to go, but he grasps her arm and she stops. He reaches up tentatively to touch her hair, and snaps his hand back as though burnt.

He tries to make sense of what his eyes are telling him. Seeing Émilie in front of him now, the way she looks, if not his wife returned to him, then a phantom of her come to haunt him.

This isn't Mireille, how could she be? His pulse slows almost to a halt, then speeds up.

André pulls her to him, his mouth impossibly close. Pausing for the briefest moment, he kisses her, softly at first, then with passion, intense and urgent.

He lifts her onto the table, kicking up flour. Her hands on his chest, Émilie pushes him, but when he bends his body against hers, she reaches behind to steady herself. He continues kissing her; she throws her head back and arches into him.

André's hands slowly slide up her thighs. She touches his face, leaving white marks from the flour. He unbuttons his trousers and pushes up her dress.

When he enters her, she exhales a soft moan.

TWENTY-FIVE

Saturday, November 20, 1943

The sign in the door is now permanently turned to FERMÉ, and André is removing the bell. He walks over to the preparation area and drops it on the worktable where it gives out a gasping tinkle before falling silent for good. André's eyes narrow at the handprints smeared in the sugar and flour, wishing he didn't recognize what they are or how they were made.

When he goes upstairs, Émilie is sewing in a slip at the table. André pulls out the accounts from the buffet. He concentrates on the figures, trying to come up with ways to multiply them by ten to survive, or five to narrowly get by, or even to double them to give the pâtisserie a slice of a chance of existing. Impossible as it is to conjure up numbers, it's just as difficult to ignore how guilty he feels. He might as well be holding a knife dripping blood.

"The Monsieur gave me a linen sheet," Émilie tells him softly. He doesn't look at her, yet she continues talking. "It'll make a nice dress, even if it isn't summer." Her voice lightens. "I found these pearl buttons in a tin at the bottom of the armoire. They're the only ones from a woman's garment—I hope you don't mind. I thought I'd use them for the opening below the neck."

André puts the accounts away and approaches her. She tilts her face up and blinks as if trying to see through fog.

"Mireille's a good woman." When Émilie looks at him with a mask-like emptiness, he adds, "She loves more than anyone I've ever known."

Émilie goes back to her work. "You needed comfort, Monsieur. We both— These are not normal times."

"I'd never betray her." André says it with a finality bordering on a threat, not caring if it sounds that way long as there's no doubt.

"I would never think that, Monsieur."

As a sign of their understanding, he places a hand on her shoulder, and she stops breathing. Let this be the end of it. When she lifts her eyes, he shows her the medallion. "Saint Honoré. Proof she's dead. Or more proof I'm a fool." André knows which he wants to believe.

Lines form across Émilie's forehead, but before she can argue with him, he returns to the buffet and drops the medallion in a drawer.

The wind and rain bang on the window with the resolve of a debt collector.

Émilie washes plates while Monsieur Durand gathers the cups from the table. She wears the dress she made—it's plain and conservative, extending below her knees and covering her arms to the wrists. The only nod to immodesty, though unintentional, is how it clings to her when she moves, the nature of the fabric. It makes her self-conscious—it needs a lining. She tugs at it every so often to correct how it drapes.

"So I see you've made good use of the bedsheet," the old bookseller says. "It's quite pretty."

He's lying—it's not her best work, given her hand. The dress is less couture than it is a stylish shroud. But she smiles anyway.

Earlier, when André told her Monsieur Durand was joining them for dinner, she thought it would be a chance to thank him again for the material, but also to gain some wisdom from him. Now she realizes that's not likely. Solutions to their predicament lie well beyond his or anyone else's reach. Yet she can't hide the worry in her eyes from the bookseller.

"Are we contemplating shadows again? You're not pleased with the news?"

"I'm grateful you've found him work. He has to keep going. You're helping."

"As are you."

She stops washing. Some decisions are no different than choosing the type of poison to drink.

"But—" he prompts, raising an eyebrow.

"Monsieur Durand, may I request another favour?" She glances towards the bed where André is tucking Frédéric in. Tell him. But any words die on her lips. As much as she wants to be honest with the old man, he might try to stop her. Or worse, tell André who won't thank her for keeping the note a secret. But he has a child who needs him. She's trapped between her obligation to Mireille and the one to André. To whom does she owe more? One duty betrays the other.

"Very well." Monsieur Durand ensures his baker friend is not watching, then pulls out his wallet, takes out a bill, and passes it discreetly to her. "It's all I have with me. If you can wait a few days—"

"Thank you, Monsieur. Thank you." Émilie quickly tucks the bill in the bodice of her dress near her left shoulder. Again, his generosity astounds her. It's been a long time since someone's shown her a bead of kindness. Normally she'd find it...suspect. There's always an ulterior motive. But Monsieur Durand has never asked for anything in return.

When the bookseller goes to the table to blow out the candles, Émilie steals a look at André. She still feels his hands on her, his lips over hers, and she can smell his scent, musky and sweet. Her body and mind remain weak from surrendering to passion and his grief.

Despite what she did with him, she isn't reproaching herself. Her words aren't any less true now: They're living in extraordinary times. In all the violent upheavals throughout history, the first casualty isn't truth, it's shame.

⚜

André reads to Frédéric just like Mireille always did. When they finished their meal, Émilie encouraged him to do it, and he almost said no, but Frédéric looked up at him with such tense anticipation, he couldn't refuse.

The boy sits with no expression save for a squint in one eye as though trying to follow along. Still, he's content enough to listen while André caresses the back of his neck. When Frédéric was two, this never failed to soothe him, although soon after it no longer worked. Yet, it persists as one of André's habits, and more times than not, Frédéric puts up with it.

Turning a page, André continues reading:

"'That's right,' the fox said. 'For me you're only a little boy just like a hundred thousand other little boys. And I have no need of you. And you have no need of me, either. For you I'm only a fox like a hundred thousand other foxes. But if you tame me, we'll need each other. You'll be the only boy in the world for me. I'll be the only fox in the world for you.'"

André pauses to see the effect of the story on Frédéric. His face opens and becomes luminescent, so much so it momentarily convinces André of the child's brilliance.

Finished with reading for the night, André kisses his son on the head. The boy was a bit more cheerful today, although nowhere near as much as before. When Mireille was here, André felt Frédéric was as happy as other children. Now he doubts the child could be sadder. Too often he stares angrily in a way that seems to accuse André for his mother being gone. It's heart-numbing. Yesterday, Frédéric started gnawing his lips to the point they bled. How to fix the boy's broken happiness baffles him.

André joins Monsieur Durand and Émilie. Standing behind her, he deliberately puts his hands on the back of her chair so there's no misunderstanding. She's wearing the dress she made, but Mireille's kerchief covers her hair. He no longer sees his wife in her—familiarity put an end to that. When he saw her first thing this morning making breakfast, abandoned somewhere in her thoughts, her face hard as wood, she looked like the gnarled tree she'll become one day. Mireille should have that same chance to grow old.

"Now we have supplies, we can open again."

Monsieur Durand gives him a broad smile, but Émilie's brow contracts. His change in attitude must seem unpredictable as a sneeze, but they have to carry on.

While André was making the meal with the rations Émilie brought back, admittedly thankful not to be cutting up another turnip to boil, he decided the man with the medallion was nothing more than a common thief, not only of money, but of hope. No one will steal that from him again. If he gives up, then who is he?

"I didn't know you wanted to stay open, but don't forget there's your new job to consider," Monsieur Durand reminds him, ever practical. "I'm keeping the *librairie* going so I have something to do to pass the day, even though there hasn't been a customer for close to a week. But for you, André, any opportunity to earn money deserves your full attention."

"I can do the baking before I leave, and Émilie can run the shop. The pâtisserie will be back to the way it was in no time."

André smiles at them, something he hasn't felt like doing in a while.

Monsieur Durand taps the table twice with an index figure in agreement, but Émilie keeps her gaze lowered as she plucks the skirt of her dress away from her legs. She's put some flesh on her bones since she's arrived. Even though they haven't had much to eat, it has to be more than what she was eating before she showed up.

André turns an ear towards the window. The storm outside is no more than a snarl, and he's confident it'll soon be over.

Now that Monsieur Durand has left and Frédéric is sleeping, Émilie remains sitting with André at the table. He reaches for her hand and tells her, "I'm glad you stayed."

She tries not to show it, but she can feel her expression alter ever so slightly.

"Not for the boy," André explains. "Not just for him, if that's what you're thinking."

"I wasn't—" She's at a loss how to respond. Her insides churn, and she desperately needs a drink of water. He's confusing her with his mercurial shifts in mood.

"We can make the best of this." What he says comes out measured as though following a recipe. "Together."

Is he offering her a lifetime? Is that his to give?

He takes back his hand to rub his head. She's oddly relieved. She hates how his touch both excites and indicts her.

"If you want," he says tentatively.

They should consider the future, even if it's only what they'll do tomorrow and the day after that. Nevertheless, Émilie feels the cutting urge to rebuke him for being emotional for no other reason than to conceal her love.

Her heart quiets to a tick.

She warns herself not to lose herself in him.

TWENTY-SIX

Sunday, November 21, 1943

Motorcars and trucks roll by, and people wend their way past each other without a greeting or even a nod. Events of the last few weeks have made the townspeople of Saint-Léry d'Espoir strangers.

Émilie sits on the windowsill, watching the street below under a clear, pale sky. Every so often, she glances at the windows opposite, ready to hide behind the blackout curtain at any sign someone is looking back. She listens for the sounds of shutters opening.

Footsteps thump up the stairs, and André and Frédéric enter. The boy runs to her making excited noises, a couple of garbled "mamans," then half of one that falters on the edge of his mouth.

"He wants to go to the park."

Frédéric hops from one foot to the other in a delighted little dance.

André yells out "Surprise!" and produces a sailboat from behind his back. The boy claps, and they look expectantly for her reaction.

It's like the last month never happened. The butcher's son. The man she killed. Mireille. Her teeth hum, and she thrusts her tongue against them to stop it. All that pops out is, "André, the cost," as if that's her only concern.

"I'm working now," André reminds her. "An unusual, little

man came in today, no taller than my hip, and showed me some carved toys. He told me they were tossed away by rich people who no longer want them. They're perfectly good, though. Well, this one has a torn sail, but Frédéric wants a sailboat more than anything. Isn't this right, Petit Prince?"

Frédéric looks back with the same wide eyes he's had since tramping in, and André nods decisively. "I paid for it with some sugar and flour—I'll buy more with my first pay packet."

The boy tugs on her clothes, his way of pleading their case. Émilie gently removes his hands, smooths her apron, and gives him an anaemic smile.

André shows her the torn canvas sail. She lets out a defeated breath before saying she'll mend it.

The sailboat floats in place, bobbing in the swell caused by boys throwing rocks into the pond. Émilie stands next to André watching Frédéric at the water's edge, overseeing his boat, possibly imagining it anchored off a mystical island where children like him bask in never-ending affection.

She and André have spoken little to each other since they walked into the park. There's so much unsaid between them, gnawing to come out, but neither will voice it.

"We must invite Durand around for dinner again tonight," André says. "We can have a little celebration."

Hasty to agree, Émilie nods. The old man will be useful as a barrier between them, as much a deterrent to frank talk and raw emotions as a moat filled with burning oil.

André leans in and grins. "And he always knows what to say to make things better."

She manages a half-smile, nearer to crying than laughter. A lock on a scream. "Yes, the war will end. Things will be wonderful again."

The baker sighs at her cynicism, straightens again, and shades his eyes. It's almost noon, and the sun beats down on everything and warms nothing.

"What's left if you don't believe that?"

Émilie turns to him. "You no longer look for her. If you don't believe the man who gave you the medallion, why have you given up?"

"I haven't given—"

"You have. I see it in you. Don't you..." Émilie searches for words, comes up with many, but dismisses all of them as too charged. As much as she wants answers, it's what they'll provoke that's frightening.

Frédéric lifts the sailboat and drops it, and the splash makes him squeal.

André shifts, planting his legs wider apart. "I breathe her every moment of every day. There's not a single thing about her I don't remember. No one else will take this empty place inside me. Don't you think I'd give anything to have her back? Anything?" Anguish smoulders behind his eyes. "Sometimes the only thing to do is to keep going."

Émilie is about to caution him not to become jaded like her, but André stops her by asking, "And your family? You never speak of them. You've never told me about your life before the war." His lips bend into an ugly arch. "Or who you love."

His words are a slap. Experience has taught her no amount of intimacy has prevented someone from turning around and using confidences in the most damaging ways.

He sighs again. "I-I'm sorry. We're as bad as each other. We both can't seem to..."

"I can't remember them—" Émilie hears herself, soft and distant as though someone else is speaking, far away as an ocean. "—what they were like, what we did. Our lives together. Just their faces. I see their faces so clearly, as if they're right...here." She wants to beg him for an explanation why this is, but has no idea how he'd know any more than she does. "I recall other people so vividly, why not them?" André gives her hand a squeeze, and she avoids his gaze. "I keep thinking when I go back home, they'll be waiting for me. I must be mad."

"No, you're brave...and strong." His expression is sincere as a cloudless sky.

Émilie looks away and blinks in the pitiless sunlight at Frédéric, who's trying to grab his sailboat that's drifted beyond reach. Before André can move to help, the child steps into the pond to save the toy, shoes and all.

André laughs and Émilie shrieks. He leans into her, his arm pressed against hers. It's tender and surprisingly welcome, different from when a man's touch feels possessive, or lecherous, or indifferent like someone elbowing for more room on a bus. His touch concedes the simple bond between them.

She warms as though slipping into a hot bath, although still wary of drowning. This kind of water may be shallow, but it's taken lives before.

Still, she lays her head on his shoulder, feeling like a fist in a glove when he puts his arm around her. They remain this way, watching the boy splash by stomping one foot after the other with all his energy, like he's marching.

"Enough!" Émilie giggles. "He'll catch his death."

André pecks her on the temple. "Come along, Frédéric. We must go home for dinner. Your uncle will be joining us."

He tries to coax the boy out of the pond, but Frédéric stubbornly faces the other way and continues to splash. In the end, André has to wade in to retrieve his son and the sailboat.

A burst of their laughter skims across the water, taunting as the key to a dungeon cell dangling just out of reach.

TWENTY-SEVEN

Monday, November 22, 1943

Scraps of coloured paper are scattered on the table as if they had floated down from trees. Émilie helps Frédéric cut them, while outside the window a light snow falls.

André comes out from behind the folding screen wearing a work shirt and trousers, pulling on a coat. He's more rugged than before. Less brittle. He doesn't so much wear his clothes as inhabits them like armour.

Frédéric shows what he's made: a cut-out marionette, a baker like his father. He wiggles it, making it dance.

André looks to Émilie for confirmation it's Frédéric's work, and she readily nods. She's been sitting with the boy for the last hour showing him how to use scissors, a pair of dull, rusty ones from deep in the buffet's drawer. She could've used them to make the dress from Monsieur Durand's sheet, having had to resort to a knife and ripping the fabric. After cleaning the tool to a mottled silver, she helped the child snip his first piece of paper. He brightened with amazement as if he'd performed magic.

Her fingers surprised her with how clumsy they were. She blamed it on her injured hand and her impatience. Countless times she had to hold herself back from glancing over at the folding screen wondering when André was going to leave.

He caresses Frédéric's cheek with a thumb, then puts on his cap. The boy raises his arms, begging to be taken with him.

"Your father's starting a new job today," André tells him. "It's very important for you to stay here and help." Frédéric's bottom lip puffs out, and André kisses his head in the hope of staving off tears. His face implores Émilie to intervene.

She picks Frédéric up and bounces him on her hip. He gives out a high-pitched screech that makes it seem he's in distress, but Émilie has come to know is his way of showing he's thrilled.

"Be careful," she says. André nods. She's worried—it's the first time he's left them alone for the day. So many dire possibilities crowd her thoughts, bringing with them equally dire emotions.

André pecks her cheek, and Frédéric giggles. Why does it sound more reproachful than it could possibly be?

Émilie and Frédéric follow André downstairs. With only a slight hesitation, the baker steps out the front door, a day of hard work on the bridge lying before him. He told her he'd only ever worked in the pâtisserie or his father's vineyard.

Before André closes the door, the smell of morning fires burning in hearths reaches her. Suddenly she misses the aroma of pastries and wishes he was back inside baking. As he passes the window, he stops to make a funny face at Frédéric, and with a wave, saunters down the street.

Émilie glances up at the light grey sky and the falling snow. Surely they're harbingers of a happier future, at least for André and his son. Each snowflake brings back a ghost that huddles around her with an obscured face she struggles to recognize. If only they'd say their names.

She puts Frédéric down and turns him to her. "How would you like to go on a journey? You love trains, don't you?" He nods, unsure at first, then with an abundance of enthusiasm. "Get your coat and hat. But we don't tell Papa, okay?"

The boy scrambles up the stairs. Émilie's expression clouds.

At the display case, she picks up a coat and hat from a chair. Her eyes are drawn to where she cowered that first day and a few nights ago when everything crashed around her. Shame claws its way up her windpipe. With two swift intakes of air, she pushes it down. She hates that feeling. It's all that's left when everything else is gone.

Mireille's note sits neatly folded in a pocket. Émilie is scared to reach in and touch it in case it becomes dust, just another cruel illusion. She doesn't relish the task ahead of her.

Frédéric clomps back down, his coat, scarf, and hat already on. Pulling on her coat, she ties his scarf, and he skips to the door. Do his parents realize how capable he is? It's like he's been saving everything he's able to do, waiting for a reason to show them.

Saint-Léry d'Espoir's railway station is a smudge of brown wood only made pleasant now by the light coating of snow. Passengers rush to the train while Émilie buys tickets, Frédéric at her side, clutching her sleeve.

The train whistles and a conductor yells, "*Tous à bord.*" Frédéric's eyes clench watching the steam billowing from its smoke-stack.

Their passage bought, Émilie takes hold of the boy's hand and moves to the train. A soldier patrols on the opposite platform, and she pulls her hat lower. The German doesn't notice her, yet her throat constricts and her heart beats louder.

On board, they walk through three crowded carriages before coming across a couple of empty seats in a compartment thick with cigarette smoke and people reading newspapers. Trying to find the man who delivered Mireille's note is a fool's errand, but how will Émilie live with herself if she gives up?

With a jolt, the train starts, stopping her from dwelling any further on questions without answers.

There's loud, boisterous laughter from the back of the carriage. Émilie hazards a glimpse and sees a dozen German soldiers, young and dirty, roughhousing. She looks out the window, but Frédéric is fascinated by them. He kneels on the seat, staring, and when a soldier raises his hand in a straight-arm salute, the boy imitates him. Émilie turns Frédéric to face forward.

She doesn't want trouble.

A couple of soldiers brazenly flirt with women sitting nearby, some of whom move away in indignation to find other seats. One decidedly Aryan soldier stalks his way along the aisle. He stops beside Émilie, salutes her, and asks in German if she wants a traveling companion. He adds, "Mademoiselle," affecting a French accent so pronounced it can only be mockery.

Frédéric gazes up at the man with both fascination and fear. Émilie focuses straight ahead, her nose stuffing up with his smell of wet dog. Whatever this soldier is about to do, and no doubt he's going to do something terrible, it'll be alright so long as she doesn't have to see him. Then when it's over, he won't exist. Not letting his face sear into her brain is one of her tactics to keep afloat and sane in a sea of bedlam.

The soldier waves to his friends to catch their attention. When they're watching, he exaggerates leering down at Émilie and makes suggestive, nasty movements with his hands. His comrades laugh and hoot at his antics.

"I'm speaking to you." Menace trumpets from the Aryan's voice. "You look lonely."

Émilie still doesn't acknowledge him, her nerves ready to break off and clatter to the floor. Frédéric sidles up to her, tears set to flow. Yet he can't turn away from the vulgar stranger hovering over them.

There's a long pause, then the soldier carries on down the aisle.

Émilie exhales with relief, but it's short-lived. Another man looms over them. She doesn't so much as twitch, stoically enduring being shackled to whatever pillory awaits her.

Frédéric cries out, "Maman!" as clearly as any child.

A ticket taker with pox scars is standing there with his hand stretched out towards her. He expels a terse, "*Billets*," impatient at having had to wait for her to see him. Émilie fumbles in her pocket and passes over the tickets. She resumes watching the snow-covered fields slide by outside the window, imagining stamping through them to somewhere serene. If such a place even exists.

The man punches the tickets and extends them to her, but she's motionless again.

With a shake of his head, he thrusts them at Frédéric and moves on.

Not far from the Argenteuil-sur-Lac station, Émilie sips water in a café and stares out the window, while Frédéric fidgets with the empty cup from his one *chocolat*. Across the street, trucks come and go through a checkpoint manned by German sentries at the foot of a road leading to a factory.

She scrutinizes a burly workman who's showing his papers. He removes his cap and smooths a shock of red hair in place. It's not him. A sentry motions for the man to pass through, and he struts up the road, his arms swinging freely—the gait of someone whose conscience must never trouble him.

A waitress comes over and scowls at Émilie. "Madame, please." They've outstayed their welcome.

Émilie searches her pocket as two German soldiers enter and sit at the next table. She pulls out a change purse she found in the armoire, her hands stiff and raw, and places money on the woman's open palm—all small coins—but drops one. The waitress snorts with contempt while Émilie picks it up.

The Germans watch Émilie as she passes the woman the last coin, grabs Frédéric's hand, and hurries to the door. One of them says, "Madame," and Émilie seizes up. Slowly she turns to him. The soldier is holding out Frédéric's scarf. Émilie takes it, nods, and leaves.

The wind cuts at her bare legs, and she tries to slow her breathing. What a waste of time this has been. What did she think she could do for André's wife? It's ludicrous to believe anyone can be saved from their fate. Once written, it's indelible. Yes, she's been an exception. So far. But doesn't that prove the rule?

She squints at the factory. There's forest surrounding it on three sides, but no fence. Guards patrol the perimeter, rifles casually slung over shoulders as if they were out for a stroll along the Champs-Élysées on a Sunday afternoon. Émilie tracks them appearing and disappearing from behind the building and counts four.

Two workmen exit the checkpoint and set off in opposite directions. One is a short, stocky man. Is that... Her memory of him has become muddled, not only by the shock of someone showing up at the pâtisserie the way he did, but by the reason why. Goose bumps prickle her legs.

"Monsieur. Monsieur," Émilie calls. She bolts across the street, pulling Frédéric along behind her.

The man stops, glances at her, and smiles. It can't be every day a woman is so eager for his attention. Then his face drops and he turns to go.

Émilie grabs his arm. He wrenches away, but she blocks his path.

"Out of my way. Let me pass," he hisses.

"Please, Monsieur. We must speak."

"I have nothing to say." His eyes dart around, making sure they're not being observed.

"You came to the pâtisserie for her."

He hustles Émilie to the side of the café.

Next to a stone wall, the stocky man takes out a cigarette and lights it. He inspects Émilie up and down, and she turns to look at Frédéric. The boy, his complexion bleached muslin, is halfway between them and the street, afraid to come any closer while he tries to figure out who this stranger is.

"Is she— Is she still there?" Émilie asks, preparing for the worst.

The man nods. "Who knows for how long? They grind them into the ground making their weapons." He peers past Frédéric to the street. "But it's of no concern to them. There are always others."

"I have money." Émilie pulls out the change purse and shows him the remaining coins and the bill given to her by Monsieur

Durand. The stocky man keeps his gaze on her and chuckles. She takes the bill out and offers it to him. "I can try for more."

He has another draw on his cigarette and leans on the wall, the sole of one of his boots up against the stone, and wipes the wet corner of his mouth with an oily black finger. His gesture reminds her of her father, a printer, fingers just as stained, always ready with a tap on the end of her nose.

A shiver runs through her. She doubts the man before her has ever been loving to anyone without expecting compensation.

The stocky man shoots her a covetous look—not that he wants her, certainly not her in particular. It's a look that says he can take whatever he desires from her, whether he wants it or not.

"You can't help me, is that it?" She puts the bill back in the purse, doing her best not to show any emotion. Her stomach is a cauldron bubbling with disgust. Before she can shut the purse, the stocky man snatches the bill and pockets it.

"It might be possible. Who is she? Your sister?" He scoffs. "You took your time."

Émilie makes sure Frédéric is alright, but he's no longer paying attention to them—he's facing the street gaping at a military truck stopped at the checkpoint. He shoves his hands into his coat pockets and his features become more pensive than an uninspired poet, probably lamenting he doesn't have a toy like that able to move without him pushing it.

"She's a good worker. I watch her while I'm making my repairs. They'll notice she's gone."

"So you won't help. Why did you bring this then?" Émilie pulls out the note and waves it at him, certain now he's been snared by the bait of sheer logic.

"She paid my price."

They stay there for a moment more, Émilie holding up the note, folded in a perfect square, a talisman meant to ward off his evil. It doesn't work. His hand swings out and moves aside the flap of her coat, and he crudely examines her. She pulls away. Any price he asks from her, a single *sou* even, will be too much to pay, even if she had thousands to spare.

Yet, she keeps standing there, still begging for his help. Oh God, why?

"Be here in two days." He snorts, and glancing at the street again, starts speaking as if Émilie is already gone. "My place is on the next street. The blue door." With a last puff, he drops his cigarette on the ground, where it sizzles in the snow.

"Don't bring the kid," he adds, and walks away.

When the stocky man brushes past him, Frédéric races over to Émilie, and she pulls him to her as she buries Mireille's note back in her pocket.

While Émilie helps his son get ready for bed, André finishes his dinner. He came in late from work, tired, but in a somewhat cheerful mood. It's satisfying to be doing something useful again.

His fellow workers are a good bunch, mostly older men and those who haven't been forced into labour by the Germans, and two young *gars* simple as *sablé* biscuits. They joke with each other as they carry blocks or mix cement, and André laughs when expected to, but only half-listens, trying not to think of what will become of them once the job is over.

Émilie sings a lullaby, and Frédéric scrunches his face, attempting to listen more closely. It's in a language André has never heard, although its rhythm sounds German to him. Her voice is pleasantly melodious, but so soft it's almost an echo.

André fights his emotions—it's good his son has her to care for him, but it's a painful reminder she's not his mother. But this is his life now—their lives. He anchors this thought in his skull, hoping it will leave no room for anything else except for the simple acts of a day. Waking. Climbing out of bed. Washing and dressing. Eating stale bread, or if Misfortune is travelling in the other direction, an egg or a piece of cheese. Trudging to work. Toiling outside for hours until he can return home again. Swallowing thin soup. Then slipping into a cold bed as though resigning himself to a coffin. So what if his mind's the first part of him rigor mortis claims? It'll give him a rest.

But none of this can smother his feelings when he turns over in bed and Mireille is not beside him.

Émilie catches him watching her, and their eyes meet. She looks away and lowers her voice to continue her song. Does she feel any guilt for having taken Mireille's place? He knows he should for letting her.

His and Mireille's life together seems so long ago, like a story about people in other lands, faraway and foreign, but familiar, as though he's heard it before. Will he ever see her again? Doubt infects André's core, spreading out the way a terminal disease does—increasingly debilitating and without hope for a cure. While certain Mireille is not dead, André no longer feels she's coming home. Who'll he be now?

He looks down and spots the paper marionettes Frédéric made: the one of him, and new ones of Émilie, Frédéric, and Monsieur Durand. Picking up the marionette of his son, a powerful affection magnifies within him.

Then he stops breathing.

Lying among the coloured paper are two punched train tickets.

TWENTY-EIGHT

Tuesday, November 23, 1943

Soon as light appears around the blackout curtain, André gets up and dresses for work. The sun rises later this time of year, and how his father likes to grumble "it's no different from a spoiled cat" comes back to him, something he hasn't thought of for years. Even the sun disappoints his father.

Émilie is still asleep, and André can't stop scowling. All night he wanted to confront her about the train tickets, resolving to shake her awake, but never putting it into action. Just before daylight, a way to pry out her secrets came to him.

He goes down the stairs, crosses to the front door, and steps outside. Yesterday's snow has melted, and the street is not yet awake. He avoids looking over at what remains of the *boucherie* and the *fleuriste*. No good will come from it. Nothing's going to test his resolve today. Whenever someone walks past those shops now, they quicken their pace.

André strides away, only able to taste the bile at the back of his throat. He glances back at the pâtisserie.

He'll find out what she's hiding if he has to wring it out of her.

Émilie readies herself to go out. She knows her deception is repugnant. It's unfair to André, unintentionally malicious and horribly ungrateful. But now it's at the point where what she owes him can't be repaid, dooming her to bear the yoke of ingratitude forever. She'll pay and be free, truly free, to leave.

She puts on the linen dress she made, feeling like a sow prepared for slaughter. Though she doesn't think André will care anymore, it's not appropriate to wear one of Mireille's garments considering Émilie must go to that man and fulfill her part of his odious deal, her chance to restore André and his family's lives. While the Alberts will never be able to carry on where they left off, they can move forward if they resolve to. Given the opportunity, she'd do the same in a heartbeat.

She wakes Frédéric and helps him dress and put on his coat, hat, and scarf. He gazes at her, sleepy and passive.

Downstairs, Émilie puts on her coat and hat, making sure to button it over her thin dress, before they leave through the front door. Locking it and pocketing the key, Émilie picks up the boy and trudges up the street towards the bookstore.

"Émilie! Frédéric! What a pleasure." Monsieur Durand's smile masks his surprise at them dropping by so early. He puts down the book he's been arranging on a shelf, and feels a creaking inside him, as if an unoiled machine is starting up after years of disuse. There were days when having nothing to do—a pleasant enough circumstance for the young, but agony for an old man like him—highlighted his waning usefulness. Now doing nothing would be a treasure.

"Monsieur, would you mind Frédéric? Just for the morning."

He hesitates before turning to the child. "Come with me, Petit Prince." He leads him to a bookcase and hands him a book. The boy readily sits on the bottom step of a ladder and starts flipping through pages, not bothering to look at what's on them.

Monsieur Durand hobbles back to Émilie, a martyr to his slashed feet. "I fear asking what this is about." He raises an eyebrow. Émilie avoids his gaze.

"'What a grand thing, to be loved!'" he says with a lilt. "'What a grander thing still, to love!'"

Her eyes snap to him. "It isn't like that, Monsieur."

"Oh?" He's ignited a fire in her. Good. Perhaps it will illuminate things. There's been too much deceit, regardless of the honourable intentions underlying them.

"He loves his wife." Émilie is adamant. Barely above a whisper, she adds, "Sometimes the memory is enough."

Monsieur Durand scratches his chin with a thumb. "Sometimes...yes."

"I'll be back in time for his meal," Émilie says. To Frédéric, she calls out, "Be good for your uncle," and moves towards the door.

"Oh, Émilie!"

Monsieur Durand opens a wooden box and pulls out bills. He holds them out to her, and after a long moment's consideration, she walks back and takes them. It's a lot of money. She looks at him, perplexed.

He taps the desk to concentrate all of his attention on that spot, waiting for her to leave before there are uncomfortable questions, as if there are any but those kind left these days.

Émilie's eyes wander to the shelf where the Hugo book is supposed to have its place of pride, but it's no longer there. She looks back at Monsieur Durand with a mix of appreciation and sympathy.

"You'll always have our love, Monsieur."

Mercifully, she leaves before tears cloud his vision.

In a row of brown and beige doors, the blue one stands out like a Moulin Rouge dancer at temple.

Émilie's trip to Argenteuil-sur-Lac was uneventful, except for her encounter on the train with a woman a few years younger, who went on about a German soldier she was sleeping with and had promised to marry her when the war was over. Émilie was surprised there were still women gullible enough to believe such lies. The woman's parents didn't approve of the relationship and had thrown her out of their home.

Émilie couldn't figure out why the woman was so forthcoming. What good does it do to tell anyone such degrading things about yourself? When the stranger finished her account as the train was pulling into the station, Émilie guessed her motivation: she wanted forgiveness. Émilie envies that—the woman's honesty is glaring in contrast with Émilie's deception. All Émilie had to bestow when she rose from her seat to disembark was a neutral, "*Prends soin de toi.*" By using the less formal pronoun, Émilie felt she was showing the woman empathy—being a friend, though one she'd likely never see again. Of course, wishing her to "take care" might be misconstrued as a warning, but she shook that idea off. Who isn't telling everyone they meet to be careful?

As Émilie approaches the stocky man's house, a woman, her head embalmed in an over-sized kerchief, emerges from next door to dump out a pail of soapy water. She draws a tattered duvet leaking chicken feathers over her shoulders and looks around.

Émilie turns away until the woman goes back inside, then walks up to the blue door and knocks. The door flies open, its frame filled by the vile man wearing an undershirt and trousers, suspenders hanging to his knees. His eyes blaze at her with lust, and his lips curve with a presumptuous familiarity. Why do repulsive men believe they're the most desirable?

Right away, Émilie takes out the change purse. The stocky man reaches out, but places his hand on her cheek. She turns from his clammy touch. He shifts to let her in, and after a long hesitation, she steps inside.

Once they're in the hallway, the man snatches the money, pushes her against the wall, and roughly kisses her throat. Repulsed, Émilie pulls away. She scrambles for a way to negotiate another form of payment, but the savageness of his brutish grunts tells her compromise won't be possible.

"No. No. No," she pleads, but undaunted, he hurriedly unbuttons her coat, then unfastens the pearl buttons at the neck of her dress, his movements clumsy and uncaring. His other hand reaches out to shut the door.

Émilie's mind withdraws—a turtle to its shell—and she goes numb. She waits the ignoble deed feeling less like Jeanne d'Arc than anyone since that woman met her end at a stake. At least flames might burn his touch from her skin.

Out of nowhere, the door is pushed open and André boulders in. He grabs hold of the man and throws him to the floor.

"What is this?" André looks at Émilie for answers, but she averts her eyes.

The stocky man tries to get up, but André lunges towards him. The man holds up his hands in defeat and stays down.

With a face like thunder, André storms out of the house.

Émilie follows, doubling her pace once she's on the street, and catches up to him outside the café.

"Please, André, I can explain." She wants to yell out she was doing it for him, but he spins back to her, angry and expectant. He waits to hear what she never wanted to say, but his patience is limited—he folds his arms and leans forward, giving her a chance to come clean.

She's hesitant to begin. How much can she say and still protect him? Already scepticism is creeping in behind his eyes. Soon he won't trust a word from her. She doesn't doubt the lies she's been telling herself have become a religion of blind faith. It's these deceptions that are distancing her from him and any possible atonement. But he'll do something rash, something that will end in things being worse than they already are.

André abruptly stands straight again. Time's up.

A tangle of nerves, Émilie pulls out Mireille's note with a shaking hand.

André glares at her before taking it. He unfolds it and starts reading while she watches—she's able to recite every syllable in the note by heart. *I am a prisoner in Argenteuil-sur-Lac.* André's expression twists. His eyes move down to the next line. *I beg you to come for me.* When he sees the signature at the bottom, his mouth purses, then peels open like he's going to be sick.

He drags himself over to the bench and sits down heavily to read the note again. His wife's words must be pounding in his brain. *I am a prisoner. Come for me.* Each one has to be a bruising blow to his insides.

How much misery has Émilie caused him? Pain upon pain upon pain. She sits next to him, wary of touching him or being too close. Often when a man goes quiet, a burst of anger follows. Even violence. She needs no reminding of this.

After André reads the note for the second time, she expects him to look at her with all the condemnation she rightly deserves, then to shout at her until she's crushed into bone fragments. Instead, he faces the factory, no doubt imagining his wife returning to him, arms wide, overjoyed to see him, as he must have done hundreds of times. Émilie knows that fantasy well. This is what you do when the person you love the most is gone: imagine one thing again and again until it becomes real or freezes you in madness.

She takes a long look at him, trying to commit to memory the André she's known until now and will never see again, before beginning her confession.

TWENTY-NINE

"I was useless to them. I'd injured my hand. When you're use-less..." Émilie stops as her body dams with ice. He doesn't need to know that. "They were taking us to Drancy. They marched us past your shop." Her muscles strain like she's making each step and every movement of that day once more.

She decides to admit everything in spite of her insides being perforated by the rusty nails of memory. She'll rescue those images for him so he'll understand, images all at once so close to the surface she can reach down and pick them up by their soggy corners. Then maybe she'll be free from one more prison.

"I was with a dozen others, thin and wretched in our dingy clothes and yellow badges. We were shackled to each other by our wrists, following a horse and cart.

"As we made our way up the street, people ran away and shopkeepers disappeared.

"Two German soldiers were leading us, one big and burly, the other wearing glasses. An officer followed behind with a rifle across his chest. He always carried it like that. I hated his ugly face—I'd seen too many hideous, detestable Germans—so I had stopped looking at it, but I knew it was him whenever he was near me because of the way he held that gun—the others carried theirs across their backs."

Why is she telling him such details? Is it to emphasize the

danger, hoping it robs him of his claim to anger?

"I was the last prisoner in line, and I purposely lingered behind. I wasn't going back to..." Again, that isn't something he needs to hear. She glances at him, his expression now one of permanent outrage.

"I stumbled, and the officer was on me at once. He hit me in the back with the rifle and told me to move. That's all they'd say to us: 'Move.' The entire night we walked from a factory not much different from this one—" Émilie lifts her chin towards the building beyond the checkpoint. "—and they kept telling us to move. If we slowed down. 'Move.' If we fell... Again, they'd order us to move. The only time they didn't say it was when we asked for water, then they'd beat us with their rifles or fists.

"An elderly man fell near the front, bringing down four other prisoners with him. He gave out a horrible screech that sounded like something being butchered. The officer yelled to keep moving, and they struggled to free themselves from the tangle of bodies, but the chains made it impossible. The other soldiers went over, but all they did was jab with their rifles. Finally, they had to yank up those who fell, back to their feet, one at a time.

"I desperately tried to extract my hand, this one, from the manacle." She holds up her injured hand. "They got everyone up, except the old man. The officer unlocked his manacle, cursing at him the whole time, and they threw him into the cart.

"By then I had freed myself. There was terror in the faces of the prisoners next to me when they saw me stagger past them. Even though my legs wouldn't stop shaking, I ran fast as I could towards the first place I saw. Your pâtisserie."

Émilie pauses to decide whether to go on. She looks at the baker again—he's still staring at the factory. Another truck pulls up to the checkpoint, and two soldiers jump out the back and change places with the sentries. It's enough now. The right thing to do isn't telling him the truth, it's walking away.

"Was she there?" André asks, his voice thin as thread. "Mireille. Did you see her?"

Émilie hesitates. "Yes."

228 | MICHAEL WHATLING

Moving closer, she fights the desire to touch his arm, having no idea why she wants to. To comfort him? To make sure he's still here? Both seem implausible.

"When she saw me running towards her, she stepped back. She was scared of me, I suppose. You know how I looked, how desperate I was. Her expression was so... I ran past her into the alley and I heard them keep going. The soldiers. The other prisoners. I thought I'd gotten away. Then there was a commotion—the officer yelled, '*Halt. Halt.*' They must've discovered my manacle hanging there empty on the end of a chain.

"I found the door to your shop open, so I went in and hid behind the display case. Loud music was coming from upstairs. I was sure someone was up there about to discover me—the woman's husband. You, I guess. I only hoped the Germans would move on by then."

Émilie falters; she can't recall what came after that. Her memory is still spotty. She's sure there was more yelling on the street, to the point she shut it out. But then she remembers, and fear shakes her.

"What happened next?" André's voice is leached of anything gentle.

Her throat dries. She swallows air. "The officer ran up to Mireille, his gun drawn." Émilie hesitates again. This part, no man would want to know.

"Continue." André's look cautions her not to test him.

"I could tell she was frightened," Émilie says, and he winces. "She turned to come into the shop, but stopped, and carried on with her sweeping."

Émilie grapples with whether to tell André more—it's too damning. But enough dishonesty! It ends here.

"I— That's not what happened—not all of it." She runs her hand across her forehead. "Before your wife went back to her chore, she spotted me through the window staring back at her, twisting in fear, pleading with my eyes not to tell them where I was hiding.

"And we locked eyes."

Émilie waits until André regains the will to look at her again. She tells him the officer said something, but couldn't make out what over the music. "I imagine it was a threat to get her to reveal where I was, but she was having trouble speaking. Her lips moved, but I'm not sure if anything came out. So she pointed...down the street away from me."

The breeze chills Émilie's neck, and she goes to fasten the top of her dress, but the button is missing thanks to that brute behind the blue door.

"She was fearless." Émilie's tone lightens with admiration. "What she did worked—they ran in opposite directions searching for me, so I remained hidden in your shop. I kept my head bowed and squeezed my eyes shut tightly as I could, hoping against hope they wouldn't find me. But they did."

André turns to her, surprised.

"The alley door opened, and a soldier came in, the large one. Even with the music, I heard a floorboard creak. I looked up, and he was squinting at me down the barrel of his rifle.

"It was strange. You'd think I'd die right there, but my fear transformed into...serenity, that's the only way I can describe it. This sudden calm to my mind, my heart, my entire being. And all I did—all I could do—was look at him straight on and say, '*Bitte*.'

"That's all it took. 'Please.' And he hesitated. His eyes grew big as he looked past me, as if something behind me frightened him. I assumed it was the officer pointing his gun, but it was Frédéric holding out his ball. The soldier started backing away."

André wipes his mouth as though he's tasted something rancid. "Go on." He adjusts his position on the bench in anticipation of what's coming next. "I said, 'Go on.'"

"I heard a gunshot in the alley." Émilie hears the resignation in her. "I thought he was shooting at—" She shakes her head. "But she was alright. I guess he shot in the air so it seemed I got away and he could claim he'd done everything to stop me." She wondered why the Nazi did what he did. Was he a father who couldn't shoot her in front of a child? Or was it sudden scruples, a deathbed conversion of sorts? Maybe he couldn't kill anyone, a peculiar trait in a soldier.

"What—" André has difficulty getting it out. "What did they do to her?"

"The soldier ran back to the officer. They started talking to each other in the street right outside."

"I asked about Mireille." André glares at her. He straightens again and folds his arms, unwilling to budge until she tells him, like he needs to suffer.

She understands him wanting answers, but it's the details mulled over endlessly that damage you, the tiniest ones sticking in thoughts like a chicken bone in a throat.

"The soldiers ran over to her. She tried to get away; she managed to push open the door; the bell rang. She must've seen Frédéric—I dared to look and saw her expression, so helpless and confused.

"But they were on her before she could step in. I lay down so they wouldn't see me, but I could make out the sounds of them dragging her off. She screamed she wasn't doing anything, begged them to let her go. When I looked again, they were in the street trying to put the manacle on her. She was flailing and kicking out. She bit one soldier's hand and he cried out in pain, and I thought: Good for her." Émilie casts her eyes down. "It was selfish, I know."

Still clutching Mireille's note, André starts walking. Émilie shuts her eyes, appealing to be given the iron determination for what's coming next.

She heaves herself up and follows him back towards the station. How can he sleep now? She hadn't wanted to say anything, fearing knowing what occurred would get him killed, but maybe now it will save him. She remembers something her father—her heart leaps—was fond of repeating: "*Quand le vin est tiré, il faut le boire.*" Yes, the wine has been opened, she opened it, so it's up to her to drink it.

Émilie stands beside André on the platform. A train pulls in, and disembarking passengers push past them, buffeting them like tree branches in a gale. She hardly notices, André even less.

She waits for him to speak. When the passengers are gone and he still hasn't said anything, she moves in front of him and looks him in the eyes. André meets her gaze unflinchingly, defying her to finish her god-awful account of what became of his wife.

Her insides ache with nauseating intensity, and she has to bite her lip against the pain before carrying on.

"The officer's patience must've worn thin. He glanced up at the sky and took in a deep breath. Then he exhaled, and in this horrible continuous motion, he turned and hit her on the side of the head with his rifle."

André flinches but doesn't look away. He's turned to stone, and she's Medusa, her lies the serpents, her curse on him irreversible.

Émilie tells him, slightly above a murmur, that Mireille dropped to the ground and the Germans picked her up and *put* her in the cart. She can't tell him they *threw* the poor woman in.

"The officer tore off her apron and flung it aside, and he walked to the front of the line with the burly soldier. The one wearing glasses ripped something off her neck and pocketed it. One of them used a whip on the horse—it was like another gunshot. I hid again. I heard them continue down the street."

"Her cross," André says distantly. Émilie is unsure what he means, then understands: the German stole Mireille's cross.

"She saved me." Émilie's voice is almost a squeak.

André stares at the factory. It must be torture for him to realize his wife's right there. His muscles go taut like he's considering storming up there and freeing her. A cog in his own fate, as predictable as rain.

"Why would they take her? That doesn't make sense. She isn't a Jew." His tone is hollow with disbelief.

"I've been asking myself that over and over. Émilie says simply, "I escaped. "Mistakes are severely punished. They couldn't show up with one of us missing. Without me." She hears the remorse in every word reverberate inside. "They took her to make up the numbers."

André turns back and pierces her with a look of abject hate.

Just before curfew, Monsieur Durand sits with André and Frédéric, watching Émilie sew a coat for the boy. She finished repeating what she told André that afternoon, and Monsieur Durand needs time to sculpt some sense out of it. He heard a few of the particulars before—Madame Bujold imparted to him what she witnessed that day from behind her shutters, as fragmented as could be expected for something seen through slats. But it's the specifics and the corroboration Émilie provides that makes hearing what happened more numbing.

Lately, he's listened to an increasing number of anecdotes chronicling the vagaries of war and its atrocities, either from customers in whispers, or in letters from his few former colleagues still at the Sorbonne, unsigned less their frank opinions be intercepted and the writers unmasked. But hearing it about Mireille, someone Monsieur Durand has known since she was a child, makes it that much more potent. Such accounts cause his aching bones to feel weak and brittle. War makes everyone old, except for those it kills.

When he brought Frédéric back from the *librairie*, André was scouring baking tins in the preparation area, and Émilie was moving around upstairs, the floorboards creaking above them. André trailed him and the boy up the stairs, but wouldn't eat. Émilie said very little until Monsieur Durand asked her what was wrong. That's when she told her story over, seemingly as resolute now to divulge her secret as she was before not to tell a soul.

André sat listening to it again, his eyes closed when he wasn't drumming his fingers on the table, grunting under his breath.

"Could you return to him?" Monsieur Durand asks. "This man at the blue door, might he still help?"

Émilie stops sewing. "I don't think he can, even if he wanted to, even if we paid him everything we could put our hands on. Smuggling out a note was probably all he could ever do."

"Yet, you didn't stop dealing with him." It comes out more accusatory than he means it.

Émilie lets out a long sigh. "I suppose I wanted to believe he could do something."

André stands, scraping his chair on the floor. "Time for bed, Frédéric."

The boy scampers over to a book and holds it up for Émilie to see.

"Of course," she says. "Just let me—"

"Bed. Now," André barks, making Frédéric whimper. "Stop that. You're not a baby anymore."

Monsieur Durand vigourously rubs an eyebrow. What an uncharacteristic manner for him to take with the child. "André, are you not being—"

"And how is it any of your business?" The baker's face contorts. "I've had enough of people meddling in my life. Enough of words, always words and more words—they mean nothing and change even less."

"You can't be clever and angry at the same time. Mireille would want you to—"

"And how would you know?"

Émilie extends a hand to Frédéric, who's lost amongst the adults' harsh tones. "Go to bed, *petit lutin*. I'll be over to tuck you—"

"I'll do it." André barges over to Frédéric's bed and pulls down the covers. Frédéric lifts his big eyes to Émilie, helpless to comprehend his father's anger. With a single tap of his foot in defiance, the boy pads over to his bed and tumbles into the sheets.

André pulls the cover up and joins them again at the table, but doesn't sit. He hovers over them, tottering in the winds of his own rage. He turns on Monsieur Durand, his voice dripping with accusation. "You knew Mireille was involved with the Resistance and you said nothing."

"I...suspected," Monsieur Durand says. "If I kept anything— I didn't mean to, *mon ami*. I was put in a very difficult—"

"And her?" André jerks his head towards Émilie. "She knows where Mireille is. She knew all along."

"No, that's not—" Émilie starts to protest.

André ignores her and spits out at Monsieur Durand, "Did you?"

The lines on Monsieur Durand's face deepen as he searches for a reply. So many confidences—why did he forget that to keep one means all of them will be broken? He strived to be a true friend. His heart rips open at his abysmal failure at doing so.

The baker explodes. "Get out!" He pulls Monsieur Durand from the chair by his collar. "Get out, you *maudite tapette*."

"André!" Émilie cries out.

He drags Monsieur Durand to the stairs and roughly pushes him, almost toppling him down them. "Don't come back."

Holding onto the wall with one hand, Monsieur Durand reaches out the other one, beseeching André to reconsider. He's at a loss how to best express his regret. A lifetime of reading and writing, and still he's reduced to saying, "Please, André. I never meant for this to happen."

André says nothing. When Monsieur Durand realizes there's only disgust left in his friend, he slowly descends the steps.

He could never hurt them. André has to know he wouldn't dream of harming as faithful a family as them. Being called that reprehensible insult leaves him devastated, no different from if he'd been pummelled by fists. He's had a lifetime of names. Cuts and bruises heal, vindictive words fester.

Monsieur Durand hesitates at the front door to look back at the shop. The wonderful times he's had here when Georges and Marie-Claire took over the pâtisserie: dinners, when they bought the display case, when Mireille was born. There were dreadful times, too: a fire that almost destroyed their shop, and when the Pellegrins died, so close together, like they never stopped holding hands. That's what he told Mireille and André to console them over the loss of her parents. He prided himself on having an aptitude for comforting others with his words.

How arrogant!

These magnificent bakers welcomed him into their family in place of his blood relatives who no longer spoke to him because of whom he loved, as if that was something he could stop like the twist of a faucet. They befriended him at a juncture in his life when carrying on was unbearable.

Fear overtakes him. Is he to end up falling into his grave without mourners? If so, he doesn't know how to change it. He feels panicked, stranded in a desert with no idea which direction to walk, unable to see his footsteps in the sand behind him.

It's nothing to die; it's everything not to have lived.

Monsieur Durand slips out into the dim street and slogs home, feeling more lonely and abandoned than ever, a comfortless shadow fading into the night.

THIRTY

Wednesday, November 24, 1943

The smell of burnt sugar lingers. Unable to sleep, Émilie crept downstairs to start the baking, and left the first batch in too long. Now those biscuits sit stoically on the worktable, their edges black.

The trouble she caused for Monsieur Durand kept her up all night wearing away the colour from her worries. She shouldn't have let André throw him out. She couldn't stop thinking about how he assaulted the old man. And that appalling name! She'd heard homosexuals in the camps called that by guards, and even other prisoners. André's in pain, and when someone can't endure their pain any longer, they wield it like a scythe, cutting down everything.

She didn't have the nerve to rouse him from his bed to talk about what took place. She rationalized what André did by telling herself he had to have been upended listening to her story, set adrift hearing what happened to his wife. It would have been better had his idea of what happened to Mireille remained undisturbed, even if it meant he'd stay trapped in a cage built with the bones of memories.

There are footsteps on the stairs. André comes in, his eyes roaming like those of a wild animal. They stop for a moment on the biscuits she baked, before moving on.

"If you knew what we made do with during Passover." Émilie gives him a tentative smile.

The OUVERT sign, turned to the street, catches his attention. He marches over and flips it around, then locks the door.

"Who said you could open? I should throw you out. With any luck, you'll land at the feet of the Germans." He expels the words like they've been marinating in the Devil's mouth. She resumes baking as if not having heard them.

There's a long silence, the air thick with challenge and hair-trigger fury, before André thumps back upstairs.

Émilie holds out a hand—it's shaking. She's glad she didn't rise to the bait; still she's riddled with shame. How easily it is to become hurt children.

The words André slung at her last night ring in her head. She shouldn't have expected this *sheigetz* to be any different. She's only known one who wasn't, her husband Claude, rare as Byzantine silk in so many ways.

Soon as André returns upstairs, he knows he has to go back to Argenteuil-sur-Lac. Pulling on his coat and cap, he races down to the shop and out the front door without glancing at Émilie. Why did he let her step back in there after what she told him?

The train ride allows him to think without being bothered, and when he arrives at his destination, he strides with purpose to the checkpoint.

André narrows his eyes at the factory up the road. The sentries give him threatening looks, but they don't confront him. Feeling his face pinch with anger and deliberation, they wouldn't be blamed for assuming there's something wrong with him, that he's not right in the head. Just in case, they watch him like mangy dogs ready to pounce on a scrap of meat.

He focuses on the perimeter guards patrolling behind the factory. Breaking in would be suicidal, and still Mireille might not be free. There has to be a way to get to her.

When a sentry starts towards him, André tips his cap and walks away.

He ends up at the café sitting next to the window. He orders a watered-down apple juice, the only thing they have to drink today, and nurses it until dusk. Then he pays and starts shuffling back to the railway station. All this time, and he's still a jumble of emotions and unanswerable questions. What a waste. Another day amounting to nothing. He should be home.

This thought depresses him. The pâtisserie no longer holds any pleasure. It's like all the good memories of that place don't belong to him anymore—they've been exorcised as thoroughly as midnight demons. Now the shop exists to mock him.

At least Frédéric will be happy to see him, but the woman will still be there. What else is she keeping from him? His blood congeals at the thought. She's a viper. And after all André did for her. He'll never forgive her for not telling him sooner about the note. How much longer will Mireille have to be there because of that curséd woman?

Again, André's as furious as when Émilie first told him about Mireille—he feels snapped at by the teeth of wolves. But he won't be weakened by anything again. At the *vignoble*, after they cut back the vines in autumn, they always came back stronger in the spring.

He glances back at the factory. Mireille being with another man would be more merciful than being held up there having to endure God knows what.

André passes the station and plods up the street. Abruptly, he turns into the forest and starts running. Dead leaves and twigs give out brittle warnings as his feet grind them into the ground. In the branches above, birds start squawking. The dankness of their droppings and the stench of decay take turns assaulting André's senses.

He keeps going until he makes out light from the factory's windows through the trees.

André crouches and scans the field between him and the back of the building. No guards. He darts to the factory's wall. There's a rapid-fire knocking in his chest, but he pushes himself to carry on. He can't waste a second. Mireille's just there, so near he feels her.

The windows are too high, and André struggles to drag over a rain barrel squatting at the far end of the wall. Thankfully, it's half-filled, a drop more and it couldn't be moved. Climbing up on it, he balances on the rim and peers through a window. Prisoners, mostly women, are working or shuffling to a side door. They look alike: the same dirty grey uniforms, same kerchiefs around their heads, the same exhausted and crushed expressions.

He hunts for Mireille, but doesn't find her. He scrutinizes each face with the meticulousness of making a dozen identical entremets.

A truck rumbles up the road, and headlights illuminate the field. André jumps off the barrel and crouches beside it. The vehicle stops next to the factory, its lights resting on André's hiding place.

The factory door opens. Prisoners file out, escorted by two soldiers, and climb in the truck without being told, submissive as whipped dogs.

André takes a cautious look and spots a woman bent over as though groaning under a load that would bring a beast of burden to its knees. She straightens to pull off her kerchief—her face is filthy and her hair's closely cropped. Mireille! Joy floods André's heart. But it's short-lived. Surrounded by Nazis, she could be as far away as the rice fields of Indochine for all the good it will do.

Mireille stops to argue with one of the Germans. The soldier forcefully shoves her, almost knocking her over. Still she persists. Her back straightens and more words are exchanged—André can't make them out over the noise of the truck's engine idling. Mireille licks the corner of her lips the way she does when her patience is being tried, and André's pulse skips. Only when the soldier raises a fist, threatening to hit her, does she climb in with the other prisoners.

André pulls out Egger's Luger. He'll be damned if he lets anyone touch her. When he takes a step towards them, lights sweep the field from behind him. Two perimeter guards, each carrying an MP40 and a flashlight, walk his way.

André ducks and crams himself best as he can into the crook between the barrel and the wall.

The last prisoner is climbing in the truck when the perimeter guards reach it. They exchange pleasantries with the soldiers, the four of them indistinguishable in the beams of the constantly moving flashlights. André has glimpses of round faces and thin bodies. One guard waves his arms, imitating swimming, then shakes them as if being eaten. The others laugh at his exaggerated gestures. The guard leans in conspiratorially, possibly to tell a dirty joke or brag about one of his sexual exploits. His pals ripple with anticipation for the punchline like children waiting to open gifts.

The humourous guard stops smiling and swings his flashlight across the field, resting its beam directly on the barrel. Another guard moves to check, but the first one lifts his hand to stop him, levels his submachine gun, and peppers the barrel with bullets. Water spouts out the holes like spitting fish.

In the forest, André gasps for air behind a tree and watches as a perimeter guard pulls out a pack of cigarettes and passes it around. The two soldiers get in the truck, and it noisily reverses and turns to go down the dirt road.

The vehicle sways away, and with it, André's hope of reuniting with Mireille. Distraught at failing to free her, his grip tightens on the Luger, his finger pressing the trigger with almost enough pressure to fire it. Coward! His insides crumble like dry cake.

He knows Mireille will forgive him, but how can he forgive himself?

André walks back to Saint-Léry d'Espoir in the dark, lying beside the road whenever vehicles approach, almost always German motorcars or trucks. Halfway home, he hears the ominous rumbling and creaking of a Panzer. André dives for a ditch and hides until the colossus passes. Too exhausted after the events of the day to make it back to town on foot, he catches up to the tank. Climbing onto its back, he wedges his foot into a notch and holds on.

Just outside of town, André has an inspiration clear as a drop of rain on a leaf: He's going to rescue Mireille with the help of the Resistance fighters.

They just won't know it.

Alone in the candle-lit gloom of Saint-Joachim, André kneels at a pew and bends his head as though in prayer. One by one, the Resistance fighters enter the church and hasten to the catacombs. André sees the mechanic stomp his feet against the cold before steaming up to the altar and slipping through the doorway beside it.

When André is sure all of them have gathered, he goes down the stone stairs and along the passageway to where they met weeks before. He's swamped with self-loathing for being at their mercy again. To drown in coffee or drown in tea? Any other time, he'd have accepted burning bridges with them meant that was that. But he won't let it stop him now.

The fighters' whispering peters out when he walks in. They gape at him with a mix of surprise and distaste. They blame him for Gilles. André feels a sharp stab of sorrow. He doesn't think they know for certain about Egger or that Émilie's a Jew, but they suspect something that happened in the pâtisserie attracted the Nazis' attention. It *is* brazen to show up here, especially with what he's going to ask.

"We thought you had forsaken us," Père Blais says, his tone friendly enough, but still wary.

"He's not welcome here," the white-haired woman snarls.

"Everyone who has our goals is welcome." The priest motions for André to step forward, but he stays rooted at the doorway.

"By now he could be one of them." The woman looks to the others for agreement. "The directive is clear on what to do if we're discovered."

They wait for André to convince them not to throw him out, or worse. He doesn't need to guess what their instructions are to deal with him. What can he say to make them trust him again? Monsieur Durand cracks his thoughts. André could use his eloquence—all André has is contrition, and what's that worth now?

On his walk home from the factory earlier, he debated about going to the bookseller and apologizing, but decided not to. Already too much time has passed. Maybe with people who aren't so close and mean less, years can go by and reconciliation is possible. *Ça vient, ça va.* Easy come, easy go. With the depth of his friendship with the old man, ironically that possibility disappeared in minutes.

When André doesn't speak, the fighters explode in discussion: the white-haired woman wants nothing to do with him, the priest and the teenage girl argue they need more help, the shy man shakes his head, unsure, and the mechanic simply glowers at him.

André lets them prattle on. He's here for one thing. They can hate him all they want as long as they say yes.

In the end, his voice booms over them. "I-I know where there's a German munitions factory not far from here."

THIRTY-ONE

Tuesday, November 30, 1943
Six Days Later

Émilie finds André at the front door again, staring at the morning. There's no point in trying to reason with him. Even saying the word "patience" seems likely to break him into jagged pieces as if cut out with pinking shears.

She watches André step out, not bothering to lock the door after him. It's not like there's something to steal. Or maybe he knows she'll lock it. This gives her a small comfort—he still counts on her. And there's Frédéric. If André's lost all faith in her, would he leave his son for her to mind? Her relief is dashed when she realizes that after his falling out with Monsieur Durand, there is no one else.

Waiting this past week to hear from the Resistance, André's fallen into a tortuous routine. Each day he goes to work on the bridge crew, but hurries home in the evening to interrogate her whether someone has shown up looking for him. When she says, "No," it angers him more. Still, he stands at the door, vigilant as Cerberus at the gates of Hell.

After speaking with the fighters, André had so much hope— Émilie could hear it in his voice when he told her about it. "They have to see how important it is. They have to." But as the days drifted away, he became increasingly discouraged. Whenever Émilie asked him a question about the pâtisserie or Frédéric, he grumbled his reply or barked at her with the hoarseness of an old man too tired to clear his throat.

His plan is lunacy. As much as she'd give for him to have a change of heart, with nothing to offer in its place, she might as well be arguing the wind out of blowing.

As soon as he's gone, Émilie walks over with Frédéric to check on how the old bookseller is, and to confide in him her concerns about the baker. She's resigned to caring for André's child and cooking their meals—thankfully there's more to eat since André has been working. The rest of her time is spent sewing next to the boy while he plays or sleeps. André won't let her near the shop to keep it going. That part of him is sealed as an urn.

Yesterday, Émilie taught Frédéric to say his name, and at dinner had him repeat it to his father. But when it came out mangled, André just carried on eating. Even small victories are galling to him.

She attempted to convince him to go see Monsieur Durand, to make things right and ask for his counsel, but André's face screwed up in response. All Émilie could do was give her head a shake in reprimand, made more useless because he refused to look at her.

The *librairie* is shut. On the other side of the window, Monsieur Durand sits at his desk doing nothing, not even reading a book, staring blankly at the middle of the shop. Émilie knocks. When he lets her in, the old bookseller tells her he'll be leaving once he can find someone to purchase his business—keeping it open is too sentimental by half—although the possibility of a buyer turning up is unlikely.

"And then where?" Émilie sees his eyes pinch with defeat.

"Abroad," he tells her, vague as the setting of an impressionist painting.

Émilie looks around at the empty shelves and the books on the floor, now stacked neatly in piles. Would they ever be read again? She'd wanted to leave, too, but reconsidered. In spite of telling herself repeatedly she should go, she can't walk away from André and Frédéric. If the old man were to ask why, and she was able to answer truthfully, she'd finally admit: Her love for them won't let her.

With nothing left to say, Émilie and Frédéric depart.

Monsieur Durand resumes gazing into the middle distance, distilling his life and how it has gone quickly as a glass falling to a stone floor.

It's late afternoon when the postman arrives at the pâtisserie, and finding it locked, slides an envelope through the crack under the door and continues on his way. When André comes home from work, he see the letter, a landmine in his mother's handwriting.

He opens it with a mixture of hope it's an attempt at rapprochement, and the sinking belief it will only contain more recrimination.

His mother's neatly penned note consists of one sentence, only four words: *Your father died today.*

André is unsure what sort of reaction he should expect from himself. He knows he isn't going to cry, though there's a numb feeling throughout him. Then sadness gurgles up inside him, not over his father's death, exactly, but for what might have been. Once he told Mireille, with a laugh, he wanted his relationship with Frédéric to be "two sides of the same crêpe." His father should've wanted the same with him.

How easy it would be to fall into a pit where André could pour scorn on the man, but he decides to show generosity to his father's memory, if nothing else. André wasn't able to overcome his past, but maybe now he can move beyond it.

He could write back to his mother and invite her to visit, but chooses not to just then, worried she'll ask him to come home to the *vignoble* and take over. Mireille, who had a wonderful childhood and couldn't imagine anyone hadn't, would've insisted he do whatever his mother wants.

His legs push him up the stairs to where Émilie is placing a bowl in front of Frédéric. André gives her the letter before he walks over to his bed and lies down. She reads it and gives out a small "Oh!" Taking off her apron, she stands, looking like she's about to come over, but thinks better of it. She carries another bowl to the table and sits next to Frédéric.

The boy makes a loud slurping sound and lets out a punch of laughter that fades like air leaving a balloon.

When Émilie attempts to give him her condolences, André silences her with a wave of his hand as though performing a half-hearted magic trick. He's relieved she doesn't push him on it. To avoid her, he plans to go to bed early and leave before she wakes up. She can't begrudge him sleep, even if it won't fool her. He doubts she believes anyone can outsleep grief.

He tries to hold on to the anger he has for his father, but finds it as impossible as grabbing mist. At least he didn't report them to the Nazis. It's a fissure, small as it is, in the dam of resentment. Despite the countless incidents André can recall when his father shamed him, and yelled at him, and, yes, beat him, the only memory that wafts to him now is when André was fifteen and had visited a cousin in Lyon. It was his first time apart from his parents, and he'd broken an arm. In exchange for a jéroboam of wine, his father borrowed a motorcar from a nearby doctor and drove through the night so André didn't have to journey home on the train by himself. This isn't something he's thought of in years. It leaves him even emptier. He supposes someone's good points are seen from far away, and their flaws from up close. The thing about when someone heartless dies, a day soon approaches when there's no one left to remember them, or care enough to, and so they die again.

Just another life that wasn't really lived.

André gives up all hope the Resistance will bring him the answer he desperately wants, so he slips out from the pâtisserie an hour before curfew to find them and make them change their minds. He walks to the garage to demand a frank reply from the mechanic, despite the man's past hostility towards him. But the garage is shut, and the mechanic is nowhere to be seen. André has no idea where to search for the others.

So he ends up where he began—at Saint-Joachim. Where else do those without a prayer go? André finds Père Blais in a hushed conversation with the white-haired woman. When André approaches them, they stop talking, and the woman blinks at him, both surprised and nervous, and immediately leaves.

Something's happening. They're planning a mission, and he's not included. André slumps down in a pew and looks up at the priest, begging for him to say what he dreads to hear. His senses are punished by the cloying smell of sacraments.

Père Blais scrutinizes André's face. "We're going to raid the factory, and God willing, free those prisoners. We'll do what we must to end the production of munitions." The priest's expression locks up. "At least there."

"Let me help." André exhales an excited puff of air. "I know I was reckless the night the train derailed. A lot has happened since then. Don't use that mistake against me."

One of the priest's eyebrows rises, and André uses this hesitation to explain his plan. When he's finished, Père Blais thinks it over, his mouth a careful line. Finally, the man of God says, "Leave it with me," and glides to the front of the church and folds into the darkness beside the altar.

So André drags himself home and waits again. When the curfew bells ring and it doesn't seem likely he'll hear back from the priest, there's a rap at the alley door. André opens it and the teenage girl thrusts a note at him and strolls away.

André reads the mission is to take place the next day—he's to be at the station two hours before sunset.

For the first time since Mireille vanished, he almost feels whole, as though all the fragments inside him have joined together.

THIRTY-TWO

Wednesday, December 1, 1943

"I'm going to bring her home." André pulls Émilie's fingers from his lapels, but she seizes hold again and suddenly looks down. She pats his chest, then plunges a hand into the inner pocket of his jacket and pulls out Egger's Luger.

"You said you threw it away." Her eyes flash with alarm. "Hasn't there been enough—"

André snatches the gun and opens the door. "Tell Frédéric I expect him to be the best Petit Prince. To always be the best Petit Prince."

Émilie moves in close. André breathes Mireille's fragrance on the kerchief around her neck. Many nights he has lain awake waiting for this scent. Well, no more. It ends today.

He shoves the gun back in his pocket and pushes his way out.

In the grey just before twilight, André sits with Père Blais in Argenteuil-sur-Lac's café, watching two sentries across the street patrolling the checkpoint. Without his black clerical soutane, the priest looks no different than anyone else in the room. André finds it disconcerting, as though any deception from a man of the cloth, no matter the reason, is a cardinal sin.

Père Blais cocks his head to indicate the perimeter guards walking out from behind the factory. André lifts a cup of weak tea, but impatiently puts it down without taking a sip. This has to work. It's been thirty-six long days, and now he's moments from having Mireille back. She's so near. A look away, really. A touch. His loss of faith in Mireille ever coming home was a shameful lapse. Now he'll rise from that pile of skulls.

Mireille will never believe who he's had to become, a man who never held a gun in his life now is never without one, sitting here with a knapsack of explosives at his feet.

When André draws his coat shut, his impatience doesn't go unnoticed by Père Blais. "They'll be here. And our country friends, the Maquis, as well. We're not alone. Messages have been passed—we have the girl to thank for that. Faith in our fellow man is never wasted."

André stifles a snort and squints at the sentries. They're sharing a cigarette and rocking with laughter. The world's gone mad if they can joke while steps away others are slaves.

"Not everyone is a monster," Père Blais says.

"Oh? Tell them that."

The priest's body slackens. "Yes. Sometimes I test myself by thinking if God made us in His image, how ugly is He?"

"Don't you priests take a vow of absolute faith? Or why bother being one?"

The clergyman's only response is to purse his lips.

"I have a question for you, *curé*," André says. Like he's about to pray, the priest folds his hands and rests them on the table, ready to listen. "If God doesn't answer our prayers, is it because we haven't asked enough, or is it because the answer's no? If you accept that it's no and stop asking, what if all you had to do was pray one more time? And if it was always no, why even pray in the first place?"

The priest itches his chin. "If only I knew. There's no lack of cruelty in faith, *mon fils*."

Irritated by the priest's words, André pushes back his chair and looks out the window. He's aware of his own breathing, heavy as though he just ran a race and lost. If the others take any longer, the war will be over.

The priest clears his throat. "If I may attempt to answer your question... We never know what God's written on each of our temples. I choose to believe mine is 'hope.' Yours is something you must uncover for yourself."

Before André can respond, the waitress comes over to fill their cups with more tepid water. Père Blais waves her off. When she moves on to the next table, he leans closer to André. "You may think you've duped us, but I know you're only doing this for your wife."

André's mouth curves while his eyes bore into the man.

"Gilles told me," the priest says. "We spoke every evening—he mentioned you quite a bit."

"So he was in the confessional that night. Did he ask forgiveness for Mireille?" It comes out thinner than what André expects, given how long those emotions have been simmering.

"That's not why he was there." The priest pauses to size André up. "I have faith you won't say anything." Père Blais lowers his voice. "There's a wireless radio inside so we can receive our assignments. In code, naturally." His face becomes troubled, as if second-guessing having told André this. He should be uneasy. André would turn him over to them in a heartbeat if it would end this travesty, God's shepherd or not.

André crosses his arms and waits for the man to order him to go home. Go ahead. If André can't rescue Mireille tonight, he'll do it tomorrow. Or the day after. One thing André has learned is doing nothing is no different from stopping breathing and expecting somebody else to do it for you.

The memory of the first time he met Mireille blossoms in his thoughts. He never told anyone about it—he and Mireille kept it to themselves fearing it would break a fairy-tale spell if shared. Back then he believed that, even though his father frequently labelled love "a sloppy blend of insanity and stupidity."

Not Mireille's love.

The priest repositions himself in his chair and pulls his coat sleeves, first the left, then the right, over his wrists. His expression settles to a pious calm, and his eyelids half-close like he's prepared for André's confession. But then the clergyman gives André a serene look, aggressively saintly, and André feels compelled to justify himself.

"I saw her outside a café much like this. She'd smile, but she wouldn't talk to me. It took two weeks to get her to speak. I waited there every morning. She would be carrying a tray of pastries and had trouble opening the door, so I'd rush to open it for her, always with a *bonjour*, hoping for an answer. Every day I offered to carry the tray, but Mireille wouldn't let me. When it rained, I walked beside her, holding an umbrella over her. She only looked more annoyed each time, but I didn't let that put me off. She told me later it was because she was angry at herself for falling so easily, too. I suppose if she'd never spoken to me, I'd still be there. I was that stubborn, she called me 'her summer flu.'

"One morning, I couldn't meet her because of a problem at the *pension* where I was staying—another resident was being thrown out for lack of payment, and had barricaded the hallway outside his room. I couldn't get past. I tried to reason with him, but he wouldn't back down until I told him why I needed to leave so urgently." André lets a hint of a grin escape. "He let me through. That was when France seemed full of romantics."

He pauses so the priest has a chance to say something, but the man remains stoically blank. He should anoint André's forehead and give him three "Our Fathers" as penance and be done with it.

Just when André decides talking to the priest is useless as whispering to Notre-Dame's spire, the clergyman rests his arms on the table and gives André a nod, encouraging him to continue.

"When I showed up at the café, Mireille was still there. Finally, she spoke to me. She'd been worried when I hadn't shown up. Her voice was so beautiful and clear it sounded like singing, and I could smell lilacs on her. I was ecstatic and nervous, all at once. It took another week before I could ask her to join me for a walk."

Père Blais exhales a puff of approval. "There you go. There's your faith: Love. If you believe in nothing else, believe that with love, stars can shine through your soul."

As wonderful a sentiment as that's meant to be, one Mireille would agree with without hesitation, André is not sure he does. "What's love when the other person's not there?"

"It's an act of faith that it exists, even when it can't be seen, like air. Some would argue it's more important whom we love and how we love than who loves us."

His words strangle André's breath. No, the mistake was not holding on tight enough.

Père Blais shakes his head. "But never mind. I won't reveal your reason to the others, but let's stick to the plan. You did right coming to us during these times of spiritual emptiness. Think of the lives we'll save from their bombs," he discreetly points at the factory, "and those wretched souls working inside."

Callous as it is, André wants to say he can only think of one of those souls. He'll leave the rest of them in someone else's hands.

A girl carrying a basket on a bicycle passes in front of the checkpoint, and even in the fading light, André recognizes the teenage girl from the Resistance.

The sentries step out of their box, and one says something to her while the other chuckles. The girl climbs off the bicycle and casually walks back. She beams with the charm of a sunrise in May as she coquettishly lifts a corner of the cloth draped over the basket to allow them a peek inside. After more banter, the teenage girl rolls open the cloth and invites the soldiers to help themselves, which they eagerly do. Like starving jackals, they start gobbling down the pastries André baked.

A canvas-covered military truck rumbles down the street towards them. The two sentries, all at once serious as pallbearers, throw down the treats and shoo the girl away.

André and Père Blais grab their knapsacks and hurry out of the café.

Suddenly the teenage girl falls, the bicycle tumbling to the muddy ground with her, right in the vehicle's path. Just when the truck's about to roll over her, rusty brakes grind, and it skids to a stop with a hand's length to spare.

A sentry helps her up while the other guard moves her bicycle out of the way. She slowly rises to her feet, then falters, stalling for time, while André and the priest cross the street and stealthily climb into the back of the truck. The smells of gasoline and musty canvas are so strong André can taste them.

The girl picks up her bicycle and the basket and carries on.

One sentry returns to the box and opens the boom barrier, as the other one waves the vehicle through. It travels up the road to the factory, where the driver, a German soldier, climbs out, stomps over to the door, and forcefully knocks.

André and his devout comrade jump out of the truck and take cover behind it.

A loud horn blows from inside the factory. A soldier with a sidearm exits, and dozens of prisoners tramp out after him in a single file to the truck. Another German follows, rifle at the ready.

Back at the checkpoint, the shy man from the Resistance creeps up behind a sentry, and in a flash, slits the German's neck in a fluid, brutal motion, in spite of having one arm. The other guard flies out of the sentry box, but before he can raise his rifle, the teenage girl pops up at his back, grabs his wrist, and flips him onto the dirt. The shy man finishes him with an expert slice.

The girl snatches a pistol strapped inside the basket and picks up the rifles, and they hustle up to the factory.

André and the priest spring from behind the truck and start shooting at the guards. Prisoners scream and scatter and dive to the ground. The driver attempts to wrestle the gun from Père Blais, but André shoots him in the head, and he falls down dead. André's mind drains until he's only aware of his physical senses. His mouth fills with the sour taste of beer gone bad, although he can't remember the last time he drank any. He takes down the guard carrying the rifle, while the one with the sidearm hides beside some rusty equipment.

The girl and the shy man dash up to André and Père Blais. The nearest perimeter guards run towards them, firing their MP40s at everything that moves. Bullets make pinging sounds piercing the truck's metal chassis.

André scrutinizes the prisoners for Mireille, and doesn't see her. He waited too long. He should've come on his own soon as he knew where she was. He motions for the teenage girl to take out the approaching perimeter guard while he fires at the guard hiding behind the machinery.

At last the guard is shot, by whom is difficult to know in the confusion—he falls to his knees before toppling over face first into mud. André uses this as his opportunity to make a break for the factory door, when another German soldier comes out, sees him, and gets off a couple of rounds before retreating inside again, slamming the door after him.

It's locked. André shoves his hand in the knapsack, pulls out a lump of plastic explosive, and molds it around the handle. Jamming in a detonator pencil, he takes cover behind the truck again. He thinks of Gilles and knows, had he had the chance, he'd be right beside them.

Another perimeter guard barrels their way—now two Nazis bastards are shooting at them. Père Blais and the girl return fire, and the guards hit the ground, popping up to snipe at them any chance they get.

The explosive detonates with a loud bang. The door falls inward and there are more screams from the building. André runs in, and prisoners scatter when he exchanges shots with three German soldiers.

So badly does he want to find Mireille, every one of his muscles burns, straining to run up to her the minute he sees her. His eyes scan back and forth searching for her, but the Germans maintain their non-stop barrage, so André has no choice but to hunker down next to a brick pillar.

Outside, Père Blais steps out from behind the truck and kills a perimeter guard, while the teenage girl shoots at the other one, keeping him occupied. Despite bullets hissing by in erratic bursts, she skillfully aims, steadies her hand with the other, and slows her breathing. BANG! The guard drops like an anvil.

André remains pinned down in the factory as the three guards move to flank him. The stink of gunpowder makes it hard to breathe. A bullet whizzes by his left ear. He finds himself praying again, forgetting his claims of no longer being religious. If he's to die, at least let Mireille go free.

The priest and the girl charge in, the deafening salvo from their guns announcing their arrival, this gun battle more ferocious than the one outside.

Now the Resistance has the Germans busy, prisoners risk escaping through the windows, but André doesn't see Mireille. He throws the knapsack with the rest of the explosives at the teenage girl's feet and bolts back through the door.

André sprints to the rear of the factory where bodies spill out windows onto the ground, then rise up disoriented, as if from a deep lake, to flee for their lives to the forest.

He searches for his wife. His heart lurches when he spots her scrambling towards the trees. He calls out, "Mireille," but she keeps to her beeline. "Mireille!" he yells again, but she doesn't stop.

A handful of perimeter guards appear from around the side of the building and start shooting the escapees—terror rises to André's throat as they drop. This can't be for nothing. It can't end this way.

He tries to go after her, but he's trapped again by a volley of bullets. Mireille glows in the truck's headlights and floats between the trees.

Out of the forest, the white-haired woman and the mechanic materialize leading a dozen men. The Maquis! The perimeter guards now concentrate their weapons on the newcomers. The woman takes out two Germans, but one of their bullets hits the mechanic in the shoulder. He stumbles back towards the trees, but is shot again, falling to the ground as though his clothes no longer have anything inside them.

The white-haired woman crawls over. She lies beside him for a moment, bullets kicking up dirt around her, and rests a hand on his chest. Then she scrambles over to the trees, and seemingly oblivious to everything, fires with a reckless vengeance at anyone in a German uniform.

André runs towards the forest. "Mireille!" he screams over and over. All of a sudden, he hits the wet ground hard. Only when he struggles to stand does he notice blood leaking from a bullet hole in his leg. He manages a few steps before falling again, his eyes not wavering from where his wife has disappeared—she's right here, not a dozen paces from him.

He feels his arms wrap around her, their lips touching, and the all-encompassing euphoria of being together pulses through him.

Then she withers away along with everything else.

Père Blais and the teenage girl exit the factory without the knapsacks, their guns firing at any Germans still able to shoot, and run like hell as the building explodes spectacularly in oranges, and yellows, and clouds of black.

The pâtisserie barely exists in the dim light of a new moon.

There's loud knocking at the alley door, and Émilie's quick to open it. André stumbles in, supported by the white-haired woman and Père Blais.

"Here." Émilie points at a chair, and the woman and the priest ease André down. He's covered in blood and mud, and his eyes are glassy and rolling back in their sockets. Her core fills with a familiar foreboding. A human being can withstand so much, yet perish over so little.

"I saw her," André mumbles. "I saw Mireille."

"He's been patched up, but there was a lot of blood." The white-haired woman's expression collapses like she's lost control of her features.

"We removed the bullet," the priest says.

The Resistance fighters go to leave, and Émilie follows them to the door where the priest nods to her. He and the woman join a girl and a young man, each looking depleted as candles on the last night of Hanukkah. They remain in the alley for a moment, oblivious to their cuts and wounds, their muddy and ripped clothes, the blood, and bow their heads. The girl is especially upset—she dries her tears with the sleeve of her coat.

Someone hasn't returned. Émilie sees the mechanic Monsieur Durand spoke of so highly when they were under the catacombs isn't here. She feels her heart close around her own grief.

The fighters go their separate ways. Émilie imagines Père Blais going back to the church, the girl to her parents, and the woman home to an ill mother waiting up for her, rosary beads gripped as firmly as her arthritic hands will allow.

The young man is the last to exit the alley. He scrutinizes the street before slinking off, hugging buildings, to a flat spartan as a crypt and just as quiet. There he'll grieve all his losses alone. Sharing them is too much like shedding clothes until you're naked and shivering.

Émilie fetches a cup of water. She brings it to André's lips, but he pushes it away. He mumbles incoherently, the only words slicing through the fog are: "Is she here? Did she come back?"

"No."

"I have to—"

"You're in no condition."

"She's free. She made it out. They couldn't have shot her, not after everything— I have to find her."

André attempts to stand, but drops back into the chair to stare off in the distance, his eyes half-shut. A moan rises from him, ripped from inside as though by a jagged hook, growing louder until it fills the shop. His body will heal, but can the same be said for his mind?

As André wails, Émilie falls to her knees and lifts one of his bloody hands to her cheek.

THIRTY-THREE

Thursday, December 2, 1943

Émilie takes the cloth, warm and clammy, from André's forehead, soaks it in a bowl of cool water set on the floor, and tenderly blots his face. He stirs, mumbles, and falls back to sleep.

She stayed next to him all night. Although she wanted to find a doctor, she argued herself out of it because of the difficult questions that would be asked about a bullet wound. She was going to go for Monsieur Durand, but André slept so restlessly, she worried if he woke and found himself alone, he might do himself harm in his delirious and despondent state.

The things he muttered in his sleep were troubling, of revenge and killing. At the stillest hour of the night when something was scratching in the walls, André settled, only to thrash around violently as though being burned alive.

Frédéric watches while she tends to his father, the boy's expression perfectly reflecting his concern, deep and sharp. Any other time, this would be welcome progress. He wouldn't go to bed and was close to tears whenever Émilie mentioned it. Fearing a tantrum, she let him stay up. Now he sits at the table like a guard at his post, clutching the Guignol to his chest as a shield. Against what, she has no idea.

What this unfortunate child has endured these last weeks. Émilie can't rebuke herself more for it. She believes the love and attention she's shown him has slightly eased whatever he's going through, but this could just be wishful thinking. And isn't wishful thinking simply diluted hope for those who've had it beaten out of them?

As she changes André's bandages, the odour of blood reaches her. The bullet hole, round and black as a dilated pupil, shows no signs of infection. Her fingers brush against his skin, its softness surprising her, while his blond hairs are wiry as a scouring brush. She fights an impulse to lie beside him and take him in her arms.

André breathes deeply, his lips slightly puffing out each time he exhales. The urge to taste him on her mouth again rises in her like a fever. She can't forget his kisses of hazelnut and vanilla. An exhilarating energy pulses through her, joining her to him, and for a second, she feels the shock of love once more.

Then it crashes down on her that André can't be experiencing it the same way—she's hiding in a fantasy. No matter what's happened, there's nothing between them. All they were doing was bleeding in each other's wounds.

Émilie picks up the bowl of water and retreats to the sink to empty it.

Since André is sleeping more soundly, she tiptoes downstairs and stands at the front door, looking out the window at the vacant street filled with birds fighting for specks under the first glint of dawn. Now's the time to bring back a doctor or the old bookseller, but she can't move. She stays there until people start passing by, although few notice her. For all those times wanting to be invisible, here's when she demands to be seen—her survival shrieks to be acknowledged. She won't be made worthless again.

She hears André struggle on the stairs, and her sight returns as if the curtain is rising on a third act.

"You should be resting."

He waves her off, shuffles towards the door, and falters. Émilie offers her arm as support. "Let's go up—"

"She's out there." André reaches for the door, but Émilie stops him.

"I'll keep watch. I promise."

He shakes his head, too weak to object more than that. "Is everyone..." he begins, but it fades in his throat. He coughs with a racking spasm and he can barely ask, "How many died?"

Before Émilie can answer, André turns his face. He knows she's withholding something from him—the smell of a lie's on her again.

She remembers her grandfather, who survived the Battle of Verdun, telling her, "Truth has killed more people than all the wars, it's certainly caused more suffering."

He didn't live to see this war.

Émilie makes Frédéric mashed *topinambours*, while André stays in bed. When it's time for dinner, the boy refuses to eat the vegetable, somehow knowing before the war it was only fit for livestock. How fast standards drop when bellies are empty. Suddenly everything's caviar. In the end, she coaxes him to finish his meal with the promise of a bonbon found in the buffet's drawer, the last one.

When Frédéric hides under the table, she joins him. She tells him to imagine they're in a castle where wishes are granted as readily as water flows, but he responds with a pucker of his mouth, perhaps realizing the frivolousness of make-believe at a time like this. When Émilie picks up his ball, hoping playing with it will please him, he snatches it from her.

Not long after, he traipses to bed willingly enough, and falls asleep almost immediately.

Émilie sits on the floor in front of the display case, in the dark, scanning the windows. She leans back, her head pressed against the cold glass, and shuts her eyes.

It's a terrible thing to want, wanting something so badly, wanting what's not here or even possible.

Out of nowhere, a shadow crosses her, and her eyelids spring open. A hooded figure is at the window, its murky face peering in.

Émilie stares back in astonishment. She rushes to the front door and tries to open it, but it's locked. She furiously searches her pockets, but can't find the key, so she bolts to the side door, pulls it open, and steps out into the alley.

No one. She dashes to the street, but it's empty as a canyon.

It's her, it has to be. Mireille has come home at last. André and Frédéric will be so happy.

Émilie closes like a jar as tears form in the corners of her eyes.

THIRTY-FOUR

Friday, December 3, 1943

The *librairie* is nearly restored to its former state—bookcases have been righted, and most of the books returned to their proper places on the shelves. Only one stack remains on the floor, looking too much like a pyre for Monsieur Durand's liking.

He's trying to read *L'Étranger*, but it's difficult to concentrate—he finds himself speeding over the words, hardly comprehending the text, and retaining little of the page once it's turned. Yet he feels an obligation to the greats who've meant so much to him to keep reading. But when pleasure has been stolen from your passion, what else remains?

The door opens, and out of habit, he hides the book—the Nazis are not fond of Camus. Seeing it's Émilie and Frédéric, he relaxes.

"That's a fine coat you're wearing today, Frédéric." Monsieur Durand does his best to sound jovial for the boy's sake. Frédéric raises his mittened hands above his head, presumably his way of calling attention to them. "Oh! They're matching!" Monsieur Durand glances at Émilie. "Your work?" She answers with a thin smile.

Frédéric looks towards the children's books, then back to Monsieur Durand, waiting for permission. He nods, and the boy runs over.

Émilie takes a step forward, a hint of tired defeat bleeding into her expression. "Monsieur, I was wondering..." She pulls on her earlobe as if debating whether to go on.

"What is it?"

"Remember when you helped me get away?"

"Of course. If only I had been more of an assistance to you." He pauses for her to collect her thoughts, but promptly works out the reason himself. "Oh! You're leaving. After all that's happened? Where will you go?"

Émilie replies with an ambiguous, "Far."

He lifts an eyebrow. "In that case, I wish you good fortune in reaching it, but I've heard there are no longer places of refuge for someone like..." His lips clamp shut. Why is he being so delicate? An obligation to courteousness? The weeds of incivility have long since overgrown every garden. What's the point of being the last courtier at the execution of Louis the Sixteenth?

"For Jews," Monsieur Durand adds bluntly.

Émilie shrugs. "How can I stay?"

"Does he know you're going?"

She shakes her head.

Monsieur Durand doubts she will make it far. Yet, he tells her, "Fine. I will make the arrangements."

She kisses him on the cheek, and hurries to the door. "Come, Frédéric. We have an entire day to spend together. We can't let it pass."

Émilie opens the door, and Frédéric starts towards her, then pauses to doff his cap. From somewhere inside Monsieur Durand's old frame, a burst of laughter percolates up that even shocks him.

"Émilie?" He looks at her with anticipation he's scarcely able to contain. "Will you give André my regards?" There has to be a way for their differences to be resolved.

"He's closed to everyone except for the one person not here, but I'll try. He'll come around."

With a nod goodbye, she departs with Frédéric.

Monsieur Durand watches them walk past the window and out of sight, confident that his friendship with the baker will be salvaged. And when Mireille comes back... That thought over-whelms his pessimistic temperament of late, a break in the storm. The ennui dissipates, clearing his mind. Everything will go back to the way it was.

He ambles over to the last stack of books and resumes reverently placing each volume on a shelf.

When André wakes, or as near to it as possible in his fevered state, he lies still, unable to move or speak, helpless as if held down by rocks.

Defeated, he eases into sleep again like he's being lowered into a cave black as a Périgord truffle. Not able to see a thing, he hears a voice, although what it's saying isn't clear. It laughs, sweet and inviting, and André finds himself running barefoot through a forest holding hands and giggling wildly with Mireille. When she trips over the root of a tree, pulling him down with her, they lie on the cool moss, arms wrapped around each other, legs entwined, looking through the lattice of branches at a sky frothing with clouds.

From the hills outside of town, an echo of a howl reaches their ears, and they imagine a giant ogre coming to devour them, and laugh some more. The clouds break open, just in time to be saved by a rain that melts the world around them.

André and Mireille lie knotted together. Soon their lips touch, linger, and soften into a kiss.

Dreamlike as it is, André recognizes the first occasion he and Mireille were alone. It's the one memory that can hold him close and promise everything will be all right.

Émilie helps André to the table where Frédéric sits patiently waiting. They pass around food in silence. She hoped it would cheer them if there's more on their plates than usual, even though she has no idea what they'll do in a day or two when there'll be nothing left to eat. On the menu tonight is tinned horse meat. Next they'll be eating rats.

She looks at André, but he ignores her, and they begin eating with little interest. Émilie takes a few bites, but it's mushy and pungent, and decisively lays down her fork.

"André? There's something I need to—"

His eyes snap up. "We'll take the boy to the park on Sunday. We missed last week."

"But you're not well enough to—"

He turns to his son. "Want to play with the sailboat?" Frédéric grins at the word, and André goes back to his meal.

Émilie tries to say what she has to, but loses her nerve. She picks up a plate with the bread, staggers to the buffet, and cuts two more pieces. She glances at the sombre baker and his child beaming up at him. Tell him, she orders herself, or be cursed forever. But she can't bring herself to do it. Disclosing Mireille has come back will cause a cataclysm no one will be able to control, least of all her.

When lying awake becomes unbearable, Émilie extracts herself from her bed, careful not to wake Frédéric, and slips past a snoring André to the stairs.

In the pâtisserie, she unlocks the door to the alley and sits in front of the display case, her arms hugging her knees.

André went straight to bed after dinner. She was amazed he ate as much as he did—yesterday, he was barely able to smell the consommé. She stood over him and implored him to tell her about the rescue and how his wife got away, but he only mumbled "I failed," over and over. His expression was so miserable, she could've cried.

She wills herself to stay focused on the windows, but soon there's a strange pull inside her, and she's back home walking through a field of irises, deep purple and soft as velvet, and she realizes it's a dream. Even asleep, disappointment spreads through her like poison.

She wakes with a start, leaving her exposed and self-conscious, unable to remember the details.

A shadow passes over her and is gone.

Émilie races to the window. Nothing.

Why did she believe his wife would return home as long as she's still here? There isn't room for both of them.

Trudging to the stairs, she turns back for another look, and the hooded figure creeps into view. It spots her and glides away.

This time, Émilie goes to the alley door and steps out right in the figure's path.

"Show me your face," Émilie commands. Its head is bent and covered by a blanket. The figure moves to leave, but Émilie blocks the way. "Show it or I'll call for—"

"Your husband?" a woman's voice asks between teeth. Her scorn is palpable.

Again the figure tries to pass, but Émilie won't let it. She pushes aside the blanket. Even though the woman before her is dirty and gaunt, Émilie recognizes Mireille from her photograph. Her eyes are two unpolished stones, cold, and unable to reflect a thing.

Émilie pulls back her hand as though it's too close to a snake's fangs. "He's not—" she tries to explain. "He's not my—"

"But you're still here. You live with him. I've seen you." Mireille moves to go.

"You can't leave. André will be—"

The woman wheels around. "Don't tell him." She spits the words. "This one thing I ask of you: Don't let him know I was here."

"But he'll be so happy. He's been—he never stopped hoping you'd—"

Passing lights warn them of an approaching vehicle, and they both instinctively move into the darkness until it passes. Émilie scrutinizes the frightened creature before her—Mireille's eyes dart with a touch of madness—and sees herself as she once was.

"You're hungry. I have food." Émilie bolts back in and pulls out the three petits fours from the display case. She spins around. Mireille is right behind her, glaring at her with equal parts curiosity and loathing. Émilie holds out the plate.

Mireille's grimy fingers snatch the pastries and she starts eating ravenously.

Émilie can smell the factory on her, stale sweat, urine, and dirt, but nowhere near the suffocating stench of the camps and the cattle trains they were forced in to get there. At a loss what to say now Mireille's standing before her, all she can blurt is, "I'm Émilie."

"I know who you are." Mireille's mouth is full, but it still comes out with undeniable venom. "Émilie Laurent. But that's not who you are, is it? I'm Émilie Laurent now." She drops the plate on the display, and it clatters loudly and almost falls off. "Want me to tell you who you are? No one. You can't be me, because I no longer exist." While her palm swipes crumbs from her lips, Mireille fixes her eyes on Émilie. Under that accusatory gaze, Émilie's body hangs from her shoulders as if on a hook. She's already held up her hand in remorse. Now for the punishment. A thousand lashes would be too lenient.

Mireille makes her way to the stairs and tilts her head up to where her husband and son are. Émilie reads her look. How she must ache with the intensity of a burning star to climb those steps and hold her family in an unbreakable embrace.

"I'll get them. André will want to—"

"He didn't come for me." Mireille's features screw into an agonized knot. "I sent a note. I begged him to—"

"He did! He was part of the raid to rescue you. He organized it! I can tell you everything he tried to—"

Mireille expels a dismissive snort, and her expression takes an even more sinister form. "I heard about you in Drancy."

Émilie involuntarily steps back. Questions inundate her, but the palpable anger in the woman's voice make her afraid to ask them. Or is it the answers that scare her?

"Someone who knows you searched me out when your name went around the barracks. An old woman, Sophie Dreyfus." Mireille softens for a moment—proof not every crumb of sympathy within her has been brushed away—then hardens again.

"I don't see how she lasted so long. Of course, she saw I wasn't you. I begged her to tell, and she promised she would, but only if I said they also made a mistake with her." Mireille emits a chilling laugh. "Who'd believe either of us, then?"

She pauses, waiting for an answer, but all the air in Émilie is gone, and if she attempted to speak, she'd only gasp.

"But I got out. Or, should I say, you did." Mireille shows Émilie her perfect hands. "You were miraculously useful again. They took me to that factory and made me work, while the others—the old and broken—ended up who knows where." She gives out a mockery of a chuckle. "One of the guards believed me. He was gentle and polite and looked as young as Frédéric, although he insisted to everyone he was eighteen and old enough to fight a war. He said he'd help me, but he got himself killed before he could."

Her eyes run over Émilie like a finger down a page. "There may be a resemblance, and I can forgive you for that, but not for how you've wormed into their lives. I don't care how you did it—I've already wasted too much time thinking about it. But you've burrowed your way in the way rodents do, just like your people do. *Maudits sales*—"

She stops short of completing the epithet out loud, yet Émilie has no doubt it finished in her head. With so little effort, hate perpetuates.

Émilie stares at her in pain, then pity. It's not her fault; she's been driven to it. What Nazis do to the innocent sometimes results in them doing the same to others. Now this woman can't allow herself to show weakness—she's thrust the knife in, all that's left is for her to twist it.

Mireille's lips peel open and she meets Émilie's eyes with rancour. "Oh, that old lady—Madame Dreyfus—knew what happened to your mother and father."

Émilie's eyes flare brighter, ignited by the remaining embers of love and hope. Is it true? At the factories where she worked, she tried to find out about her parents, tried to send notes to Drancy on the off chance they were still there, but her path never crossed with anyone who knew them, and there was never a reply.

"They were sent to a camp in Poland," Mireille tells her. "No one comes back from there."

Émilie stands straight as tears slide down her cheeks.

A begrudging silence roosts between them even Mireille won't break.

"Some do," Émilie finally whispers.

"Then they're ghosts."

Émilie walks to the front door and opens it. The air smells of wet leaves and banked fireplaces.

She only did what she had to do to survive. Mireille must understand this now. Émilie didn't want this—she never imagined she'd be here. But she is, and she's endlessly appreciative for what André has done for her. And more than that, Émilie is thankful to this woman for what she had to endure in her place.

Mireille persists mercilessly. "Sophie Dreyfus told me you were sent to Auschwitz first." She moves closer, her mouth near Émilie's left ear. "How did you escape?" she growls, and draws back, not in retreat, but in disgust. "Cunning? No, it would be by deceit—it had to be. Certainly not good fortune. You're not deserving of that mercy."

Émilie glares at her and defiantly wipes her tears. With great effort, she fights hiding behind her hands.

Mireille's chin juts forward. "I heard your daughter was with you."

Émilie flinches.

"Yes, Dreyfus told me about her and how she came by *her* freedom. They say by suffering we become angels." Mireille scoffs. "When all we really do is trade hells." She takes a few steps to the alley door. "I have to wonder—did you escape before or after they killed your child?"

Everything stops. Émilie feels unable to move, impaled on this one spike of time.

Mireille turns to her again, and the two women face off: one fierce and cruel, the other broken and robbed of all words. One tightens her spine with determination, while the other's flesh falls from her.

"I want my son." Mireille demands, final as Solomon's verdict. "I want Frédéric. Have him here tomorrow night."

THIRTY-FIVE

Saturday, December 4, 1943

Émilie stays up with Frédéric, watching him as he plays with the paper marionettes, trying to remember every detail about him.

Excited about going to the park the next day, the boy wouldn't go to bed after dinner, not even when André repeatedly told him to with a steady patience that surprised her. Finally André gave up, and unable to keep awake much longer, hobbled to his bed, saying Frédéric would follow him soon enough.

That afternoon, seeing André wasn't in the shop, Monsieur Durand ventured in. Émilie asked about leaving, but the bookseller shook his head and said, "They're everywhere." She decided to wait two more days. If there's no news from him by then, she'll go on her own.

Frédéric becomes bored with the cut-outs, and having nothing else to do or to think of, nods off. She envies him that. She carries him to his bed and lies down next to him. She listens to André sleeping on his side of the folding screen making disgruntled noises like he's arguing with himself. All day she deliberated—not if she's going to tell André about Mireille having been there, but how.

Her thoughts shift to Mireille's cold-hearted revelation. Émilie needs to mourn, but to succumb completely to sorrow will asphyxiate her. Saddled with uncertainty about her family's fate for so long, she was already walking around wearing half of her grief like sackcloth. Now that the worst has been confirmed, she's ready to don its full coat, oversized and oppressive.

Émilie allows herself to silently cry until André calls out in his sleep, loudly as if he were warning of approaching danger. Given the chance, she would weep endlessly. She worries if she starts again, she won't be able to stop until she's desiccated.

She has never spoken of Auschwitz, and hopes never to have to. She escaped; she did what she had to do to live. For fourteen months, she worked diligently in the tailoring workshop, mostly mending clothing for prisoners and the SS. Sometimes she made outfits for officers' wives, even party dresses.

Over time, she hid parts of German uniforms that couldn't be repaired. When she had enough for a complete one and had obtained a forged pass, she convinced Jakub, a Pole who unloaded the bolts of material off the truck from Ravensbrück, to don the uniform and escort her out the gates. Of course, they were stopped. Jakub showed the pass and explained, in perfect German, he was escorting Émilie to the villa of Frau Höss, the commandant's wife, for a dress fitting, calmly as though he was informing them of the hour. Émilie held up a craftily folded scrap of fabric as proof.

The gates opened, and Émilie and Jakub strolled through. They walked to the commandant's house and kept going until they reached the nearest town, where they parted company, forever grateful to each other. Émilie made her way west, marvelling at how more vivid the colours of everything around her were and the crystal clarity of the quiet. No one was groaning in pain; no one was weeping in despair. When they took her from her home, Émilie quickly forgot what the world was like, believing that outside the camp nothing existed.

Yes, she escaped. When she had a chance to be free, she grabbed it. She smelled the smoke. She saw the sky flaked with ash and knew what it meant. Being there a minute more would've meant death.

In Drancy, when they wrenched her Esther's little hands away at gunpoint and dragged Émilie to the train, she frantically begged her mother and father to take care of her child, assuming they'd end up with her in Auschwitz. Every day for months, Émilie asked around the camp if they arrived. Often she heard a two- or three-year-old girl matching Esther's description had come in. Émilie would contrive to be where she could see the Nazis lining up the new arrivals. She'd search the face of every child, as she told herself, *Oh, God, let me find her*. Émilie was well aware what becomes of the young ones, those Esthers who weren't hers. It made finding her child more crucial than the beating of her heart.

But she never saw her daughter or parents again.

There's thunder inside her brain, a continuous hammering on a drum. She remembers Esther riding on a chocolate-coloured donkey, the time she and Claude took her to the beach, the child's small face opening up like a field of wildflowers in the morning light. Émilie was never more gratified as a mother than when seeing that joy in her daughter. The deepest happiness you can experience is to know your child feels loved. Émilie heard the satisfaction in Claude's voice when he remarked she and Esther sported the identical untroubled smiles and laughs.

Claude! She feels every tremor of her pulse. He came for her and lost his life. Knowing that will forever be a tightening garrote of guilt around her neck.

No, she hasn't spoken about any of it. What's the use of telling someone? No amount of sympathy can right a horrendous wrong or dull a cavernous pain. It only reminds you of your loss. How can she make anyone who hasn't lived it understand? They'd only hide behind the thought that they had no part in it coming about, as if these camps sprung up from the ground. Well they didn't. And neither did Nazis.

As a distraction from dwelling too long, Émilie thinks of ways she'll occupy herself during her last day with the Alberts: cleaning and dressing André's bullet wound, showing Frédéric how to print his name, and making mashed carrots with bits of yesterday's meat for their evening meal.

She slides out of bed and picks up Frédéric, cradling him like a newborn.

Then she'll be gone.

The alley beside the pâtisserie once held fond memories for Mireille. Her father bouncing a ball for her to catch while her mother clapped. Sitting on a crate with André on humid days, hoping for a breeze. Frédéric tirelessly running from one end to the other in a race with a finish line always out of reach. Now such thoughts taunt her and reveal her to be empty as an eggshell.

She leans against the wall and waits. Ever since she was taken, Mireille has constantly imagined wrapping her arms around him again, and it fills her with a magnificent love. She should have gone upstairs the night before and scooped up her son, but she was afraid André would stop her...and make her stay.

But now she'll take her boy away from here, and André can have his other woman—she can't think, let alone say, her name. Mireille rubs her cheeks and finds them close to bone. She knows her bitterness is no more real than the saccharine they refused to use as an ingredient. But she can't return to him. Not after what she's had to do—what she's been made to do. What she did to others. How can she ever look André in the eyes again? Her foolish moment of passion with Gilles pales in comparison to the sordid humiliations she's endured since she's been gone. Yet it compounds it. She'll leave with Frédéric and never have to think about any of it again.

Her plan is to follow a route between Saint-Léry d'Espoir and the coast, one of those the Resistance relies on for the messages she used to send and receive for them. It'll take a day or two. Boats leave all the time. Long as Frédéric is with her, who cares where they go?

She hears the door crack open, and pushing it wider, walks into the pâtisserie and cautiously scans the room. There's no aroma of baked goods, not even traces of cinnamon or anise. It makes the shop as disturbingly unfamiliar as lying on someone else's bed or wearing their clothes. She turns and sees Frédéric sleeping in the arms of that woman.

With the sound of her own deep breathing filling the silence, Mireille bites her lip and reaches out to touch her son, but stops. What if this isn't real? What if her hand touches nothing?

"Here." The woman motions for Mireille to take him. He stirs, wakes, and gapes at Mireille, not a flicker of recognition in him. She takes a step back. His look is seven daggers through her.

"Say *bonjour*, Frédéric." Despite the woman's words, everything becomes confused behind the boy's eyes.

Mireille whispers, "*Bonjour*, Petit Prince." Even in the dim light, she sees his cheeks and nose are still dusted with summer freckles, the last touch on a lovingly made cake.

Frédéric frowns. Surely he remembers her. He can't have forgotten her so soon. Mireille kneels and stretches out her hands to him, but he buries his head in the woman's dress.

"Remember the lady in the photograph?" The woman puts Frédéric down and gives him a nudge. His eyes crease a little before his head moves, no more than a quiver, from side to side.

His rejection lodges in the stillest part of Mireille's soul where it will rot for as long as she lives. Her heart withers, and she's left with a cutting emptiness. She lowers her arms and shuffles towards the alley door.

"Frédéric, it's your maman," the woman yelps.

Hearing "maman," Mireille looks back. Frédéric still clings to the woman, and when she tries to drag him over, he starts to cry, tears dripping from his lashes.

"Shh. Shh. What's the matter?" The woman turns her sorry face to Mireille. "He has to get to know you again. You'll see. Come to him."

Mireille moves forward. Frédéric screeches so piercingly loud, it rises to the ceiling like a flood. She reaches out again, but he turns, and his left leg stamps up and down on the floor as if crushing any memory of her.

She glares at the Jewess with contempt. "A mother's embrace

is made of love. Who'd be so evil to deny a child that?"

Mireille backs away and shrivels into the alley's gloom.

Émilie hugs Frédéric—it's soft and familiar. She picks up a sweet scent on him, although she's sure he hasn't had a bonbon all day. Now his mother is gone, he stops crying as easily as if he's forgotten how. He reaches up and runs a finger across Émilie's top lip, then along the bottom one, tracing their shape.

André comes in from the stairs. He freezes when he spots the open door.

The anguish creasing Émilie's forehead contrasts with the tiny chortle Frédéric gives out at seeing his father.

André wraps his arms around his son and holds him close.

"Will she be back?" André pushes aside the blackout curtain and peers at the street below.

"She didn't say."

He moves to go, and Émilie grabs his arm. He's not sure if it's trembling with anger or anticipation.

"André, no. The curfew. Your leg. When it's light out, you can search for her. We'll both—"

"Why didn't you call out for me? I could've made her stay." He gazes over at Frédéric asleep in bed. Hopefully he's dreaming of as many sailboats as will bring a smile to him again. "Was he happy to see her?"

Émilie withdraws her hand.

"I'm asking you: Was he happy to see his own mother?"

She shakes her head, and André snorts.

"She wants to take him." Émilie's words are grating, stones being crushed in her mouth.

André's stomach contracts. Mireille's only come back for their son. Why would she... He glares at Émilie and his expression hardens to iron. Any feelings he has for her, any emotion, even friendship, has slipped away like sugar between his fingers. What he did for Émilie was the right thing to do. And as thanks, she's brought nothing but bad luck.

"I'll convince her to see you," Émilie says, shedding desperation. "She won't take him from you."

André sorts through a dozen acid thoughts while his emotions totter on a brink. Émilie deserves the wrath of all of them. But he only chooses one.

"Durand stopped me in the street today to tell me you're leaving. So much for the last of your secrets." With an ugly hint of menace in his voice, André adds, "If you need money—if all it takes is money for you to go, to be rid of you—you can take everything I have."

THIRTY-SIX

Sunday, December 5, 1943

Saint-Joachim's bells summon parishioners to the eleven o'clock service, though few are willing to heed the call. It's unusually sunny for how close it is to winter, the kind of morning to temporarily forget your troubles.

Carrying Frédéric, André humps down the stairs and over to Émilie, who's packing a small basket at the display case. Its glass has never glistened so brightly, even with the crack, as if in rebellion for its shelves being shamefully bare. The sailboat perches on top, waiting for the park. The instant André lowers Frédéric to the floor, the boy tries to grab the toy, but it's out of reach.

Anyone would think it was a day no different from any other. Inside, nothing could feel less routine for André. Last night in bed, before his mind was shaken out like a rug, all he could think was: *I just want my family back.*

"Put these on first, Frédéric." Émilie passes the child his coat and cap as André hobbles over, picks up the basket, and starts towards the front door. He's hurting, but he won't show it, at least not to her.

They haven't spoken since yesterday. They ate their godawful dinner in an uncomfortable silence and went to their separate beds coated in the molasses of animosity. At breakfast, when the day ahead looked to be another one spent in resentment, Émilie asked if they could still bring Frédéric to the park. André didn't object.

"We don't have to," she says now.

André exhales through a clenched jaw. The bullet hole in him, the atmosphere between him and Émilie, and the possibility Mireille might show up again are good reasons not to go. Only his leg has a chance at healing. Going to the park is a diversion, not only for Frédéric, but from what's consuming his brain. What can he do to make Mireille stay? And if she insists on... A heaviness builds in his chest.

"It's Sunday. The boy looks forward to this all week."

Frédéric is having trouble putting on his mittens. "Here, Petit Prince," Émilie says. Not having the strength to conceal his irritation, André glares at her while she helps his son.

There's a loud knock at the door. Three Germans are outside: an older officer, his face stained with grey, and two undernourished, young soldiers, clumsily holding rifles. Beside a truck are more Germans, not much older, weapons at the ready.

Before André can reach the door, the two soldiers storm in like they're taking a hill in a battle. Émilie stiffens, and Frédéric hides behind the display case. André's teeth clench, then his eyes open wide.

A soldier drags Mireille into the shop.

André's pulse skips a few beats as dread pools inside him. The German gives Mireille a push, and she almost falls at André's feet. His bones ache not to be able to defend her.

"Heil Hitler." The officer delivers a straight-arm salute, his other hand clutching a wooden swagger stick topped by a plain brass knob.

"Monsieur Albert?"

André barely nods.

"Obersturmführer von Aschenbach." The man sizes him up before continuing. "We found this Jewess eating out of your garbage." The swagger stick swings out towards Mireille, stopping short of hitting her in the chest.

"I'm not a—" Mireille begins, and Aschenbach slaps her with the back of his hand. She recoils, and whimpers like an injured dog. André sees blood on her lips and hatred blisters through him. The *sale boche* will pay for that.

"Normally, I don't bother," the Nazi goes on, his tone measured in contrast to his violent eruption, "but I was intrigued. She tells quite a fanciful story." He flashes a brutal smile. "Do you know this woman?"

André looks at Mireille as if trying to recognize her, scrambling for a way out of what he fears is coming. She's thinner now, and her hair is short, almost the same as Émilie was when he first saw her.

"I don't understand." He feigns ignorance. His legs wobble like he's standing on the ledge of a building, his feet sliding forward. "What is this—"

"It's simple. She says she's your wife. Do you know her? Yes? No?" Aschenbach stares at him cold and piercing as a raven. Unlike Egger, there won't be any feeble attempts at friendship from this German.

Mireille's eyes plead with André as a ferocious longing to go to her and take her in his arms racks him with pain as agonizing as a thousand bullet wounds. Still, he remains mute. It only takes one wrong word.

With a tap of the swagger stick against his boot, Aschenbach reaches for the picnic basket. "May I?" Without waiting for a response, he opens it and roots around. "If I must, I'll take in all of you and we'll sort it out one way or another. I won't be wasting my time." Finding nothing, he drops the basket on the floor, causing Frédéric, behind the display, to jump. The Nazi rests the stick lazily on his shoulder, rubbing it back and forth like it's scratching an itch, while he scrutinizes André again.

"A woman claims she knows you, but you won't say if you know her. She claims she's your wife," Aschenbach pauses to inspect Émilie, "but I notice you already have a woman." The look he gives her is unnerving.

Émilie blanches, but holds her hate-filled expression. She's going to go down fighting like she's given up all hope of being free again.

To distract the German, André clears his throat, but Aschenbach doesn't even glance at him. The Nazi removes his cap and runs his fingers through his wiry white hair. An arc of his hand is enough of a signal for a soldier to spring forward and seize Émilie.

"Your papers. Immediately," Aschenbach barks. He puts his cap on, adjusting it so it sits low on his brow.

Émilie looks to André, begging him to intervene, but he keeps staring straight ahead, trusting she'll obey the officer.

She fishes in her coat pocket and pulls out the papers. Aschenbach snatches them and holds up the identity card. Émilie brazenly removes her hat as he compares the photograph to her. At last, with a pronounced grimace, he passes them back.

"The other one," he commands the soldiers.

They push Mireille to the door. She screams, "No. She's the Jew. She has my son. She has my boy." Her fingers dig into the doorframe, and the Germans have to fight to pull her loose.

André is helpless to do anything but make matters worse. Be clever. Think. Every breath he's about to take feels crucially life-altering for all of them.

Aschenbach raises the swagger stick. Everyone stops. "A boy? Where is this boy?" He glowers at André, who gives nothing away, so Aschenbach starts walking around the display case.

Frédéric crawls away to avoid being seen.

André's arms become rigid, he forms fists, and he takes a step towards the Nazi. He could reach him before the other sons of bitches can stop him. But before André can lunge forward, Aschenbach points the swagger stick at him. "Yes?"

André claws to control himself. "You're scaring him."

The German tilts his head slightly, then turns and squints at the toy sailboat, before continuing to circle the display.

"Come out, come out, *Dreikäsehoch*."

Frédéric runs to Émilie, and wraps himself around her.

Mireille bursts past the soldiers and tries to take her son in her arms, but he holds onto Émilie with everything he has.

"Frédéric. It's me. Maman. Your maman."

The soldiers are on Mireille at once. They haul her back to the door as she fights to escape. They finally subdue her by clamping their paws around her wrists and twisting. Every move she makes is torture.

André's eyes stay fastened on her, petrified at the thought this could be the last time he'll see his wife. They won't let this go unpunished—they'll take it out on her. His insides are riddled with panic, and he starts to sweat.

"Strange," Aschenbach says to no one in particular. "She knows the boy's name. How do you explain this?" He bends towards Frédéric. "Hello!"

"Go upstairs, Petit Prince," André orders his son, but the frightened boy is frozen where he stands.

"GO UPSTAIRS."

Aschenbach pulls his sidearm and points it at the child.

Mireille stops struggling and gapes wide-eyed. Émilie looks away, fearing what's next as Frédéric buries into her hip.

As if being tugged on by a rope, André takes another step, and the German turns the gun on him. "I'm speaking to the boy." Aschenbach points the weapon back at Frédéric, leveling it at his forehead, daring André. This *espèce de connard* won't hesitate to do the unspeakable, but what can André do? Everything's a trip wire tangled around his legs.

Trying to diffuse the situation, he extends his arms from his sides, palms facing out, and slowly raises them. Aschenbach scoffs at the attempt. André has never felt more useless.

Aschenbach flips the gun around and offers it to Frédéric. "Do you want to play soldier?" The boy doesn't look. The German sighs, holsters the pistol, and tries another tactic.

"Frédéric?" The Nazi's light and friendly. "Do you want a bonbon?" He pretends to search his pocket, and Frédéric is curious enough to take a peek. Instantly, the man drops his ruse. "Is this your maman?" Aschenbach's waxy finger jabs at Mireille.

Frédéric does his best to recognize her, but gives his head a violent shake and disappears in the folds of Émilie's dress again.

Turning to André, Aschenbach asks, "Is your son some sort of imbecile?"

André sneers at the man, and Aschenbach stiffens. As the German swells with anger, André says, "Monsieur, may I speak with you?" He suppresses any trace of revulsion in his voice. "Perhaps there can be an arrangement."

Aschenbach studies him with suspicion, but then relaxes and moves closer. "Yes? Yes?"

"I don't have much money—"

"Then you have nothing." Aschenbach scowls at the obviousness of the statement.

"No, Monsieur. The shop. This." André sweeps a hand over the room. "You can have it."

The German surveys the pâtisserie, entertaining the idea. André inflates with hope. They're all corrupt, but he can use that. Then Aschenbach's expression firms. "What am I to do with a pastry shop?" He steps back and straightens his tie. "Someone will talk. Take the child!"

A soldier grabs Frédéric by the collar, and the boy shrieks. Émilie holds onto him past the point when her arms should shatter, so the soldier knocks her to the floor. He tries to pick Frédéric up, and when the child bashes him with the small ball of a fist he's made, the surprised soldier lets him go.

Before the German can think of touching Frédéric again, André moves to intervene, but Aschenbach aims his gun between André's eyes.

"Monsieur Albert. I will ask you for the third and last time." The German points the swagger stick at Mireille. "Is this your wife, the mother of that child?"

André turns into a pillar of salt. The only thing more threatening to Mireille and Frédéric's lives than saying something is saying nothing.

He exhales and is about to reply, when Mireille shakes her head ever so slightly. What's she trying to tell him? In a rush of clarity, André sees what she does, what'll happen if he confesses: Frédéric will be taken from them—or worse—and neither

André nor Mireille will be around to see their son again. Émilie will certainly be killed. All of them will be trapped in an ending that can't be retracted.

When André's face slackens, Mireille gives him a nod as confirmation of what she wants: Make sure Frédéric survives.

André couldn't love her more than right now.

"This," he manages to get out, "is the mother," his throat narrows, "of my son." Shards of his heart stab at him yet again as he points to Émilie.

Émilie rises to her feet while Aschenbach mulls it over, not entirely convinced he's being told the truth. He humphs and signals to the soldier to release Frédéric. The boy scampers back to Émilie.

The Germans march Mireille out. She goes willingly, almost serene now.

With a *"Sieg Heil"* and another straight-arm salute, Aschenbach leaves.

As she's escorted to a truck waiting on the street she grew up on, Mireille looks beyond the rooftops to a sky with no clouds, wide and open. Damn everyone else. Damn them all to Hell. They'll never be able to imprison her love for her child.

André doesn't know what to do next. The world has stopped, and will only begin moving when he resumes breathing. He's a tangle of emotions, messy as grapevines left untended. He flips through words and actions and combinations of them, hoping to stumble on the one that might change where they find themselves. Mireille is finally home, yet they're right back to that day she went missing.

He focuses on Frédéric, reassuring himself he's still here. The boy's brow wrinkles like he's asking, "Now what?" He's no more upset his mother's gone again than having lost an eyelash.

Émilie's gone pale as a porcelain plate. She hangs onto the display as though it's a life vest and she's drowning.

André picks up the basket, passes it to her, and sweeps Frédéric up in his arms. He moves to the open door with a weary fatalism, but Émilie doesn't budge. She stares out the window at Mireille fenced in by German soldiers.

"No. I can't..." Émilie lets go of the basket—it makes an abandoned sound when it hits the floor and tips over. Any glint of hope for happiness was stripped away when Mireille told her the fate of her family. Émilie's heart flaps helplessly as a newly caged bird.

There's still André and Frédéric—they're all that matters now. She starts towards the door, but André's fingers hook around her wrist. He pulls her to him, his shallow breath against her cheek.

"Think of the boy."

Émilie glances at Frédéric. His eyes, once clear as the sea, are filled with fear. No child needs love and caring more. She turns back to André.

"Think of his mother."

Beside the truck, Mireille hears the rattle of chains, and panics. "Noooo," she moans, the way wind gusts through a tunnel. Being their prisoner again hits her with the force of a boxer. "Not that. Please," she begs, but the soldiers don't listen. When they grab her arms, she fights back, and falling to the ground, she viciously kicks them as they try to pick her up.

Émilie attempts to break away from André, but his grip on her tightens.

"They won't let her go just like that," he hisses.

"I'll make them. I'll show them the tattoo."

"Then they'll take all of us."

Her body goes slack, and he lets go.

There's an ungodly screech outside as the soldiers shackle Mireille.

André's face contorts. He presses Frédéric's head against his chest to block his hearing and covers the other ear with a hand. André's heart clenches, then unclenches with decisiveness. An excruciating clarity stirs within him.

It's the only way, their only option.

"You have papers," he reminds Émilie. "Go as far from here as you can."

She forms words in protest, but nothing comes out.

André sets Frédéric down and kneels before him. "You're going to hide, Petit Prince. Be quiet as a fox. Hide and don't come out until you hear your name."

The boy claps his hands, pleased to be playing again. Then his mouth arches, his eyebrows slant, and there's the tinniest crease in his forehead. André searches for any sign Frédéric is making sense of what he's being told. He has to understand. Surely the promise André sees in the boy is there, the one Mireille has always seen. But Frédéric's face goes blank, as if washed clean.

André hugs his son. He has to believe in him. That's what a good father does. He's encouraged by how stoic Frédéric is—there's only a slight quiver in his upper lip.

Émilie touches André's shoulder. "You can't— Please—"

"Get word to Monsieur Durand." André's eyes dart to the boy so Émilie grasps his meaning. "I'm asking you this one thing. Make sure Monsieur Durand comes for him soon as he can."

Émilie slowly nods. She has to grant him this one thing. All his trust is in her. God help him.

"Lock the door after me," André directs her. "And run!"

He lingers a moment more to reach out and brush away the tears dripping down her cheeks.

André turns and walks out the door.

Émilie wants to object, outright refuse to do it, tell him to leave with Frédéric—they could all go—but seeing his chisel-carved resolve, she can say nothing. There has to be some other way, but her mind is a muddle of noise.

She tracks André as he crosses the street towards the truck, and she becomes an empty spool of thread.

Maybe they'll meet again even if it's an eternity away. She hopes he'll keep a small place for her in his thoughts, if not his heart.

Claude. Esther. Émilie's mother and father. Soon there'll come a point when she'll have loved them longer without them being here, than she did with them. Émilie resigns herself to endure life like it's an affliction, anticipating nothing more than the bittersweet comfort of memories. One day. All those times she couldn't find an answer to why she survived, now she knows: to mourn those who didn't.

Frédéric's arms tighten around her, and she bends to hug him. She looks out the window. The Nazis are stunned when André approaches—even Mireille stops struggling. Aschenbach draws his gun.

"This is my wife," André announces. He moves towards her, but a soldier bars the way.

Émilie can't bear any more. There's been enough senseless endings to humble lives. But the finality of André's decision covers her in a smothering pall, and all she can do is justify it to herself. What other choice is there for him? For them? This is how it has to be, as atrocious as it is.

She locks the front door and places a tender hand on Frédéric's head. "I'll see you soon, *mon cœur.*" He clings to her until there's nothing left inside her. She slowly pries his little fingers away. "Listen to your father. You have to hide. Do you hear me? Go hide." The boy merely blinks.

Her eyes smarting with tears, Émilie forces herself to the alley door. If she stays a moment longer, she'll never leave.

She shuts the door and looks back at it. Her hand feels along the pâtisserie's stone wall, making sure it's solid enough to be here if she ever passes this way again.

And now?

She could leave and send a message to the old bookseller, as André wants. Monsieur Durand will keep Frédéric safe until the baker returns. Then she'll be scratching for survival again, wandering alone and laden down.

Or she could go back in and stay with the boy and protect him, regardless of what that'll mean for her. But for how long? The Nazis won't leave without hunting for her.

Then it comes to her like rain from the sky—she could just take Frédéric with her. She'll care for him as though he's... She pushes that away. They'll be on the run until she can bring him home, and that might be a long while. And if they're caught, they'll either be shot on sight or brought to a camp. Children are sent to the right when they arrive, and quickly don't exist except in the memories of their parents, who soon no longer exist either.

Émilie's hands are numb with panic. All her choices are cliffs with only rocks below.

On the street, Achenbach's lips curl in exasperation. "So now you're telling another story?"

"She's Mireille Albert." André looks at her the way he did the first time he saw her outside the café, giving undeniable power to what he's saying. "She's my wife." The truth releases his soul, and his entire being becomes weightless.

Mireille thanks him over and over until it's a Gregorian chant.

Achenbach pokes André in the chest with the swagger stick. "You will pay for lying." He nods, and a soldier hits André in the gut with a rifle butt. André doubles over and falls to the ground.

The German officer starts beating him, wheezing louder with every blow, as André tries to protect his head with his arms.

Monsieur Durand watches from outside his bookstore. The taste of cognac in his mouth becomes sand.

A door slams shut across the way. His eyes snap to the right to catch someone peering at him from between a crack in the curtains, another of this street's craven spies. He turns back to the imbroglio outside the pâtisserie.

Mireille's returned, but so thin and dirty she's almost unrecognizable. She bites and claws at the soldiers, who slap her mercilessly in retaliation, while André spits blood. What those beasts are doing to them! She's like a daughter; he's like a son.

The past crashes around Monsieur Durand with astounding vengeance, bringing his soul to its knees. He thinks of his precious Alexandre and the overpowering helplessness felt back then. He should march over and demand they release André and Mireille. It's not only an obligation to his friends, but a moral duty, as well.

Just when he's set to go to their aid, a debilitating futility washes over him, and he lowers his eyes. Dread, and shame, and acrimony squeeze him. All the good intentions imaginable amount to nothing if one's resolve is fragile as a bird's wing.

With a last look, Monsieur Durand steps back into his shop and closes the door.

André rises to his feet, leans against the truck, and wipes his bloody mouth with his sleeve.

"Where's the Jewess?" Aschenbach snarls. André ignores the question, so the Nazi knocks him down again. "Speak up. You can't hide her any longer." He boots André in his mid-section for emphasis, but André only spits more blood.

"Tell him," Mireille pleads. She turns to Achenbach. "If you find her, you'll let me go, won't you? Please. I've done nothing."

The German waves away her appeal.

He scans the area, then motions for his men to search the pâtisserie. Several soldiers hurry across the street, weapons at the ready, eager to punish someone.

"Where is he?" Mireille begs André. "Where's my boy?"

André glares pointedly at Achenbach, hoping Mireille doesn't give away their son's hiding place. She asks him again to tell her where Frédéric is, and when he doesn't, implores him to tell her if her child is safe.

André wants her to have this assurance, but seeing a soldier pounding on the pâtisserie's front door, knows he can't give it. He says under his breath, "If any of us get out of this alive, let it be Frédéric."

The soldier tries the handle—it's locked. His comrades break down the door and smash the windows, shattering them into thousands of pieces. While one German bounds up the stairs two at a time, the others search the shop, knocking things onto the floor and purposely stomping on them. Frédéric's sailboat is the first casualty. Added to the noise of their destruction are sounds from upstairs of cupboards and drawers being opened, the contents tossed on the floor, beds being overturned, and the folding screen being broken into kindling.

Three soldiers work together to overturn the display case. It crashes forward, and the glass front splinters into jigsaw puzzle shards.

As André is being thrown in the back of the truck, he hears the noise of the display meeting its end. His stomach heaves with a pain more intense than any of their kicks could inflict.

Aschenbach watches the ransacking of the pâtisserie as dispassionately as if viewing a Baroque painting. A soldier steps out of the shop and shakes his head. Aschenbach look around, and his tongue flicks out to taste the morning air. Pistol still drawn, he strides to the alley fast as old legs can go, and raises the weapon, intent on shooting anyone he finds there.

But the alley's empty.

Mireille sobs with a despair bordering on madness. André's expression softens while he takes one more look at her. She's everything he's ever wanted. When Mireille passed near him that first day he saw her, even though she hardly glanced at him, André caught a gleam in her eyes he'll always believe allowed him to see into her soul. No one's as loving.

Seeping frustration, Aschenbach doubles back to the truck with the soldiers. The vehicle lurches out, leaving Mireille there like a discarded tin.

"I'll come home," André calls to her. "I promise. No matter what it takes, I'll find my way back to you." She'll be alright. She's back to her beloved pâtisserie. Frédéric is waiting—the Nazis didn't discover his hiding place. André seizes with a devastating thought. Or is it because he's no longer there?

When the truck passes the Alberts' shop with its broken windows and hanging door, André bows his head, not wanting to witness the remains of what used to be his life. He wants to preserve in his mind the way the pâtisserie was the day Mireille brought him home to meet her parents, her presence making every surface glisten even brighter.

As desperately as he wants to see if Frédéric is inside, he doesn't look. He's all too aware of the soldiers being jostled around him, and doesn't want to tip them off. The German sitting next to him lights cigarettes and passes them out to his buddies, rewarding them for a job well done.

Wringing out the last drop of faith, André says a silent prayer for his wife and son's safety. He only asks for this one thing. He can't imagine there'll be anything he'll ask God's intercession for again.

As the truck drives away, Mireille screams, "Where is he? Where's Frédéric?"

Her voice roars across the street and through the pâtisserie.

Inside the shop, her words fade, and a quiet stillness overtakes everything. There's a sound from the overturned display case, faint at first, like the scrabbling of a mouse, then growing louder and more sustained, as though the majestic piece of furniture is giving out a last groan.

One of the bottom doors, now turned to the ceiling, slides open, and Frédéric emerges from the pastry boxes.

Mireille watches the truck in anguish until it's out of sight. She scours her brain for what to do, but it's gone dark, her emotions stumbling blindly. Her arms and legs are limp, her body hollowed out.

A movement catches her attention. Her heart soars when Frédéric steps out of the pâtisserie as if sleepwalking. "My beautiful, beautiful boy." He searches the ground, attracted by the glass at his feet sparkling brilliantly in the sun.

Frédéric lifts his head to check if the stars are still in the sky, but stops when he sees the distraught woman in chains, kneeling on the empty street.

They stare at each other for the longest time.

Finally, he smiles.

About the Author

Michael Whatling began his career as a technical writer for engineering firms in Canada and Japan. Leaving to teach at the secondary and university levels, he returned to writing by penning *A Vigil for Joe Rose*, a collection of young adult short stories, based on his doctoral research, that made the American Library Association's Rainbow List.

He's the writer of the award-winning independent film, "The Dancing Dogs of Dombrova."

The French Baker's War is Michael's first novel.